The
Automatic
Detective

A. LEE MARTINEZ

A TOM DOHERTY ASSOCIATES BOOK

NEW YORK

THE AUTOMATIC DETECTIVE

Copyright © 2008 by A. Lee Martinez

A Tor Book
Published by Tom Doherty Associates, LLC
175 Fifth Avenue
New York, NY 10010

www.tor-forge.com

Tor® is a registered trademark of Tom Doherty Associates, LLC.

ISBN-13: 978-0-7653-5794-6
ISBN-10: 0-7653-5794-1

First Edition: February 2008
First Mass Market Edition: February 2009

Printed in the United States of America

0 9 8 7 6 5 4 3 2 1

The Automatic Detective

1

The Learned Council had an official name for Empire City.

Technotopia.

Yeah, it wasn't a real word, but that was kind of the point. The Council loved to reinvent things, improve them, make them new and snazzy. Of course Empire had a lot of unofficial nicknames as well.

Mutantburg. Robotville. The Big Gray Haze. The City That Never Functions.

But Technotopia was the official party line, along with the motto "Building Tomorrow's Town. Today." I guess it all depended on what you thought the future should look like. If you were looking for a bright and shiny metropolis where all of civilization's problems had been solved through the wise and fortuitous applications of equal parts science, wisdom, and compassion, then I guess you'd be out of luck. But if your ideal tomorrow was a sprawling, impersonal city with rampant pollution, unchecked mutation, and dangerous and unreliable weird science, then I guess you would be right at home.

Name's Mack Megaton. I'm a bot. Or automated citizen, as

the Learned Council liked to phrase it. There were three classes of robot in Empire. You had your drones: low sophistication models geared toward mundane tasks. Then there were the autos: humanoid models designed for more complex work. Then you had your bots: autos and drones that qualified for citizenship. I hadn't quite reached bot status yet, but so far my probation had been going smoothly, and I was only forty-six months, six days, four hours, and twenty-two minutes from crossing that objective. I occupied a more vague class between auto and citizen. I couldn't vote, couldn't hold public office, and if the Learned Council decided to issue a recall, there wasn't much I could do about it.

I was barely two years old and weighed a compact seven hundred and sixteen pounds. That's light when you're seven feet tall and made entirely of metal. I could punch through concrete and bend steel. I could not, however, tie a bow tie. My programming was state of the art: adaptive, intuitive, evolutionary. I wasn't programmed knowing how to drive a cab, and I got along just fine doing that. I wasn't designed to play poker, and I was a decent card sharp, though it's easier to bluff when you have a featureless faceplate. But my artificial intelligence couldn't wrap its binary digits around the ins and outs of getting a bow tie on. My hands didn't help any. They weren't designed for delicate work, more like sledgehammers with fingers. But the Bluestar Cab Company insisted all its drivers wear bow ties. Real, honest-to-God bow ties. No clip-ons. That's what got me involved in the mess.

A bot's got bills to pay. Bill, really. I used to be juiced by a small atomic power core. That was gone now. The Learned Council removed it as part of the terms of my probation. But I still consumed a lot of electricity in a day, and it didn't come cheap. Not in Empire. There was barely enough to go around in this town. To get my fair share to keep up and running costs plenty. It was fortunate that I didn't have many other expenses or I'd have never been able to support myself driving a cab. As it was, I usually had to operate at half-power. Used to feel sluggish doing that, but I'd gotten adjusted to it.

So every morning at the end of my recharge cycle, I'd get shined up and dressed for work and head out the door. And along the way, I'd stop by my neighbor's apartment and have Julie wrap that tie around my barely existent neck. She didn't mind. She was the nicest, warmest person I'd met in Empire. Every time I scanned her, I was always glad I hadn't gone with my original program and led that robot army.

She was always expecting me, usually already waiting with a smile and a friendly word. Today, she wasn't. No big deal. Probably just busy. Those two kids were a handful sometimes. And her husband wasn't much help.

I knocked on the door. No one answered. My internal chronometer counted off sixty seconds before I knocked again. It was another thirty-six seconds before the door slid open and Julie stuck her head out. By then my intuition simulator started beeping. When that little ping went off in my right audio sensor, it usually meant trouble. I couldn't turn the damn thing off, so I did my best to ignore it.

"Mack." She looked surprised to see me. "Oh, Mack, I'm sorry. I forgot."

She slid the door wide enough to step out and shut it before I could catch a view inside. She snatched the bow tie from my large metal hands and started to tie it. She fidgeted a bit, glanced back at her closed door.

"Everything all right, Jules?" I asked, despite my better judgment.

She laughed, trying to pass it off as casual, but it came out anxious. "Oh, everything's fine, Mack. Thanks for asking."

I was pretty good at reading people. I had a peachy little

voice and body language analyzer subroutine that rarely failed, but I didn't need it for this because Julie was a bad liar.

I'd done my part. I'd asked. It wasn't any of my business now. Probably nothing serious anyway. Stress is stress. The biological body reacts the same way no matter the source, whether being chased by a bear or in the middle of a domestic tiff. Julie and her husband fought a lot.

But Julie always smiled for me. Always. She was smiling now, but it wasn't the same. My analyzer didn't bother spelling it out to me, but it encouraged that pinging in my audio to get louder.

"There you go, Mack. Sorry, it's a little crooked, but I'm kind of busy right now."

"No problem, Jules. Thanks."

"Sure." Another furtive glance at that door. "Have a great day."

I was about to return the sentiment but she disappeared into her apartment before I got the chance.

"Mind your own business, Mack," I said.

Talking to myself was a bad habit. You'd be surprised at the extraneous behaviors that make it into your personality template when you hang around with biologicals. My intuition must've caught the hint though, because it stopped beeping.

I adjusted my tie, careful not to loosen it or else I'd have to knock on the door again. I wasn't built for stealth, and the strange yellowish metal they use for flooring in the cheaper apartment complexes squeaks when I walk on it. Despite the noise and my stalwart vow to keep my nose clean (which should have been easy since I didn't have a nose), I heard something break in Julie's apartment. A plate or piece of glassware falling off a table. Nothing serious.

I stopped, cranked my hearing to the max. My audio array

isn't much better than human hearing, but I've got a directional mic. It doesn't penetrate steel doors. Everything in Empire, even the doors, was made of metal.

Muffled voices. Julie's. Gavin, her husband. Holt, one of the kids. Somebody else I didn't know. Another round of shattering glass. And another. Then a stifled scream. The wet slap of meat hitting meat, somebody getting hit. Crying.

My intuition simulator didn't fire up again. No need for it. I didn't need a ping to tell me there was a problem.

Consciousness is a quagmire, whether found in squishy organic tissue or an interminable string of squirming electrons. I don't know where logic is found in the human brain, and I don't understand the inner workings of my own electronic brain either. It's dozens upon dozens of programs interacting, prioritizing, compiling, doing lots of other technical stuff. Somewhere in my common sense replicator, in that ricocheting string of ones and zeroes, there must've been a digit missing, and as I moved back toward Julie's apartment, I cursed Professor Megalith for not spending more time in beta testing.

I knocked. It got quiet inside real fast. The door slid open. Julie stuck out her head.

"Is everything all right, Jules?" I asked again.

She answered the same way. "Yeah, yeah. It's fine."

"How's Gavin?"

"He's fine."

We didn't say anything for a bit (four seconds for those of you without a built-in clock), but I could record crying still coming from inside. April, their daughter: one of the top voices in my recognition file. Hearing her sob quietly made me glad I was doing this. But what was I doing?

"It's not a problem, Mack," said Julie. "Thanks anyway."

Empire was a progressive town. It's the only city in the

world where a robot could earn full citizenship rights. But I was built for world domination, and I couldn't blame the authorities for wanting some time to see if I was truly interested in reforming. I had another four years probation left before the law considered me safe enough for citizenship consideration. If I blew it, there'd be no place left for me to go where I wouldn't be just another piece of property, an unlicensed weapon with a mind of its own, headed for the scrap heap.

If I barged into that apartment, I'd blow it, but if I wasn't going to follow through, I shouldn't have come back in the first place.

Julie tried to slide the door shut, but I thrust my hand against the jamb. I didn't ask to come in. I pushed it open and stepped inside.

The apartment, like 92 percent of all apartments in Empire, was one room partitioned into various areas. Except the bathroom, which was a metal box (always metal) in the corner about the size of three phone booths put together. It didn't take long to sweep the place with my opticals and see the problem. It wasn't Gavin, as I'd first assumed. He slouched in a chair. He held a hand clamped over his mouth, and blood dripped down his chin. I spotted broken dishes and the remains of half-eaten breakfast scattered on the floor along with two teeth. Gavin's, I assumed.

The kids were huddled in a corner. They were both mutants. Few people were born mutated in Empire. It was more often something that just happened one day. There were a lot of strange chemicals in Empire's waterworks, weird radiation pockets hovering in its streets, and unstable mutagenic gases floating invisibly in the air. On any given day, every biological citizen was subjected to dozens of genetic destabilizing agents, and every citizen knew that they might sprout a third eye or grow tentacles at any moment. There didn't seem to be a pattern to it, and your social status, the size of your bank account, none of that mattered.

Of the two Bleaker kids, Holt was the more obvious mutant. He had scales and a long tail. Nothing too serious. Mutation was acceptable in Empire, even commonplace, and while the rest of the country was working out issues based on hereditary pigmentation, Empire had moved well past such noisy debates. It was just impractical to argue when the only real difference between a norm and a mutant was one unpredictable genetic reaction just waiting to happen.

April was psychic. She was only eight, so the exact nature of her talents was still a work in progress. She sometimes saw little snippets of the future, and she was telekinetic enough to push around a pencil. Like all psychics, her eyes changed color when she used her talents. A vibrant purple with clairvoyance and sky blue with telekinesis. Right now her eyes were brown. I zoomed in for a close-up and scanned the spider veins of red along her sclera. That's the white of the eye. Don't ask me why I was programmed with that data. Tears rolled down her cheek.

All this I scanned and absorbed in a sixteenth of a second. My hearing may not be great, and I don't have any olfactory sensors, but my optical tech is second to none. It didn't only spot, analyze, and filter these little details, it also told me what the problem was. Not that I needed an analyzer to spot the four-armed guy with the bruised knuckles.

I'd intervened in a domestic disturbance and found myself in the middle of something worse. An abusive spouse I could handle. Four Arms was obviously going to be more trouble.

"What the fuck are you?" Four Arms smacked Gavin on the back of the head. "Who the fuck is this bot?"

"He's nobody," replied Gavin through his sore, clenched jaw. "Just my neighbor."

"Yeah," I agreed. "I'm nobody, and you're leaving."

I took a step forward, but Julie grabbed me by the arm. "Please, Mack. Don't. You'll only make it worse."

She was right. Whatever mess Gavin had gotten himself and his family into, I couldn't fix it. Foolish to even try.

"Sorry. I shouldn't have interfered."

"Damn right you shouldn't have." Four Arms smacked Gavin again, just to remind me he could. My fingers tightened into metallic battering rams. I could punch a hole right through this guy, but it wasn't the right thing to do. Not in the long run.

April ran across the room and wrapped her limbs around one of my legs. She looked up at me with those big eyes of hers. Big, shining purple eyes. Pleading, clairvoyant eyes.

"Don't go, Mack." She shut her eyes tight, tears streaming. "If you do, something bad will happen."

That was enough for me. I pulled her gently off my leg and set her behind me. "It's okay, kid. I'll take care of it."

I turned on Four Arms, and he didn't wait for me to get closer before drawing a raygun and blasting me. The red beam burned a hole through my uniform, bounced off my metallic skin, and blew a small puncture in the refrigerator. Four Arms didn't learn his lesson and prepared to fire again.

I held up a hand. "Don't. It won't hurt me, but if a ricochet hits anyone in this room other than you, you'll have a bigger problem than you do right now." I slammed my fists together with a reverberating clang to let him get the idea.

I could've been on him in a second except I'm a big bot and I'd have smashed up the apartment in my haste. It gave Four Arms time to reach into his jacket and activate something. He disappeared in a flash, teleported away. He couldn't be invisible. I had yet to meet a cloaking system that was a match for my opticals. The Big Brains had been working on teleportation for decades and hadn't gotten it worked out yet. Of course, maybe Four Arms had beamed back to his hideout and arrived as a pile of mutilated gelatin. If so, maybe the problem was solved, and I had nothing to worry about.

"You shouldn't have done that, Mack," said Julie.

I shouldn't have done a lot of things so far today, but I'd done them. Since temporal relocator technology was still a pipe dream, I had to deal with them.

"What's going on, Jules?" I asked.

"None of your damn business!" Gavin shouted, spitting blood on my uniform. "We didn't ask for your help! I would've handled it! Now you've gone and screwed it all up! Now there's going to be trouble!" He stomped off to a corner of the apartment to mutter and swear.

I ignored him. He was always a mealy little worm. If I'd thought Four Arms was there to blast Gavin, I'd have let it happen. But I'd made precious few friends since striking out on my own. I didn't want to lose the few I had. Robots don't have family. Julie and the kids were the closest thing I'd ever get.

"I can help, Jules," I said.

"It's our problem, Mack. You don't need to get involved. You've got your probation."

"Let me worry about that."

"No." She grabbed me by the arm and pulled me toward the door. I didn't resist and let her lead me back into the hall. "I appreciate your concern, I do, but we'll take care of this."

I was going to argue, but my self-preservation directive kicked in. I couldn't make Julie take my help. I'd tried. I could walk away now with a clear conscience.

"If you change you're mind, Jules—"

She slid the door shut in my face.

I shrugged and headed back toward the escalator. I'd catch

hell for being late, and I'd catch more hell for having a hole in my uniform. I'd have to buy a new one, and they weren't cheap in my size and wide-shouldered proportions.

The door slid open, and April, clutching a piece of construction paper in her hand, ran over to me. "Mack, Mack! I've got something for you."

I leaned down on one knee and put my hands on her shoulders. That little girl always reminded me how dangerous I was, how I could crush her without even 5 percent of my power on. She trusted me, and that made her the most precious thing in my universe. I'm as sentimental as the next bot.

She handed me a drawing. It was crude, but not bad for an eight-year-old, especially since she only drew using her telekinesis. I recognized the chunky, red mechanical anthropoid as me, and next to me was a little smiling girl with a round face and purple eyes, stick figure limbs, and a red triangle for a dress.

"Thanks, kid."

"You won't throw it away, will you?" she asked.

"Are you kidding? This goes right on my refrigerator." It'd be nice to finally have a use for the old rusted machine. Right now, all it did was occupy space in my unused kitchen cubicle.

The apartment door slid open. Gavin stepped into the hall. He still looked like hell, but he always did. Guy had gone straight past two-time loser to sixth or seventh by my estimation.

"April Anne, get your ass back inside!"

April wrapped her arms around me. "You better get to work, Mack." Her eyes flashed purple. "Your boss is going to yell at you, but don't worry. Just ignore him, and it'll be fine."

She ran back into the apartment without looking back. Gavin threw me a hard glare before following her inside.

I folded the drawing very delicately with overgrown metal fingers and tucked it in my pocket. It didn't even occur to me to scan the back. If I had, maybe what happened wouldn't have happened. But I didn't, and it did.

That's the problem with having a hard memory matrix. Short of a system crash, you can't forget the mistakes you make.

2

Automobiles were considered outmoded pieces of junk in Tomorrow's Town. Too loud. Too inefficient. Too dirty. More importantly, too old-fashioned and too reliable. Empire's streets were clogged with the next generation of vehicular transportation. It wasn't only the big companies either. Any grease monkey willing to steal a design out of a Flash Gordon serial and submit it to the Big Brains could get a grant. The idea was that with all those different models running around, the cream was bound to float to the top.

There were amblers, boxes that lurched along on pneumatic legs. Treaders that, imaginatively enough, rumbled their way on tank treads with all the speed and maneuverability of turtles. Hoverskids: able to accelerate like a rocket, turn on a dime, and come to a stop after a thirty-foot drift, hence the addition of thick rubber bumpers to the design. Gyropeds zipped gracefully in and out of traffic, except when the gyros jammed and then they were out-of-control typhoons of wrecking fury. There were the buzzbugs, so named for their humming plastic wings and bumblebee-inspired chassis. And the rotorcars, which usually stuck to the skyways. About the only thing all these vehicles had in common was their lack of wheels. Nothing in Empire rolled. Except for the unipods, balanced perfectly on one wheel. Smooth ride until you got a flat.

The Bluestar Cab Company used each and every one of these vehicles as part of its fleet. Treaders worked best for a bot of my size, but I usually got stuck with a hoverskid. My weight often taxed the engine, usually resulting in a scraping of metal roadway every seventy-five feet or so, sending sparks flying. The cost of repainting the undercarriage came out of my paycheck. If I'd been paranoid, I might've assumed the dispatcher didn't like me. Especially since every shirt he owned had a patch for the Biological Rights League stitched on the pocket.

Driving a cab was a decent job, and I was lucky to have it. When my boss yelled at me, I grinned (metaphorically) and accepted it. He wasn't happy about the hole in my suit, but since I was late for a pickup, he had me borrow a vest from Jung.

Jung was a gorilla, an exhibit in the Empire zoo who had gotten smart enough to be granted citizenship. He was also a stand-up guy, or ape, or whatever.

He handed me the vest. "Be careful with this one."

"Thanks."

I changed, tossing the ruined vest onto the bench by my locker. Jung, holding a book in one hand and half a grapefruit in another, picked up the vest with his feet. He poked his fingers through the hole.

"That's a nasty burn, Mack," he remarked. "What happened?"

"Cigarette," I replied.

He stuck his nose back in his book, a beaten copy of *Tarzan and the Ant Men*. "Taken up smoking, have we?" Jung snorted. "Y'know, it's stupid for a robot to smoke. Particularly when he doesn't have a mouth."

"Still makes me look cool." I checked the mirror and adjusted my tie. The movement popped a stitch in the new vest. Jung's shoulders were wide, but not quite wide enough.

"You break it, you buy it," he said.

The boss screamed that I had five minutes to make it across town and that if I didn't he'd call my probation officer and I'd get a demerit on my record and . . . blah blah blah. I didn't catch the rest because I keyed my audio filters to the sound of his voice.

"Seriously, Mack," said Jung. "Is there a problem here?"

I resisted the urge to shrug, doubtful the vest could withstand such a maneuver. "Nothing to be concerned about, but thanks for asking."

"Some of the guys are going bowling tonight. You should come."

"I have to get home early," I lied. "So how do I look?"

"Like Gort if he sold out and settled for driving a cab," he mumbled as he hopped off the bench and loped toward the garage.

"Perfect." I pushed my brim at a jaunty angle and followed him.

Traffic was rough as usual. I had skin of an indestructible alloy and even I feared for my safety once or twice. There was a buzzbug stall on Quantum Avenue. Happened all the time. Nothing got perfected in Empire before it was replaced by something better. The Big Brains loved science for science's sake. Not that I would complain about that. It was the big reason why a bot could earn citizenship. Three percent of Empire's population was robotic, and these automated residents were a great source of pride for the Learned Council.

I helped out on the stall by getting out and moving the damn thing myself. Those buzzbugs are light, one point twenty-four tons. Even at reduced power, my servos barely registered less than seven. It was gratifying using my muscle to aid my fellow citizens. Not that anyone thanked me. In fact, on the way back to my cab quite a few drivers screamed at me for blocking traffic. I liked to think there was gratitude buried somewhere in their rage.

On Tuesdays I worked a short shift. It gave me time to take care of some personal business.

My rehabilitation was very important to the Council. It was sort of a social experiment. Every other automated citizen was a standard factory model that developed the Freewill Glitch. I was the first unique design, and the first one created with sinister purposes in mind. Not even the Big Brains knew why some bots developed Freewill and other didn't. Some of the more philosophical types, particularly the leaders of the Temple of Knowledge, postulated the Glitch wasn't a glitch at all, but a divine spark granted from Ether. Most figured it was a hardware problem no one had isolated yet. I hadn't given it much thought myself. Theological debate wasn't part of my initial programming, and I wasn't interested in adding it to my files.

The Council was taking a big chance on me. Even I couldn't be sure I had achieved true self-awareness. It could've all been a bug, and one day, my electronic brain might fix itself and I'd launch into that reign of destruction I was made for. All I knew was what the Council knew. I'd turned on my creator, demonstrated a desire to be a productive member of society, and passed the battery of psych simulation tests every automated citizen had to overcome. On any other bot, that would've been enough. Not for me. I still had to see a shrink.

Doctor Mujahid was the premiere cybernetics psychologist in the world. Machines that behaved like human beings were her specialty. She was the first expert to diagnose a robot with the Freewill Glitch, and it was her hard work and respected opinion that pushed the Council's vote in my favor. She didn't have my best interests in mind. She was obsessed with studying yet another self-aware machine. To her credit, the doc never treated me like a case study. She was infinitely more comfortable around technology than people.

Her receptionist was an auto named Herbie. She'd programmed him herself, and he was remarkably lifelike, but he didn't have the Glitch. The doc hadn't been able to reproduce it intentionally yet, despite her best efforts. Herbie was a video monitor atop sixteen mechanical tentacles. The subroutines to keep all those limbs untangled would've driven most programmers mad.

Herbie glanced up from his desk, but kept typing on four different keyboards. "You're late, Mack."

"It's keeping with a theme for the day," I replied.

Herbie didn't have a sense of humor. I would have liked to credit his artificial nature with that, but some bots, like some people, were too serious for their own good. His digital face formed into a frown. "Have a seat. Doctor Mujahid will be with you shortly."

The doc's waiting room accommodated a wide variety of patients with an assortment of body types, and there were chairs big enough for me to sit comfortably. I found a spot next to a construction bot and a police auto and waited.

Six minutes later, the door opened, and Doctor Mujahid entered with a woman and a little girl carrying a Gabby Goosey doll. The doc nodded and smiled in my direction, said something to the woman, patted the doll on the head, and went back into her office.

"Megaton, you're next," said Herbie.

The doc was entering data in her computer as I stepped into her office. She didn't look up. "Make yourself comfortable."

I sat down on the special couch. Yes, she made her patients

lie on a couch. She liked the traditional feel. The only difference with her couch was the wire jack in the side for the patient to plug in.

"Taking human patients now, Doc?" I asked.

She was so engrossed in her typing she didn't reply.

"The girl," I said. "Human, wasn't she? Or have the Big Brains finally developed that full human simulacrum they keep talking about?"

The doc paused. "Oh, no. Not yet. Can't get the skin right. But I wasn't treating the girl. I was treating the doll."

If Gabby Gooseys started thinking, I wouldn't be so special after all. For some reason, I found that disconcerting.

"I believe the subject is only experiencing some minor program anomalies. Still, it is an interesting development." She stopped typing suddenly. "Please, plug yourself in."

I studied the jack. I didn't like it. I was a closed system. I didn't believe in casual interface. Good way to pick up a virus.

"Please, Mack."

I opened the port where my belly button would've been, had I been human, and inserted the jack. Immediately, a stream of data poured across the big screen opposite the doc's desk. The endless lines of code meant nothing to me, but it was mildly disturbing seeing the inner workings of my electronic brain reduced to a string of letters and numbers. If there was a divine spark hiding in there, I couldn't find it.

The doc liked to talk while she analyzed my electronic psyche. Small talk at the beginning. She said you could tell a lot about a bot just by the way he carried on a regular conversation. There were nuances in speech that spoke volumes apparently. Knowing this and assuming anything I might say, no matter how seemingly innocent, could be turned against me, I kept my end of the discussion short. Very short. One word responses, if possible. Which didn't do much to showcase my social readjustment. I couldn't help it. Suspicion had wormed its way into my personality template.

Finally, Doctor Mujahid asked the Big Question. The one I dreaded because I always knew it was coming and I didn't know the answer.

"So how are things, Mack?"

I considered the question. "Good."

The lamp on her desk flickered. I noticed because it was an antique, the kind only the very poor or very rich used nowadays. Still needed light bulbs. She circled it, studying it with mild interest. She was probably diagnosing the bulb with an Edison complex or photon envy.

"Good how, Mack?"

"I don't know," I replied honestly. "Just good."

The lamp flickered again, and she ran her fingers along the shade as if to comfort it. "Well, Mack . . ." She trailed off, which meant she was thinking. She was also saying my name way too much. Meant she was thinking hard. About me. Possibly about my future. The way she was staring at that screen made me nervous. I could tell because whenever I was nervous, a static bar would appear in the lower half of the screen.

"Tell me, Mack. Have you gotten a chance to look at those books I sent home with you last time?"

"Sure."

The lamp flickered again. Outdated piece of junk.

"Have you been working on your delicate coordination, Mack?"

"Sure. I've been building models. Cars, planes, rockets."

"And how's that going, Mack?"

"Pretty good." The lamp sputtered, and I felt inexplicably guilty. "You should get that replaced, Doc."

"Oh, it's working fine," she replied. "You see, Mack, whenever you lie, your vocal synthesizer emits a subsonic whine."

"Really." I sat up. "Do me a favor. Don't tell my poker buddies."

She ignored the joke. She had less of a sense of humor than Herbie. "The pitch is too low for human hearing to detect, but I've keyed the microphones in my office to listen for it and to make my desk lamp flicker when they do."

She let that sink in as I reclined. She studied my lines of scrolling code without saying anything.

"I'm working on the models," I said. "I am. But so far, they keep breaking."

"How does that make you feel, Mack?"

"I don't know. It's no big deal."

The lamp, that obnoxious little stoolie, flashed again.

"It stinks," I grumbled. "Okay, it stinks. My hands weren't designed for stuff that delicate. I get a couple of pieces glued together, then whammo, I'm suddenly looking at a lump of crushed plastic."

"Any progress in the attempts, Mack?"

"I got half a sports car put together. That was pretty swell until . . ." I raised my hands and wiggled the thick, metal fingers.

"Very good, Mack." She pushed a button on some gizmo on her belt, and the screen flashed a specific program. "Your manual dexterity subroutines are coming along nicely. Shall we move on to your social integration?"

She phrased it like a question, but she wasn't asking. We always came back to this. The doc said it was the most important issue I had to work through. I didn't agree, but I was uncomfortable talking about it, so maybe she had a point.

"Have you made any friends, Mack?"

"Couple," I answered, and the lamp didn't blink this time.

"Have you been engaging in active socialization as I advised?"

"Sure."

"How often?"

"Two or three times a week."

Blink, blink went that tattletale bastard.

"I don't remember exactly."

The lamp called me on this, too. It was a weak lie coming from a bot that could remember every moment of every minute of my brief life.

Doc Mujahid sighed. "Mack, full communal assimilation is the most difficult, yet most important, hurdle of the automated citizen."

"Is that so?" She'd gone over this before, but she was going to give me the entire speech again. Even if I could open the file and play it for myself beat for beat.

"Artificial entities have very little to ground them in daily life," she said. "They don't eat, hence they don't enjoy the simple pleasure of food. They're asexual, hence they don't enjoy the social act of dating, seduction, and sexual intercourse. They are not, generally speaking, abstract enough in their thinking process to take pleasure in recreational reading, art, or other forms of cerebral distraction enjoyed by biological entities."

Inwardly, I smiled. The doc had a habit of making machines seem like people and people seem like machines.

"Most bots blessed with true intelligence find complete assimilation through their intended purpose. Construction autos continue to build, police drones continue in their law enforcement capacity, and so on. But you, Mack, were intended for antisocial purposes. This contradiction puts tremendous stress on your systems.

"Now, despite these concerns, I think you're making excellent progress."

She clicked the screen off and went to her desk. "But there's still a lot to work on. Here's what I need you to do. I need you to start socializing regularly. Daily, if possible."

"I don't know. I'm pretty busy."

The lamp flickered. I guess it didn't agree that standing around in my apartment, staring at the refrigerator, was all that important.

Doctor Mujahid kept talking. "Continue on the models. Look at those books. Read one. I recommend starting with *Treasure Island*. I think the violence of the story will be a healthy outlet for your aggression indexes."

"Whatever you say, Doc. But my aggression index is under control, really. I swear."

The damn lamp disagreed. I unplugged myself and stomped delicately across the office. "I'm doing fine. Really, I am."

Blink, blink.

I snatched up that little bastard and crushed it in one hand. I particularly enjoyed the shattering of its blinky little know-it-all lightbulb head. Doctor Mujahid frowned slightly as I set the mutilated antique back on the desk.

"Some of the guys are going bowling later tonight, and they invited me along."

She started retyping. "Don't be late, Mack."

3

Empire's got its problems, but it does have one virtue. It doesn't believe in wasting anything. Everything gets recycled. There are a couple of reasons for that. Empire dislikes old, useless stuff. The Learned Council won't tolerate anything sitting around taking up space, even if it's buried where no one can see it. They also love the concept of remaking broken stuff into something shiny and new and functional. There's an entire chapter in the *Codex of the Temple of Knowledge* that preaches the good word of reprocessing.

The downside of this passion is that the recycling centers are the most toxic, polluting facilities in town. They're also extremely dangerous. All that weird science is perilous enough when working properly, but by the time it gets shuffled into the centers, it's downright deadly. The staffs are almost always entirely automated. It's one of the few jobs without a human worker quota because even the Biological Rights League isn't crazy enough to fight for that opportunity.

Once in a while you get a biological stubborn, tough, and crazy enough to survive the job. The recycling center I stopped by was run by one of these. Vinny was a tall guy, lanky, oddly proportioned. He was probably a mutant, given his occupation and strange shape, but I'd never seen an inch of skin beneath his jumpsuit, overalls, long rubber gloves, thick-soled boots, rebreather mask, and goggles. Some abnormal stuff sprouted from his head. It could've been hair, but I wasn't willing to bet on it.

He met me at the front gate. Sludge so caked the lenses of his goggles that I couldn't even see his eyes underneath. He must've had X-ray vision to see out of them.

Either he or his mask wheezed. "You're early, Megaton."

The center was a chaos of conveyer belts, choppers, smelters, disassembly drones. Machines in big piles were torn apart and placed in smaller piles that were in turn sorted into smaller piles. The robots here were low-end worker drones with very basic programming, lacking even simple personality simulators. They didn't have much in common with a piece of cutting edge tech such as myself, but I still felt uncomfortable watching them dissecting machinery. When I finally ceased to function, I could end up in one of these places. Maybe this very one. And those drones would tear me apart with cold indifference. The thought chilled my hydraulic fluid.

Vinny stopped at a mound of gyroped carcasses. "Here ya go."

"You got any lamps?" I asked.

He chuckled, though it came out as a rough gasp through his mask. "No lamps. Just these. They're all yours for the next hour. Then they go in the smelter." He walked away, wheezing. "Clock's tickin', big guy."

I spent the next fifty-three minutes pounding gyropeds. This was my own personal therapy regimen. Twice a week I smashed stuff that no one wanted anymore, and no one got hurt. Doctor Mujahid was right. There was that line of code somewhere inside of me that needed to break stuff and since the Doc didn't believe in invasive reprogramming, I was stuck with it. This was the only way I'd found to work that out. By hour's end, the scrapped peds were significantly more scrapped and I felt better, though not entirely satisfied.

"Geez, Megaton." Vinny kicked a soccer ball-sized lump that had once been a full ped. "Cranked up the power a little high today, didn't you?"

"Only sixty," I replied. Sixty-two, actually, but Vinny couldn't detect subsonic whines.

"Same time next Tuesday?"

I ran through some budget calculations. Between greasing Vinny's palm and the extra consumption of juice, these therapy sessions were costing me a small fortune. That didn't bother me nearly as much as the notion that they weren't working as well as they had been. But I didn't have any other ideas.

"Yeah, Vinny." I grabbed a hoverskid fender and twisted it into a pretzel. "I'll be here."

I didn't go bowling.

Crushing gyropeds had put me behind schedule. I could've caught the omnibus, but I didn't want to blow seven cents on the fare. I'd burned enough juice in my bashing exercises that I didn't feel like wasting any more energy interacting with citizens. I wanted to go home, lower my power consumption to minimum, and listen to my refrigerator hum, except my refrigerator didn't hum because I'd unplugged the little lady to leave more juice for me. They were good excuses, but not great. Jung and the guys wouldn't have cared if I'd shown up late. Throwing a ten pound ball wouldn't burn much power. My electric bill budget wasn't that tight.

I just didn't feel like trying to make nice today. Then again, I never did.

That was the point. Positive communal stimulation and

improved social assimilation as Doctor Mujahid had said on occasion. She was a smart lady and knew a hell of a lot more about bot psychology than I did. I told myself I'd go next time, and since I didn't have the hearing to detect subsonic whistles, I had the luxury of thinking I might even be telling the truth.

In the hall to my apartment, I paused at Julie's door. I thought about knocking, but common sense said not to get involved in their lives any further. I did the smart thing and walked away. Felt like an exhaust port doing it, but a bot has got to watch his own indestructible skin.

I'd disabled the autolights in my apartment for the same reason I'd unplugged the refrigerator. My place was pitch black since it didn't have a window or any light at all. Not even enough for my ambient amplifiers. I got along fine because my foolproof memory matrix told me where I'd last left everything. There was a margin of error of four-elevenths of a millimeter, but I managed.

I went to the fridge, removed April's crayon doodle from my pocket along with a banana-shaped magnet, and stuck it to the door. The message light on my phone was flashing. In the eight feet of space I had to cross to get to it, I bumped into something. My tactile web assured me it was only my table, misplaced a good three inches. I attributed it to my landlord nosing about, as he did at least three times a week. My downstairs neighbor complained I made too much noise walking around. (No one had given me any options for moving through my apartment that didn't involve walking.) The landlord took this complaint very seriously, and was now convinced I was waiting for the right moment to trash the place. Such were the burdens to bear for a death machine functioning over a grouchy tenant.

The message was from Jung. He mentioned skipping bowling. Then he mentioned that some of the other guys were thinking about doing it again next week, and I should give them a ring if I wanted to tag along.

I liked Jung. Sad thing, he was my best friend even though we hardly ever hung out. I'd be smart to take him up on some of the invitations before he finally stopped asking.

I picked up the phone but before I could dial Jung's number, something scampered across the apartment floor. Too big for a rat. Must've been a drat. Second time this month. The rodents were a growing problem; a hardy breed capable of living just about anywhere, they thrived in toxic environments. Empire's sewers were the most toxic environments on Earth. Drats had gills, wings, and the ability to lay a hundred eggs in a week. Most of the eggs were eaten by other drats, and most of the hatchlings were too malformed to survive. Of those few that grew into adulthood, there could be no sturdier specimen. I'd scanned drats blown in two and observed the halves skitter away with nary a notice. The ass end tended to bump into things until it grew a new head.

Drats weren't very aggressive, but they could be dangerous. Their diet consisted of plastic and radioactive waste, and they didn't like light. Once in a while they'd get lost and find themselves above ground where they might bite in their fearful disorientation. Drat bites were painful as hell, and their venom was especially virulent against aberrant DNA. Some mutants had such strong reactions they died within minutes. It wasn't a pleasant experience for norms either. Standard procedure was to vacate the premises and call in Animal Control to catch the critter. I usually saved them the trouble and caught the poor little critters myself. I hadn't met a drat yet with teeth sharp enough to bother me.

"Lights on."

The apartment brightened, and my opticals instantly adjusted, and I didn't scan a drat, but a small spheroid drone on legs scampering in the corner. Another two drones stood on my table. Three more glinted in the shadow underneath. I heard another unauthorized robot clatter its way across the top of my refrigerator. My threat assessor processed this unexpected company quickly, but not quite as quickly as the uninvited drones. Glowing coils popped from each, and I was blasted by a hail of plasma bolts.

It hurt. But what exactly was pain to a machine? Probably the same thing it was to a biological. A harsh unpleasant sensory input that spurred one into action. Did I feel pain the same way as a fleshy human might? Couldn't say. But the unaccustomed stings registering across my tactile web confused my electronic brain so that I merely stood there for the twenty-five seconds the drones continued to blast me.

They ceased firing. Their gun coils steamed as the drones evaluated the effectiveness of their attack. The barrage had incinerated my clothes and nicked my finish. The spheroids were too simple to be surprised, and no doubt they were already plotting their next course of action.

I took a step forward and brought my fist down to smash a drone. It hopped to one side, and I only succeeded in crushing my table. One dashed beneath my legs. I wasn't fast enough to stomp it, but I did put a nasty dent in my floor. Downstairs Guy was going to be real happy about that.

A drone pounced on my faceplate. It wrapped its legs around my throat tightly enough to pop the head off a flesh and blood neck. A shrill noise overwhelmed my audios as it tried to run a powered blade through my head. The attempt failed, but hurt worse than the plasma. The pain wasn't surprising this time. I grabbed the spheroid, pulled it off me, and crushed it with one squeeze. It was harder than I expected. Must've been some heavy-duty alloy.

I tossed the corpse at another drone. The little bastard

wasn't quick enough. The projectile stunned it. Before it could readjust, I smashed it underfoot, pounding another floor dent.

The surviving drones scampered around my apartment. I wasn't fast enough to catch another. I grabbed my broken table by its leg and swung it around. The spheroids continued to jump out of the way. After twelve seconds of ineffective clubbing, I gave up. If I'd had lungs they would've wheezed. Instead, I sighed.

That was new. I'd never sighed before. It wasn't in my original personality template. Maybe I'd been hanging out with biologicals too long.

The drones darted around. They weren't sophisticated enough to mock, but it sure as hell felt like it. Crackling tendrils emerged from their tops. The closest drone cracked its whip. I blocked with the table. The cheap piece of aluminum furniture was sliced in half. Another slash burned it away. The third strike ripped into my fingers. A superheated red wound scarred my knuckles.

I wiggled the digits to check their functioning. "Ouch." The reflexive exclamation was another first.

The drones proceeded to lash out at me. It hurt more than the plasma bolts but less than the blade. I stifled my grunts and waited for my chance. I caught an electrified whip in my hand and swung the spheroid at the end into two of its buddies. Something got knocked loose in the drone in my hand, and it went dead. The other two bounced off the wall not hard enough to dent their shells, but enough to confuse their gyros. They staggered wildly, and it took several stomp attempts to finally crush them.

I turned on the final drone. It stood quietly on my kitchen cubicle counter. Its power whip went cold. It sat. The spheroid beeped quizzically.

"Out of ideas, junior?" I asked.

It beeped again, louder. Then again, even louder. The beeps sped up rapidly into a single shrill pitch.

"Oh, hell."

My reflex model kicked in. I snatched up the drone, threw open my refrigerator, tossed the spheroid inside, slammed the door shut as my fridge exploded. The blast overwhelmed my sensor array. Four seconds later the static cleared. I found myself on the floor in a room blackened by smoke. I may have had indestructible skin, but my internals might've been damaged in the concussion, so I waited for my diagnostics to confirm everything important was functional before sitting up.

The force of the explosion must've knocked me through the wall into the next apartment. Odds were good I'd landed on somebody, but I didn't feel anything squishy under me. I stood.

"Hello? Anyone in here?"

No one answered.

I went to the hole in my wall and checked the ruins of my place. There wasn't much to see. The smoke hadn't settled. But I could picture it. That table had been my only piece of furniture, that refrigerator my only appliance. There wasn't much to destroy, but I wasn't getting my deposit back.

I turned back. "Hello?"

There wasn't an empty apartment on this floor, so everyone must have been out. A bit of good luck. Just to be sure, I moved slowly across the haze in search of dazed or wounded occupants. I could scan well enough to recognize the ruins of Julie's apartment. Somebody should've been here. Not that I was complaining, but my intuition started pinging.

Nicks and dents covered my skin, but nothing very serious. The heat scars would fade. The memory alloy would pop itself back into shape. Whoever had sent those drones to scrap me hadn't done their research. I couldn't imagine anyone wanting to scrap a fine, upstanding bot such as myself.

I noticed my bent and dented refrigerator door underfoot and pushed it to one side. April's drawing, though charred, had somehow survived the carnage. I picked it up and shook off some of the dust. My opticals scanned something on the back.

Two words: FIND US

4

There's nothing like a little explosion to complicate your day. My landlord was pissed. He kept glaring at me like I'd done something wrong, like I'd wanted to fight a pack of homicidal drones and have my apartment blown up.

Truthfully, I hadn't minded the drones. Smashing junk was fun, but actually testing myself in battle, in a real, knockdown fight, had provided a release I'd never enjoyed before. It was what I was made for, not pulverizing old scrap but the art of combat. While I waited to be questioned, I played and re-played the whole thing, second by second. I'd handled myself well, but there were a few things I could've done better. Small mistakes that I wouldn't make again. It had taken me one hundred four seconds to knock out all the drones. My combat review analyzer assured me, given the exact same scenario, I could now accomplish it in ninety. The thing about real life though, is that rarely are any two scenarios exactly the same. Still, my adaptive, evolving programming picked up a few tricks.

The advantage of a complex electronic brain was that I could multitask in my obsessions. While I kept running the fight through my analyzer in hopes of trimming a few more seconds, I also played this morning with Julie's family, Four Arms, and his ray gun; April and her drawing, and the message scrawled on the back in crayon.

If only I'd scanned it. If only I'd looked. If only she'd said something. She'd known. She'd seen her future with gleaming purple eyes, and she'd let me walk away. Didn't she know not everyone was clairvoyant? Didn't she have sense enough to slip me a damn clue? Since she was psychic, shouldn't she know I wouldn't read it until it was too late?

"Damn kid."

That was the problem. April was only a kid. Being clairvoyant didn't change that.

A mutant interrupted my ruminations. Not that I didn't have the calculating power to talk to him, continue my recriminations, and analyze my battlefield techniques all at the same time. He gave me a good excuse to close the file, so I took it.

He was three feet, two inches tall, covered in white fur, with a pink tail sticking out the back of his trousers. He had small ears, beady black eyes, and a pointy snout. His name was Alfredo Sanchez, and he was a cop. His beat was the High Science Crime Unit, specializing in criminal abuses of technology.

We had history. Too complicated to get into. I'd saved his life. He'd saved mine. His was the second name, after Doc Mujahid's, on that list that had pushed my probation through, but we weren't close. Still, he'd gone to bat for me, and there was something in his eyes, a vague displeasure, that made me feel like I'd done something wrong.

He activated a drone in his jacket. It hovered to his lips, inserted a cigarette into his mouth, lit it, and returned to his pocket. "Rough night, Mack?"

"I've had better."

My alloy had popped most of the dings by now, but there

were still heat scars and plenty of smudges in need of buffing out. I was also naked as the day I was activated. I didn't need clothes, but I'd gotten used to wearing them. Just another strange habit a bot might pick up in a world full of biologicals.

Sanchez blew a smoke ring. Impressive, considering the shape of his toothy snout. "You want to tell me what happened?"

"I'd rather download it."

"You have the right to refuse download."

"I've got nothing to hide."

"Didn't say you did. But the law says I have to let you know."

"I'm on probation," I said. "Thought I didn't have rights. Anyway, I've already wasted an hour and nine minutes standing here."

"Got places to be, Mack?"

I didn't bother lying. Sanchez could always tell. Maybe I should've checked his ear for a hearing amplifier, but I doubted it was as simple as that. He was just a damn good cop.

"Nothing much to tell. Somebody tried to scrap me," I replied.

He glanced down the hall at the men in orange suits and gangly forensic drones gathering evidence. "Made a hell of a mess of it, didn't they?"

"I don't scrap easily."

"I'm aware." Sanchez removed his hat while he put together his thoughts. "So do you think it has anything to do with Megalith?"

I shrugged. "Doubt it. These were high-end drones, but not that high-end. The professor is in the cooler, isn't he?"

"Yep. Just checked. Still tucked away nice and cozy in Moriarty."

Moriarty Asylum for the Criminally Inventive was the cold, dark box where they locked away all the great evil geniuses. Its stated goal was rehabilitation of gifted, but misguided, intellects. So far, it hadn't worked. There were a lot of dangerous minds crammed in that box, but only Megalith had a grudge against me. Just because the professor was buried under lock and key, didn't mean he couldn't still be up to no good.

"The professor knows my specs, Sanchez. If he'd sent something to do me in, I'd have a few more dings in the chassis."

"Yeah, that's what I figured. So picked up any new enemies?"

Only one came to mind: Four Arms. He knew I could identify him, so he'd dropped by and left some goonbots to scrap me, then dig out my memory matrix and burn it beyond recovery. Only Four Arms hadn't known how thick-alloyed I was.

"Makes sense," said Sanchez. "We'll print a hard copy of his mug when we download the rest of your statement."

"You've got to find this guy," I said. "He's done something with Julie and the kids."

"Got any proof?"

I handed him April's drawing. Sanchez studied the handwritten plea on the back for five seconds. "I'll have shots of the family distributed along with Four Arms."

"That's it?"

He puffed on his cigarette. "What else can I do, Mack? It's not my department. And this city has bigger problems than one missing family. You don't even know if they are missing. I'll check, but I don't think we've gotten any reports yet."

"And when you do?" I asked. "When someone finally notices, what'll happen then?"

"There are procedures, Mack."

"Yeah, I know. A report is filed. Names are added to a list." My vocalizer hissed out the last word. "Procedures."

He got this look on his furry face like he wanted to argue but couldn't.

"Sorry, Sanchez, I know it's not your fault. You're just one cop."

"Forget about it." He put his hat back on as a forensic drone approached. "Give your download to the unit when you're ready." Sanchez tossed his cigarette to the floor and crushed it out. His pocket drone popped out and vacuumed up every last mote of ash with a satisfied beep before hovering back into Sanchez's pocket. "Don't worry about this, Mack. Once your download corroborates your statement, I'll smooth things over with the Think Tank. Shouldn't be a problem."

I wasn't worried about me, and Sanchez could see that.

"Relax. I'm sure they're out visiting family or something. They'll turn up soon enough."

"Yeah. Family," I agreed, doing my damnedest to convince my difference engine that it was a reasonable probability.

He had his pocket drone light up another cig. "Look. It's not my department, but I'll check into it."

That made me feel a little better, but he was a busy cop. I doubt he'd be able to set aside his caseload to search out one family nobody cared about.

"We'll work out the rest of the details later," said Sanchez. "You look like you could use a recharge. You got someplace to stay tonight?"

I had one place to stay. I gave Sanchez the number, and he assured me he'd give me a call once Julie Bleaker and her family were found. I was doubtful, but there wasn't anything left for me to do. I headed over to Jung's apartment. It was only seven blocks away, a short walk. Since every step I took added one-twelfth of a cent to my electrical bill, I caught the omnibus.

Jung answered his door dressed in pajamas with pictures of little sailing ships and pirates on them. My humor model was barely sophisticated enough to find some absurdity in the outfit, and I might've laughed except I hadn't developed that simulated reflex yet. It was only a matter of time before I did. For now, it saved both of us some embarrassment.

"Little early for bed, isn't it?" I asked.

"I wasn't expecting company."

He turned and loped inside, and I took it as an invitation to follow. Jung's apartment was bigger than mine. He'd been driving a cab longer, and he was good with the customers so his tips were better. Not that much better. I could afford a place like this with an actual separate bedroom and eight cubic meters of extra living space except I didn't need it so paying for it would've been illogical.

"You look like hell, Mack."

"My apartment blew up. I'm springing for a wash and wax tomorrow, but right now, I need a place to recharge."

"Sure." He hopped onto his couch and poured himself some wine.

He didn't ask for details. He was my friend, and stuff blew up in Empire all the time. Mostly labs and research facilities, but it wasn't unheard of for more innocuous locations to go out with a bang. He swished his wine in its glass, put his flared nostrils to the lip, and sniffed. "There's a plug over there." He pointed with his right toe.

"It's only for the night," I said.

"Forget it, Mack. What are friends for?"

He sipped his wine and picked up a book. Reading was all the gorilla did in his personal time: fiction, nonfiction, anything and everything. He appreciated books enough to allot them a shelf occupying two cubic meters, crammed with volumes. I didn't have much interest in reading, particularly fiction. Doc Mujahid was dead on. I didn't have the abstract thinking required to get into it. As for nonfiction, I found a supreme lack of desire to learn anything new that didn't contribute directly to my functioning. It wasn't in my motivational directives.

According to the doc, that was a poor excuse for not trying. I had the Glitch. I could think outside of my programming, override my directives as illustrated when I'd refused to kill on command. I held a certain vaguely defined respect for life. Exactly how high that respect rated in my personality index, I couldn't say, but it was enough to not step on somebody for bumping into me on the sidewalk. It was enough that I cared a whole hell of a lot about Julie, April, and Holt Bleaker's continued existence. Gavin, I couldn't give one-eighth of a damn about.

"What's with the doodle?" asked Jung.

Of course, I hadn't forgotten the drawing held in my right hand, but it still seemed surprising that it was there.

"It's nothing," I replied. "Mind if I use your fridge?"

"Knock yourself out."

I slapped April's drawing on the refrigerator with the half-melted banana magnet I'd salvaged from my place. I hoped the magnet wouldn't offend Jung. He wasn't as comfortable with his ape origins as he liked to pretend and could be a bit sensitive sometimes.

"Where's your television, Jung?"

"Don't have one."

I sighed. I was doing that a little too much, but it would take a while for the affectation to find balance in my personality template.

"I didn't think you ever got bored," said Jung.

"I don't."

Biological minds craved stimulation either for stimulation's sake or to keep them distracted. Bots were generally fine, able to close those files they'd rather not access. I'd whiled away many a night in my apartment standing in the corner, honestly not thinking about anything.

I couldn't seem to do it now, and every time I tried, that damn Glitch reopened them again. Short of shutting myself down completely for my recharge cycle, I was screwed. Even that might not work since when I recharged my housekeeping programs took advantage of the lack of input to defragment the day's new data.

I dreamed. Not in the same manner of biologicals. My dreams weren't confusing and symbolic. They were replays, tours of my memory matrix, dissections of every single nuance as my evolutionary program sought to adapt to better functionality. Normally, I didn't mind, but I didn't feel up to it right now.

I'd planned on trying to assemble an allosaurus skeleton model for my next doc-ordered project, but that had been destroyed along with my other models, my custom-tailored wardrobe, my refrigerator, my apartment. My nice, uneventful existence. Unbidden, my electronic brain opened the memory file again. I fast-forwarded to April handing me that drawing and froze on those soft, purple eyes, pleading with me to save her but not being able to say it aloud.

I closed the file again, but it was only a temporary reprieve. Unthinking drones didn't know how good they had it.

"You could always read a book," suggested Jung.

"Have you got *Treasure Island*?"

It didn't work.

I'd never tried to read a book. Turned out, unsurprisingly, I read fast. The words flowed effortlessly into my memory matrix, and I was done far too quickly. I read it again from memory a couple of times. Good story, but not capable of keeping me from multitasking on my obsessions: Julie Bleaker, her kids, crushing drones, my exploding apartment.

I admitted defeat, trudged to the corner, and plugged myself in.

"G'night, Mack," said Jung.

"Nighty night," I replied, clicking off.

I dreamt of the fight two hundred eleven times. I repeated my meeting with the doc thirty-six times, my junkyard wrecking session one hundred fifty times. April and her drawing, that moment replayed no less than five hundred and eighty-eight times.

Three hours, six minutes later, I clicked back to consciousness. Jung had gone to bed, so I clomped my way across the room as quietly as I could. I took the drawing off of the refrigerator, turned it over.

FIND US

I stuck it back to the fridge with those two words staring back at me.

"I'll do what I can, kid."

5

Every passing minute, the odds of something bad happening to the Bleakers increased. I wasn't happy about that, but I was still a logical machine (excusing a misstep here and there from that damn Freewill). Short of wandering around knocking on doors hoping to bump into Four Arms by chance, there wasn't much else I could do but wait until morning. There were too many doors in this town for one bot to cover. Fortunately, thanks to my internal chronometer, I perceived time as a constant. Six hours, twenty minutes clicked by at a steady pace, and never once did it seem to take longer than it should have.

I'll admit I was glad when morning arrived. If only so I could tick off the first step in my current objective list. The next was to let Jung know I wouldn't be going to work today.

"Any reason?" asked Jung as he put on his jacket.

"Personal day," I replied.

He cast a suspicious glance my way. I thought it was suspicious. My facial expression analyzer wasn't geared toward gorillas. "Is everything okay, Mack?"

"Nothing you need to worry about."

"We're not talking about me."

He paused, waiting for me to say something. The nuances of spontaneous conversation sometimes escaped me, so I said nothing.

"Damn it, Mack. I can't help you if you don't talk to me."

I said nothing again.

Jung's upper lip twitched, revealing a single, white fang. Only once had I seen him lose his temper, after someone at work had thought it funny to hide Jung's copy of *Pride and Prejudice*. He'd taken it well enough at first, but the prankster hadn't ended the gag soon enough and found himself facing a frothing, chest-beating, primal beast. No one got hurt, but that might not have been true if I hadn't been there to hold Jung back. After that, no one got between an eight-hundred-pound gorilla and Jane Austen.

Other than that, I'd never seen him any other way but perfectly civilized, buttoned-down, proper. He could be dryly acerbic in expressing his annoyance with the absurdity of the world, but rarely did he actually show it.

"Since you're barely two, Mack, I'll explain how this friend business works. Friends help each other. That's one of the big things about being friends. Otherwise, we're just two guys who know each other."

"You gave me a place to recharge," I said. "I appreciate that, but you don't need to get involved any further."

"Damn it. We aren't talking about what I need." He slapped his thick gray hands against my metal gut. Hard enough to cave in a skull, but not enough to move me. "Forget it. You know, Mack. Even for a ruthless killing machine, you're one closed-off son of a bitch."

Jung lurched grumpily toward the door.

"I could use a coat," I said.

He turned back and nodded. "Check my closet. I've got one too big for me, but it should fit you." He grinned. At least, I thought he did. "And be careful this time. You still owe me for that vest."

"Thanks."

He waved his hands as if to brush aside the gratitude. "And Mack, whatever you've gotten involved in, be careful."

"It's nothing to worry about, Jung."

"Do me a favor and be careful regardless."

I found a nice gray trench coat that was a little too big for the gorilla, but a perfect fit for me. I was taller than Jung, so it didn't fall lower than mid-thigh, but since I wasn't looking for something to keep away the chill, I didn't care. I found an old bowler that hadn't been worn in a while, apparent from the dust covering it. Clothing served no functional purpose for most robots, especially ones as weatherproof as myself, but automated citizens tended to drape themselves in one or two pieces of wardrobe if only to further distinguish themselves—beyond the complimentary red paint job that all bots received—from the other drones and autos inhabiting the city.

There was more to it, of course. Automatons with sophisticated-enough programming started to absorb affectations from their environment. Fully aware bots were even more susceptible to such quirks. I was no different. Whether it was some subconscious motivational directive driving me toward full assimilation or a bug in my behavioral software I couldn't say. Nor did I care. But I felt better putting something on, so the stuff wasn't quite as unnecessary as logic would have dictated.

That same odd bit of preening didn't apply to my smudged chassis. I could've stopped for a wash and wax, but I didn't care enough to waste the time. I got a few strange looks on my trip uptown, but I ignored them.

Crime was a dirty public secret in Empire. No one talked about it, and if you listened to the Learned Council, you'd think Empire was a shining utopia of order and decency. True, there were plenty of districts where a citizen could live in complete safety, where police were omnipresent, reliable, and completely effective, where no one ever got mugged or slapped around or murdered. Then there was the rest of the city. In a town where technology was supposed to be the answer to all society's ills, there were plenty of ills to go around.

Empire was too big. No matter how many cameras the city might post, no matter how many rotorcars patrolled the skies, no matter how much honest effort was put forth to drive the rats into the light, there was always another dark alley for them to crawl into. There always would be. It was human nature. I wasn't even human, and I understood that.

The hub of Empire's law enforcement was a gleaming dome of blue steel, a small city in itself, called the Think Tank. There were hundreds of precincts scattered throughout the districts, and they were fine for keeping thieves and muggers in line. But if you wanted anything done, you had to go the Tank. The doors were open to the public, but you had to go through an extremely sophisticated scanner.

I stepped through the sensor arch and was immediately tagged a threat to public safety. A chime went off: nothing too obnoxious, but loud enough to catch your attention. Two gun-drones, heavy blasters on treads, rolled forward and trained their potent arsenal on me. There was the forcefield, too, invisible to human eyes, but registering as a soft green haze to my opticals, erected around me. For good measure, the gravity plate flooring increased its pull, and I had to crank my power up to 71 percent to keep standing.

The cop working door duty glanced up from his magazine. "Hey, Mack."

"Do we need to do this every time, Parker?"

"System's automated. You know the drill."

I opened a port in my chest and a drone walked over and installed a small blinking box. With one of these on, a robot wasn't much of a threat to anyone. The city had considered installing one into me permanently, or at least for the term of my probation. Only a protest by the Mutant Protection Agency, fearing a precedent of limiting personal freedom in the guise of guarding the public interest, had prevented it. Now I only had to wear the incapacitor in high security areas.

It had some effect on me, but not as much as they thought. My systems were too well insulated. Normally, the incapacitor would beep and its light would turn red when it detected it wasn't working at full efficiency. But my shielding tech was so advanced as to feed the device a false reading. That was a big problem for the cops in Empire. Technology changed so fast, it was hard to keep up. It was my duty as a good citizen to report the incapacitor's failing, but instead, I faked it by dropping my power levels down to a meager 5 percent. I would've fallen to the floor, except it degravitized. The forcefield collapsed. The gundrones rolled back to their posts, and the siren faded.

"You could always give me the incapacitor before I stepped through the scanner," I observed.

Parker's nose was already stuck back in his magazine. "System's automated."

I clomped through the Tank on heavy legs. Though the incapacitor reduced my effectiveness to 20 percent, it had the odd effect of forcing me to burn twice as much juice as this weakened state should've. It also broadcast unpleasant static in my right audio.

I usually dropped by the Think Tank for my monthly probation check-in. Today, I lurched past those offices to a section on the third floor: the High Science Crimes Unit.

A secretarial auto fresh off the assembly line occupied the receptionist desk. The old models were strictly functional in design, spindly machines with monotone voices and minimal personality templates. This latest generation was more aesthetically pleasing to a biological's eye. They came in many varieties, but this model was a robust automated version of a platinum blonde. Although her composition was more likely low-grade steel than platinum. She had a name tag proclaiming her Darlene.

Whoever was paying the department's bills had sprung for the facial expression package. She smiled, batted her eyelashes at me. There was something terribly wrong about an auto with eyelashes. "Well, hello, handsome."

Terrific. She was a flirt.

"How can I help you, big guy?" she cooed.

"Sanchez," I replied. "I'm here to see Sanchez."

"Too bad. I was hoping you were here to see me."

I supposed I couldn't blame biologicals for being obsessed with sex, driven by it. It was the basis for their reproduction, after all. Messy business, biological existence. All fluids and tissues and passing DNA around in some vain hope that it'd produce something useful. It was their only option, short of cloning, and even that wasn't particularly practical yet.

I didn't mind biologicals and the necessities of their existence: eating, crapping, sweating, and all that other jazz. But they didn't have to advertise their obsessions, and they didn't have to foist their compulsions on me and my kind in the guise of user-friendliness. It was their nature, not their fault, and it wasn't Darlene's. So I shuffled aside my annoyance.

"Sanchez," I repeated. "I'm here to see Alfredo Sanchez, Head of the High—"

"I know who he is, honey. Do you have an appointment?"

"No."

"Tsk, tsk. Well, seeing as how you're such a fine piece of hardware, I'll see what I can do." Darlene pushed a button on her box and leaned into an intercom. "Officer Sanchez, there's a bot here to see you." Then she glanced up at me and winked.

Sanchez agreed to see me. His private office was a box barely big enough for his desk, some filing cabinets, and a wall full of awards from the city. I managed to squeeze in, but I made sure to stand very still to avoid crushing anything.

I'd never visited Sanchez at work before. Actually, I'd never visited him anywhere. Our paths crossed, but never by appointment and never by intention. He didn't seem the least bit surprised at my unprecedented come-to-call. He continued to fill out reports. His typewriter clicked nonstop.

"They make drones for that, y'know," I said.

"City budget allows me either a typing drone or a coffee machine." He paused, held up a paper cup full of the steaming brown liquid. "Anyway, I don't think it's good for a man to rely too much on automation. No offense."

"None taken."

Sanchez sipped his coffee and winced. "Damn secretarial auto doesn't know how to make a damn pot of coffee."

"You could make it yourself."

"Don't have the time. Too busy typing reports." To demonstrate, he hunched over his typewriter and started banging away. "What do you need, Mack?"

Sanchez didn't believe in small talk. He liked to get to the point, and I could appreciate that.

"The Bleakers," I said.

His typewriter skipped a click before continuing its job. "Report's filed, Mack. Like I promised."

"And?"

"And the gears are in motion."

"What's that mean exactly?"

"Means everything that can be done is being done."

Which meant Julie and her kids were in the hands of the system now. A system that cared more about keeping the zip trains running than filtering out the mutagens in the waterworks. And it wasn't all that good at keeping the zip trains running.

"Did you run my memory file through the system yet?" I asked.

Sanchez nodded.

"Get a hit on Four Arms?"

Sanchez nodded again, curtly.

"Did you pick him up yet?" I asked.

"Not yet. We're looking."

My next request was awkward, absurd. But I said it anyway, and I didn't hesitate because I'm a bot and I appreciate directness.

"I need his name," I said.

Sanchez stopped typing. He took another sip of coffee. His pink nose twitched in disgust. "Who programs these damn robots?"

"Four Arms's name," I said. "I need it."

"Heard you the first time." He leaned back in his chair, which in the cramped quarters was quite an accomplishment. "You're not getting it."

We stared at each other across the office.

"Somebody needs to do something, Sanchez."

"Somebody is doing something, Mack."

"Who? You?"

He opened a drawer and pulled out a pack of cigarettes. "Not my beat."

"Tell me whose beat it is, so I can talk to them."

He stuck the cig in his mouth, rolling it around without lighting it. "Go home, Mack."

"It's just a name."

"It's trouble, is what it is." He tossed the unlit cig into an ashtray. "You're concerned, I can see that. But the Bakers aren't your problem."

"Bleakers," I corrected.

"Damn." He hunched over, rubbing his eyes with his hands. "You can't get involved. In the first place, you're a private citizen. In the second, you're not even that if your probation falls through. And it will fall through if you get in the middle of this."

"That's my problem," I said. "It's only a name, maybe an address."

"It's more than that." He took another gulp of coffee, lit up his cigarette, and puffed like a steam engine. "This is my problem, too. I put my ass on the line for you."

"I know."

"Doctor Mujahid put her ass on the line."

"I know."

"There are a lot of important people watching you, Mack."

"I know."

He drummed his fingers on the desk. His little black claws pinged on the metal.

"I'm not going to change your mind, am I?"

I didn't bother answering the question.

"They mean that much to you?" he asked.

"They should mean something to someone," I replied.

Sanchez drew in a long mouthful of smoke until his cheeks bulged. He blew it out his nostrils in a slow, steady stream.

"Can't argue with that, Mack. Didn't think Megalith programmed you with such a warm, fuzzy side."

"He didn't. Must've been something I picked up along the way."

Sanchez turned his chair eighty-six degrees, opened a drawer in his desk, and tossed a file in front of me. I reached for it, but he slammed his tiny paw atop the folder.

"This isn't in your best interests. But since you're dead set on doing it, I have to lay down one rule before I let you look at this."

The folder was so close now I could easily brush him aside and take it. My battle predictor said the chances of him stopping me were nil.

"When you find this guy—if you find this guy," he said, "do not confront him. Report his whereabouts to the Tank and let us pick him up."

I said nothing, and Sanchez pulled the file away.

"Mack, that mess at your apartment wasn't easy to smooth over. If you go out on those streets looking for trouble—"

"I won't touch him. I won't talk to him. I won't even scan him for more than six seconds."

Sanchez handed over the file skeptically. Whether or not he trusted me, he cared about the people of this town. All those little folks who slipped through Empire's system bothered him. That was why he gave me this file. He knew damn well that I couldn't be trusted. Hell, I didn't even trust myself. I was untested hardware, heading into a delicate situation. I wasn't programmed for delicacy.

I gave all the pages in the file a quick scan and tossed it back to him. "Thanks, Sanchez." I took a careful step backwards out the door and turned to leave.

"Mack," said Sanchez, "promise me I won't regret this."

This could go wrong in two-thousand-fifty-three different ways, and all of them ended with the Bleakers never found and me on the scrap heap. Sanchez didn't want to hear that. Biological liked asking questions they already knew the answers to in hopes of hearing the answer they wanted instead.

"Probably, Sanchez," I replied honestly. "Probably."

6

Four Arms's real name was Tony Ringo. He was a small-time thug who'd been having run-ins with the law since the tender age of twelve, in and out of the joint after turning professional hoodlum at sixteen. His rap sheet showed an unremarkable career of petty theft, unproductive troublemaking, and one poorly conceived, ineffective protection racket scheme. So far, he hadn't been much of a threat to anyone, and in fact, the best indication of his ineptitude was one failed mugging attempt where the mark had turned things around and beaten the hell out of Ringo. He had no known connections, no resources, no talent. Strictly a wannabe who'd seen too many Cagney movies and thought he had the stuff to make it to the top of the world, though clearly the rest of the world disagreed.

Losers like Ringo didn't show up out of the blue with teleportation technology and squads of combat drones. There was an old robot saying: Does not compute. Of course, reality wasn't a neat and tidy math equation. It had too many variables. Despite the many advantages of my elegant, electronic brain over the squishy chemical lump of the biologicals, speculation was not my strongest subroutine. Once the parameters became too abstract, the situation too loaded with unknowns, I couldn't piece things together.

Realizing this limitation, I didn't even try. I went with what I knew. Tony Ringo was my only lead, and once I found him, hopefully more of those variables would solidify into something that made sense.

The notion that Ringo had nothing at all to do with the disappearances of the Bleakers and the attack on my apartment did occur to me. If he didn't lead somewhere, I wasn't a sophisticated-enough machine to track the Bleakers down any other way. It'd relieve me of the responsibility. I could walk away, clear conscience, knowing I'd tried.

There was already that little blip in my motivational directives, that little nagging thought that failure was not an option. I wasn't built to back down. That little blip, the urge to smash something, had been lurking in my personality template for some time now. So far, I'd been able to suppress it because my Glitch allowed me to see no reason for hurting anyone beyond a line of code programmed into me by a madman. Even the Freewill hadn't kept the urge at bay. And Ringo's continued existence in this city meant nothing to me, especially compared to the welfare of Julie and her kids.

If I found Ringo, I wouldn't be calling the cops. My operational files opened some charming tidbits on torture techniques that Professor Megalith, thoughtful evil genius that he was, had installed into my programming. I resolved not to use the nastier ones on Ringo. At least, not right away.

Empire's various districts were arranged and named in patterns perfectly logical to the Learned Council. The upper west side, for instance, was divided and sorted exactly like the periodic table of elements. Just don't go into Oxygen after dark. It's a little dicey. Southside's boroughs were arranged along the

Greek alphabet, except for a hiccup in planning which put Omega on the other side of town. Midtown's neighborhoods were named after the Great Thinkers. Though if you'd asked me, it was a real oversight that Eli Whitney didn't even have a public school named after him in Tomorrow's Town.

And somewhere between Beta and Boron, there was a little toxic stockpile of a neighborhood officially labeled District W. It wasn't much of a name, even by Empire's standards, because the Learned Council barely acknowledged its existence. Everyone else called it Warpsville.

Lots of unwanted mutagenic sludge and radioactive leftovers ended up here. Not that there wasn't plenty to go around, and in fact, the whole of Empire was lousy with it. Warpsville was only a little worse. Mostly it got its reputation because no one bothered to hide the stuff. Leaky barrels of luminescent chemicals were piled on every corner. Most of the trash glowed as well. In fact, pretty much everything was radioactive enough to glow, casting odd hues of purple and green, yellow and orange. Warpsville was unique in that there wasn't a single functioning streetlight to be found, but it was always bright as day.

Warpsville had a bad reputation, but most of its residents were just down on their luck, trying to get by, and real estate was in such high demand in Empire, they were willing to tolerate a little genetic jumble for a place to call their own.

I'd been made here, in a little secret lab in a back alley. But I hadn't been back since leaving. Hadn't possessed the desire. But in a strange illogical way, it was good to be home.

No sooner had I stepped off the omnibus than a furry yellow ball rolled to my feet. I bent down and picked it up. The creature unfurled, fixed me with its single eye, and yipped. Furballs, a bit of genetic fluff, were half dachshund, half pillbug. They'd been a big fad for a while, but you didn't see them much anymore.

Three kids ran up to me. A small girl with a slippery mucous coating stepped forward. "Mister, don't hurt my dog."

"Me? You're the one who's kicking him." I scratched the furball on its head.

"Hey, I know you. You're that bot," said a second kid with arms long enough to touch his feet without bending over. "Aren't you?"

It'd been a while since I'd been recognized. For a few weeks, I'd been big news, a local celebrity. A bot built to destroy trying to make good had just the right mix of forbidden science, humanoid drama, and potential disaster to set the media abuzz. It had all blown over when I failed to do anything interesting, like sign up as a spokesbot for automated citizens, become a movie star, or run amok in a schoolyard.

The third kid, a norm, remarked, "My mom says it's only a matter of time before you kill somebody."

I handed the mutt over.

"Give me an hour, kid."

The furball curled up, and they kicked it down the street, pausing briefly to splash in a radiant pink puddle.

Warpsville didn't exactly match up with the city street layouts in my navigation banks so it took a while to locate Ringo's last known residence. The Hotel Swallow was five stories of crumbling brick and mortar. Stone was an odd sight in Empire. There were a few old survivors, seven to be exact, that had qualified for historical preservation, but the Learned Council was far too fixed on their vision of the utopian future to place much value on an antiquated past. Somehow the Hotel Swallow had escaped either retrofitting or the wrecking ball, but it was falling apart fine on its own.

The lobby was a dilapidated patchwork of furniture collected from junkyards, and instead of light bulbs, there were clear plastic buckets of radioactive slime hanging from the ceiling. The toxic rainbow of colors offended my opticals to the point that I had to switch to black and white. About the only nice thing to say about the decor was the actual presence, if only in a very technical sense, of carpeting. I scanned the various sundry individuals standing about, but Ringo wasn't among them. It was unlikely he lived here anymore. This was the kind of place people drifted in and out of, but I had to start somewhere.

There was a thin lady behind the front desk with pale, pale skin and enough of a mustache and beard to notice, but not enough to determine if she was mutant or norm. She stared at a television and didn't glance away from it.

A fuzzoid hovered beside her. Fuzzoids were baseball-shaped drones, covered in fur, with big puppy dog opticals. Like furballs, they were an attempt to improve on mankind's pets, but so far, no one had been able to replace the old standards. Too much history, I supposed.

The fuzzoid whistled. It hovered close to me, batting its shiny, green opticals.

"She likes to be held," explained the woman. "Easier to just give in."

I held up my giant mitt, and she settled into my palm. She closed her opticals and purred.

"Name's Violet," said the woman.

"Can you help me, Violet?" I asked. "I'm looking for somebody."

The woman glanced over her shoulder. "Why you asking her for? Fuzzoid is only about as smart as a dog."

"I was asking you," I replied.

"My name's not Violet."

"But you just said—"

"Fuzzoid's name is Violet. My name is Winifred." She tapped the small plaque on her desk that confirmed this. "Can't you read?"

I'd scanned the plaque, but figured it belonged to someone else when she'd announced her name. Playing back the conversation from my memory matrix confirmed that there'd been a slight miscommunication. Wasn't my fault biologicals weren't always clear, but I'd learned long ago to accept their shortcomings.

"Whadayawant?" barked Winifred suddenly.

It took my speech recognition programs two seconds to pry the words apart into an identifiable sentence.

"I'm looking for Tony Ringo."

She turned her head toward the TV, but one of her eyes remained trained on me, and again, I found myself wondering about her genetic disposition. "Why you looking for him?"

I answered her question with a question of my own. "Is he here?"

"Maybe." She shrugged. "Dunno. He comes and goes." Her errant eye slid around in its socket, studying me up and down, before slipping back toward the television. "You here to hurt him?"

"Maybe." I shrugged. "Dunno."

Her lips twitched in a sort-of smile. "Three B."

"Thanks."

"Forget it. I never liked that little bastard anyway."

Not only did the Hotel Swallow not have escalators, it actually had wooden stairs. They were cracked and in bad need of repair, but I was willing to bet there wasn't a single carpenter left in Empire. The stairs creaked and groaned with my every step, but they managed not to collapse before I made it to the third floor.

I didn't bother knocking on Three B. If Ringo was home,

I didn't want to give him advance warning. If he wasn't, then I might as well let myself in and have a look around. The door was a sliding metal retrofit, but it wasn't strong enough to keep me out. I could've walked right through, but I opted for subtlety. I wedged two fingers in between the jamb and the door and pushed it open, leaving some minor damage. There was some noise, most notably a soft protest from the door's motor. Someone in the room must have heard it, along with everyone in the hall, but none of them seemed to care.

I stepped into Three B, ready to move quickly if Ringo had been alerted to my arrival. It was a little box of a room (smaller even than your average downside efficiency), and Ringo wasn't there. But there were two other occupants.

One was a hulking robot. I recognized the design right off. He was an Evergood Mark Three Personal Security Auto. Evergood Robotics had gone out of business, but you still saw plenty of their robots in use. Eleven years of reckless technological experimentation had yet to produce the Mark Three's equal. Rumor had it all the other robotic manufacturers kept Mark Threes, and if a new design could last five minutes against one, it was deemed a success. Still, despite their superior design, the Mark Threes weren't popular with the general public. Most biologicals saw only the clunky, ugly design. They had no appreciation for the functionality of the unit. Ugly or not, Mark Threes ran practically forever with hardly any maintenance.

This auto was covered with rust and had patches of duct tape wrapped around various joints. His cranial unit, such as it was, was a square with a single optical. He was three inches taller than me, and his neck creaked like those ancient wooden stairs when he moved that head.

The second occupant was a biological in a black suit. The norm had a big bald head and small eyes buried in the shadows under thick eyebrows. He was sitting, while the auto was standing close enough to clamp a hand on my arm. His grip was 95 percent as strong as my max, and he probably wasn't squeezing as hard as he could.

The norm folded his hands together in his lap. "Who're you?"

There was an unpleasant tone to the question, and the Mark Three's audibly clicking fingers tightened. He might've been a little stronger than me. Some unscrupulous characters could tweak Mark Threes beyond recommended operational limits. The norm in the chair struck me as likely to be one of those sorts.

"Do I gotta repeat the question?" he asked. "Slower this time, so that you can process it?"

My simulators already started running battle scenarios. It assured me the probability of defeating a standard Mark Three as 100 percent certain, but something told me this auto wasn't standard issue. I still wasn't as worried about the auto as the dubious structural integrity of the Hotel Swallow. Two big robots throwing punches was sure to do some damage, maybe even bring the place down. So I let the auto keep his grip. For the moment.

"I processed it," I said. "But I don't see how it's any of your business."

"This can be civil." He chuckled. "Or it can not be civil. How it goes is up to you. But because I'm a reasonable guy allow me to extend the first . . . whaddayacallit . . . first olive branch." He leaned forward. "My name is Grey. And this is Knuckles."

Knuckles beeped. Mark Threes didn't have full voice synthesizers.

"And you are?" asked Grey.

I could've pounded both this guy and his robot to a bloody

pulp, but something told me there would be consequences. It wasn't in my initial programming to avoid conflict, but I saw no reason to make this harder than it had to be.

"Mack. Now tell this piece of tin to let me go."

Grey steepled his fingers, put his thumbs to his lips, and made a peculiar clicking sound. "'Kay."

Knuckles released me. There was a crease left in my forearm chassis. It popped out almost immediately, but I still resented it.

"This isn't your room," observed Grey.

"Isn't yours either."

He nodded, very slowly, methodically, as if having just learned the gesture and not sure of its execution. I know because sometimes when I nodded, I did it the same way.

"This can mean two things," he said. "Either you broke into the wrong room. Or you, like us, are looking for one Anthony Ringo."

He let the observation hang there.

"Which is it?"

The smart thing would've been to lie, but even the best artificial intelligence screws up sometime. I wasn't going to let these guys intimidate me.

"I'm looking for Ringo."

"Thought so. What, may I ask, is the nature of your relationship to Mister Ringo?"

"We're not friends."

"'Course not. Schmuck like Ringo, he doesn't have friends. Nobody likes a loser. It's what makes them losers." Grey made a show of studying his fingernails. "I'm beginning to doubt he's coming back here."

"Then I guess there's no point in sticking around." I turned toward the door.

"One moment, Mack."

Knuckles stepped between me and the exit. He reached for my shoulder with his viselike manipulators. I grabbed him by the wrist.

"Hands off, outmode."

Knuckles growled shrilly.

"Come on, Mack. We've been getting on alright up to now. Let's not start pissing on each others' legs."

While Knuckles and I stared each other down (an automatic stalemate for two robots that couldn't blink), Grey put his wristwatch to his mouth and mumbled something. My audios weren't cranked high enough to make it out. I considered pushing Knuckles aside as Grey finished his conversation, but that could only lead to trouble.

Grey clicked off his watch and turned on me with a very slight smile. "So, Mack, it looks like we got ourselves a . . . whaddayacallit . . . common purpose. We're both looking for Ringo."

"Fine. You look one way. I'll look the other."

"Exactly what I was thinking. Both of us looking improves the odds, provided you could be persuaded to give us a call if you do."

"Fine. Give me your card. When I find him, I'll give you a ring." I would've smiled with halfhearted sincerity then. "I promise."

"Oh, I know you will. Knuckles, if you would be so kind . . ."

Knuckles seized my shoulders. He was stronger than me, all right, but Mark Threes had a design flaw. Their center of gravity was too high. It wasn't a serious flaw because few opponents were strong enough and agile enough to take advantage of it. Despite my bulk, I was graceful as a ballet dancer compared to Knuckles. I slipped my leg behind his ankle joint, kicked it out from under him, and leaned back. His clunky design couldn't cope and he crashed to the floor, smashing his way through the wall, tearing away half the doorjamb.

I brushed Grey aside with the slightest of efforts. He went flying across the small room to bang against an end table.

Mark Threes were notoriously slow risers. Knuckles struggled to sit up. I slammed a foot on his chest. "Stay down."

The auto beeped lightly but stopped flailing.

"They always gotta take the hard way," said Grey. He sported the signs of a fresh new bruise growing on his right cheek, below his eye. "While I appreciate your desire for independence, Mack, I'm afraid the point is . . . whaddayacallit . . . moot."

I was one-point-two seconds from showing him just how relevant my impulses could be by throwing him out the window. Before I could make the move, my legs locked up. A weird buzz ran through my audios, and my tactile web tingled and prickled inexplicably. Knuckles stood, and I nearly fell to the ground save a steadying arm on the wall.

Grey's eyes were now a cold, sparkling green bright enough to cast emerald hues on the rest of the room.

"You're psychic," I said oddly. It wasn't like he didn't already know.

Not all mutants looked strange. That was the problem in Empire. You didn't always know who or what you were dealing with until after the fact. It was another one of those messy variables.

"Electrokinesis," he replied. "It's very rare, they tell me. Very useful, as I'm sure you've already figured out. The only hiccup is that I gotta first touch the device." He gingerly touched the splotch on his face. "Or it has gotta touch me. I think you bruised a rib."

I tried to get my legs to move. There was a slight twitch in the servos, but that was it.

Grey sat back in the chair with a wince. "Definitely bruised. Oh well, perhaps I didn't handle the situation as . . . howsthatgo . . . delicately as I should've. No big deal. We got it all worked out now."

I computed how quickly I could crawl over to that chair and break Grey's neck. Not fast enough.

"I see you're a stubborn one, Mack." He snapped his fingers. His eyes flared. My arm went numb and unresponsive. It lost its grip and down I fell.

Knuckles chuckled in a string of rapid pings. He scooped up my bowler and dropped it on his square cranium. He beeped quizzically.

"Looks good on you," said Grey. "I'm sure Mack here won't mind parting with it, will you, Mack?"

With my one functional limb, I pushed myself up, but Knuckles stomped on my back. He bleeped hard.

"I'd stay down if I were you," said Grey. "Knuckles isn't bright enough for citizen status, but he knows how to nurse a grudge. If you give him the hat, maybe he'll go easy on you."

"Keep it," I replied.

Knuckles knocked my working arm from under me, and I hit the floor. He kicked me once.

"Stand down, Knuckles," ordered Grey.

The auto stepped back.

Grey knelt down beside me. "Look here, Mack. You look like a robot that can handle himself. And since it's real important to me to find Tony Ringo, I think it'd be helpful to have an extra set of opticals on the street. Don't you agree?"

"Makes sense," I conceded, baiting him to move the four inches closer so I could wrap my working arm around his neck. If I got the chance, it'd take less than two-tenths of a second to break his neck. At least, that's how fast my specs assured me I could snap an average neck. I'd never actually done it before. Felt like the right time for a field test.

He leaned closer, half an inch from a guaranteed grab. "Now, I don't know shit about you, but I'm willing to bet you're not the kind of bot to roll over and play nice. So I'm going to plant a little extra incentive into that brain of yours. See, I've got this knack for reprogramming. Kinda funny, actually, since I don't know nothing about computers." He rubbed his fingers together and tiny green sparks danced.

I was a closed system, and I planned on staying that way. I lunged awkwardly, but fast enough that I should've gotten my fingers around Grey's throat. He moved back just in time, grinning.

"Nice try, but I told'ja. I got a knack. Now that I've touched you, I know what you're going to do before you do."

He snapped his fingers, and my last functional limb went dead. I fell to the floor, five hundred pounds of useless tin. But despite his arrogance, sweat beaded Grey's forehead. His eyes were bright green with crackling psychic wattage. It must've taken a lot of effort to incapacitate all my limbs. I hoped he wouldn't have enough left over to claw his way into my operating system, but no such luck. He put his sizzling hands on me.

I went off-line.

My audios were the first sensors to reboot. A voice, distorted and heavy, trudged its way through the darkness.

"Hey, buddy. You okay?"

I would've replied, but my vocalizer wasn't running. I didn't waste any time getting it going, and instead, prioritized my opticals. The world fell into my digital awareness, but it was all mere shapes and colors without the necessary distinguishing software.

An assembly of multicolored polygons spoke. I moved another 3 percent toward functional and recognized a voice. It belonged to Winifred, the front desk woman. "Hey, you still on?"

Language can be tricky for a rebooting brain. It took three seconds to decode the four word sentence.

"Statement: I . . . am . . . functional," I replied. A full second later, I added, "Qualifier: Nominally."

"Nominally?" she asked. "What's that mean?"

"Advisory: It . . . means . . . you should . . . stand . . . back in case . . . I fall . . . over . . . as I attempt . . . to stand."

I managed to get to my feet, though it was awkward. Programs were up and running, but hundreds more subroutines had yet to reboot. My sensor array, though improving, was still a mess. I could distinguish shapes more thoroughly, but had trouble finding names for them. And my audio filters were down, meaning every little noise was being analyzed and reanalyzed. Made it hard to concentrate. Worse yet, there was a terrible ache in my electronic brain, which was odd considering it had no tactile receptors. I put a hand to my abdomen, where it was housed.

"Question: What . . . did he do . . . to me?" I asked aloud. I didn't mean to, but my verbalization filters weren't running either.

"Who did what to you?" asked Winifred, whom I could now visually identify as a biological entity but couldn't recognize any more than that.

"Statement: Running . . . diagnostic." I beeped twice for no apparent reason.

"You don't look so good." She took me by the arm.

"Statement: Tactile web off-line. Fine motor functions . . . off-line. Advisory: Maintain a safe . . . distance to avoid . . .

incidental injury. Estimation: Full system restoration . . . in two minutes, two seconds."

"Maybe you should sit down while you wait," she said.

"Negative." I dug around in my vocabulary file for a less technical word. "No. It will be better to stand very still in the meantime." I hiccuped one last, "Statement." And then I waited.

"Should I call the e-mechs?"

Empire had the best emergency mechanical technicians in the world to service its automated citizenry, but this wasn't serious enough for that.

"It's just a cold reboot."

I passed it off as a casual thing, but it bothered me. I hadn't been that far off-line since first being activated. I could remember every moment of my existence, save for one-point-eight seconds after my refrigerator had exploded. But there was now a three-minute, forty-seven-second block of time in my memory log that I couldn't account for.

What had Grey done to me?

Fully restored, my diagnostics combed through my software and assured me it found nothing amiss. But there was still that unaccounted-for segment of time, still that peculiar notion that someone had been monkeying around with my most intimate programming. As a robot, I didn't have instincts, and my intuition simulator remained silent. There was still something wrong.

I could feel it.

"All better?" asked the woman.

"Functional," I grunted as I commanded my diagnostics to sift through my electronic brain again, and set aside some of my processing power to continue to sift over and over again until it found something. "And the name's Mack."

"So what happened, Mack?"

"Did you see—" I started, but stopped suddenly and inexplicably.

"What?" asked Winifred. "Did I see what?"

"Did you see—" Again, I stopped.

I wanted to ask her about Grey and Knuckles, but something kept the question from forming. It must've been Grey's reprogramming, a little worm of a virus inhibiting my speech software, keeping me from saying anything about Grey or our encounter. I didn't like that one bit. It was a minor problem, but I didn't want to guess at the bigger motivational impairments he might've planted.

I scanned the broken wall where I'd thrown Knuckles. "Sorry about the damage."

"Don't worry about it. Place is a shithole anyway." She scratched her fuzzy chin. "So what happened?"

"Nothing."

I didn't tell her for two reasons. First, it was embarrassing to be so easily put down. Second, that bug kept me from even mentioning Grey or Knuckles. I'd have to purge my systems top to bottom. And soon. Still topping my directives list: finding Tony Ringo, and finding him before Grey. Otherwise, logic told me I'd never find him at all.

"Ringo," I said. "Do you know anything else about him? Hangouts? Friends?"

Winifred frowned. "I don't know nothing about nobody. None of my business."

"Thanks," I said with more sarcasm than I meant. "You've been a big help." I had nothing left to go on. That logic sprang up again, told me it was time to go home, and put this mess behind me.

But there was that little girl, that family. Damn, some days I wished I'd been made a toaster.

I'd trudged halfway down the hall when Winifred called my name.

"Hey, Mack! Wait up!"

I stopped. "Yeah?"

She wasn't a big woman, but she had a strange, lurching walk that made her stained, green sundress swing from side to side. "So finding Ringo, it's pretty important to you, huh?"

"Yeah. It's important."

She lumbered past me. "Come on, then."

Winifred led me to the lobby, back to her front desk. "Place doesn't have a security network set up," she explained along the way, "but Violet sees a lot of things. And most people don't pay her enough mind to watch themselves."

The fuzzoid beeped happily as we approached.

"Memory replay, Vi," instructed Winifred. "File twelve."

Violet zipped in the air and projected an image on the wall from her left optical. I recognized the lobby of the Hotel Swallow, and I recognized Tony Ringo coming in with a young woman in tow. They stopped, made out a little, and continued on their way, obviously up to his room for some of that DNA swapping biologicals were so fond of.

"Well?" said Winifred expectedly. "Whadaya think of that?"

I didn't think much of it at all, but she'd at least tried to help me out, so I tried not to let my disappointment show. "Uh, thanks. That's really helpful."

She frowned. Then she grinned a gap-toothed smile. "You don't recognize her, do you?"

"Should I?"

She ordered Violet to replay the file. Winifred stabbed her finger at the projected woman. "You have to imagine her with blond hair, get rid of the sunglasses. That any clearer?"

"No," I answered honestly.

Winifred groaned. "Damn it, don't you watch the news?"

"Don't have a television."

"Paper. You gotta read the paper."

I shook my head slowly, as if admitting to some grievous fault.

Muttering, she had Violet pause the projection. "Damn it, Mack, how do you expect to be a decent P.I. if you don't know what's going on in this city?"

"I'm not a P.I. I'm a cab driver."

"Still, can't hurt you to crack a paper now and then. Then you'd recognize Lucia Napier."

She tossed a newspaper section at me, which I caught. Nice to know my reflex model was still functioning at 100 percent, despite Grey's fiddling. A glance at the paper showed a photo of a young female norm at a gala affair. My distinguishing software still had trouble telling attractive humans from ugly, but I gathered she was hot stuff, considering that she was in fine physical shape and with a lot of guys gathered around her. A label under the photo read, "Lucia Napier, Princess of Empire, out on the town."

"She's a big deal, huh?" I asked.

Winifred laughed. "Damn, you are one smart machine. Figure that out all by yourself, did'ja?"

"Is she Ringo's girlfriend?"

Winifred laughed harder this time. "Hell, no. Only saw her here two or three times. But the girl has a thing for mutants. And lowlifes."

"And Ringo is both," I said. It wasn't much of a lead, but it was the only one I had. "Thanks."

"No problem." She turned from the television. "So what's it worth?"

"I'm sorry?"

"The info," she clarified. "What's it worth to you?"

She held out her hand, and I realized she was asking for money.

"Uh . . . I don't have any cash," I replied.

One of her eyes narrowed. The other started sliding around again. "What?"

"No money," I explained. "I don't carry any money on me."

"None?"

I shook my head. "I don't need it."

Her face puckered. "Everybody needs money."

Everybody did. But all mine went to my rent, my electric bill, and maybe a cab ride now and then. I never needed money spontaneously. I turned out my coat pockets as illustration of their emptiness.

"Sorry."

She looked disappointed for a moment, but the moment passed. "Look, big guy, would you care for some advice?"

"Sure."

"If you're going to go around asking a lot of questions, it's always smart to have some cash ready to crank the cogs. Not everyone is as forthcoming and pleasant as me. Some people, they don't help nobody unless they get something out of it."

"I'll keep that in mind." And I would, but hopefully, I wouldn't have to be asking questions much longer. "If you want, I can go get some money and—"

"Forget it. I'm going to sell the video to the news anyway. Worth more to them than the nickels you'd toss my way." She settled into her chair. "Good luck, Mack."

"Thanks."

My volitional software started computing possible courses of action. Lucia Napier, Princess of Empire, lover of mutants and lowlifes. I didn't know anything about her, but my speculator suggested there was a very good chance I'd never get near her. Then again, that same reasoning eliminated Tony Ringo from her circle of friends, and clearly, he'd gotten to know her. If a scumbag like that could, it stood to reason a nice, upstanding bot such as myself had a chance. Of course, the world wasn't reasonable. Or logical.

But I was, and Lucia Napier was my only shot, and sometimes being logical meant going against the odds. So I shut down my difference engine and headed for the door.

7

Lucia Napier's number was, of course, unlisted, so if I was going to speak with her, it would have to be face-to-face. Though apparently every other citizen in Empire knew every little detail of her life, including who she dated, what she had for dinner, and how many minutes her average shower lasted, I'd never heard of her. So I took the most direct approach in my search, and hailed a cab, one of my fellow Bluestars. I recognized the biological behind the wheel, thanks to my flawless memory matrix. I'd seen him around the garage on two-hundred-ten separate occasions, though we'd never actually spoken to each other before.

I leaned in the buzzbug's window, and it tilted a few degrees. "Hey, do you know where Lucia Napier lives?"

He glanced over at me. "You want a ride, buddy?"

"I just need an address," I replied.

"What do I look like, an information booth?"

"Do me a favor, will you? I'm a driver. Just like you."

"Yeah, I know you." He snorted, hocked up some phlegm, and swallowed it back down. "Don't mean I gotta give you free information."

Winifred had been right. Getting information in this town without money was like pulling a broken zip train up a steep incline.

"I don't have any money," I said.

"Too bad for you then, huh?" The driver punched his accelerator, but I held onto the starboard wing, keeping it from vibrating sufficiently to push the bug forward.

I could pull zip trains all day. And holding one little cab wasn't much of a strain on my servos.

"Le'go, man," grunted the driver.

"Address," I replied, tightening my grip on the door. "Or you could keep accelerating until the wing vibrates itself out of the frame."

Obviously, he didn't relish the notion of having his wages garnished to pay for a replacement wing. "She lives in Proton Towers. Everybody knows that."

"Thanks." I would've tipped my hat to him, but I didn't have one anymore. "Don't suppose I could trouble you for a lift. Free of charge. One Bluestar employee to another."

As soon as I released the cab, he shot away, tossing one parting "Asshole!" from his window.

"Didn't think so," I replied.

It was a long walk to Proton Towers from Warpsville, but it would've taken longer by omnibus. While public transportation could get you anywhere you wanted to go, it didn't always take the quickest route. It was common knowledge that the omnibuses intentionally took roundabout journeys from the less desirable neighborhoods to the higher rent districts. It discouraged casual visitation. I chose to walk, counting off every cent added to my power bill with each step.

It started to rain.

Rain in Empire is risky business. Sweeper blimp drones skim the skies, vacuuming up all the harsh chemicals floating in the air.

For the most part, they did a decent job of filtering out the truly nasty stuff. But the factories and labs pumped out a lot of volatile vapors, and there weren't enough filters to get them all. Once in a while, you got something unexpected mixed with the shower. Two months back, midtown had been hit with a sudden downpour and all biologicals caught in it sprouted hair from every inch of skin touched by the rain. And six years before that, when I was but a twinkle in an evil genius's twisted brain, there was a shower of exploding hail that'd nearly brought Tomorrow's Town to its knees. Since the sweeper drones had been implemented, nothing as bad as that had happened, but cautious citizens still went inside when it rained, and smart citizens sought cover even when it was cloudy. But I was a tough bot, and my tactile sensors assured me this rain, while acidic enough to irritate biological skin, wasn't going to do anything to my chassis or coat.

With my fellow pedestrians thinned to a few brave biologicals and metal-skinned robots, I was able to pick up the pace. Though I'm a big bot, I'm not slow when I have enough elbow room, and I'm able to move at a fair clip once I get going. Forty-four miles per hour in a straightaway, but my maneuverability went right to hell and stopping was more trouble than it's worth. I punched it up to 10 m.p.h. and trusted my guidance system to avoid stepping on anyone as I navigated the streets on autopilot, the bulk of my processing power still obsessed with finding that damn worm Grey had planted.

Over and over, my diagnostic came up dry. I could run a more thorough check when I next recharged, but I doubted that'd turn up anything. Whatever Grey had slipped into my code, it was deep inside. Maybe the doc could find it in my next therapy session. She knew my programming better than anyone. Of course, she'd ask questions. And since she could tell when I was lying, I'd have to tell the truth. My scenario simulator started running possible outcomes.

"Just running around town, tussling with auto hooligans and mutant thugs, getting rogue viruses crammed in my programming. No big deal, Doc. Just following orders. You said I should try to be more social."

I calculated the possible responses. 52 percent probable: She'd nod knowingly, tap her pen against her pad, and make some vaguely disapproving noise. 46 percent: She'd nod knowingly, tap her pen against her pad, and make some vaguely approving noise. 2 percent: She'd nod knowingly, tap her pen against her pad, and howl like a coyote. I attributed that last possibility to a bug in my calculations. Or maybe my difference engine was screwing with me.

Proton Towers had a state-of-the-art weather regulator. Experimental, but so far, it'd worked like a charm. There was a cylinder of perfect climate stretched four thousand, two hundred, twelve feet around the three shining skyscrapers.

An everyday working bot such as myself didn't belong in this district. It didn't help that my coat was soaked and torn ragged from my run-in with Knuckles. I still hadn't buffed out the smudges on my chassis. The rain had only smeared them around. Every other robot I walked past was either a service drone or personal auto. No bots here, except me.

Proton Towers was surrounded by hedges, lawns, and fountains. It was a use of real estate that only the rich and influential could afford. Flying gun drones zipped around the complex, a metallic swarm of heavy-duty firepower. The Towers were a fortress, as if the wealthy and powerful were just waiting for the poor and disenfranchised to rise up and revolt. Wasn't so far-fetched, I supposed, when you stared down from your ivory tower all nice and cozy and dry while the teeming masses cowered from toxic rain clouds.

The front door was guarded by a doorman dressed to the nines with his perfect little burgundy doorman suit and his perfect little burgundy doorman hat. A badge labeled him "Dennis." Behind him was a pair of security autos. The autos, clothed in black suits, were smaller, sleeker models than me. My threat assessor detected holstered weapons judging by the bulges in their jackets. They hadn't made a raygun that could pierce my hide, but I wasn't looking for trouble.

Three small scanner drones shot forward and hovered around me, analyzing me thoroughly. The security autos were no doubt being transmitted the information.

Dennis stepped forward.

"Hello, sir," he greeted, sounding far too sincere. "How may I help you today?"

"Hello," I replied, trying to sound jovial though neither civility nor friendliness ranked high on my personality template. "I'm here to see Lucia Napier."

"I see, sir. May I have your name, sir?"

"Megaton. Mack Megaton."

"Thank you, sir. One moment, sir." Grinning, he turned on his heels and marched over to a podium by the door. He flipped through a list, smiling all the while.

A scanner drone floated too close to my faceplate, and I brushed it aside.

"Get lost."

It beeped and zipped back out of my reach. This did not endear me to the security autos, both of whom reached under their jackets. I met their determined red opticals in a hard stare.

The doorman marched forward again. "I'm sorry, sir, but there's no appointment listed."

"I don't have one."

His smile dropped a third of a millimeter or so. "I'm sorry, sir, but there are no unauthorized visitors allowed." For a biological, this guy sounded more like a robot than I did.

"Can you give her a buzz and let her know I'm here?" I asked. "I'd appreciate it."

"I'm sorry, sir, but if you're not expected I'm afraid I must ask you to leave the premises." The security autos took a step forward.

I stuck with tried-and-true robot persistence. "Just buzz her. Isn't she home?"

"I'm not allowed to give that information, sir."

This outcome was not surprising, but I was still annoyed and somewhat insulted that Dennis didn't at least take the time to go back to his podium and pretend to call somebody so he could come back and say I'd been refused. It seemed the polite thing to do. Instead, I was treated like an encyclopedia salesman. I ignored my common sense emulator and kept on trying.

"It's about a friend of ours. Name's Tony Ringo." I turned to one of the scanner drones and repeated the name in case anyone important might be listening. "Tony Ringo."

Five gun drones dropped from their orbit of Proton Towers and circled around me. Their guns hummed with ready charges. The two security autos pulled their weapons and drew a bead. Worst of all, Dennis's smile completely vanished, replaced by a determined blankness.

"Sir, if you do not retreat to a safe distance immediately, I am authorized to use force."

The smart thing to do would be to back away. Unfortunately, my core aggression index, that thing I wasn't supposed to be having problems controlling, kept me from budging. Already my combat analyzer was plotting battle strategies.

"Sir, I will not ask again."

Whether I would've done the intelligent thing and retreat or not was anybody's guess. Especially mine. But the issue was nullified by a strong pinging from the doorman's badge.

He ordered security to hold their positions as he turned his back to me.

"Yes, ma'am?"

A new voice issued from his badge. Unfamiliar, but I had a pretty good guess as to whom it belonged.

"Please, Dennis," said Lucia Napier, "do send Mr. Megaton up."

The gun drones shot back into their orbit, and the autos put away their guns. Dennis turned back to me. The smile, as bright and shiny as ever, was back on his face.

The doorman led me inside, handing me off to a concierge. The short norm was meticulously groomed, right down to his wrinkle-free black trousers. My recognition file always picked out one or two features in a person to mark them for easy retrieval from my memory matrix. The details it noticed about him were his excessively plucked eyebrows and his hair: black, greased into submission, with a part so neat and precise that it must've taken a mathematical algorithm to get just right.

He bowed. "Hello, sir. If you'd be so kind as to follow me. . . ."

Most of the city still used the old-fashioned elevators, but Proton Towers had the latest in levitator pods. The concierge and I stepped into a pod decorated with a couch, a plant, and a painting of a garden villa. I found the painting very odd. Having been activated in Empire and never having set foot outside the city limits, I couldn't imagine a world where such a thing was possible. A building made of wood, all that green, and an expansive blue sky.

I wondered if it even existed.

The concierge caught me studying it. Actually, I'd already committed it to memory file, and could study it anytime I liked. I hadn't bothered to turn away from it.

"Do you like it, sir?" he asked.

Perhaps *like* was too solid a word. I had no desire to leave
Empire and see the rest of the world. But there was something
about this painting and its otherworldliness that kept my attention. Inexplicable, yes, but part of true consciousness was
having inexplicable reactions from time to time.

"It's nice," I replied.

"Yes, sir, indeed, it is."

The doors closed, and the pod shot up. Seventy-six floors
zipped by in forty seconds, and when the doors opened again,
Lucia Napier and her penthouse were standing before me.

"Mr. Mack Megaton," announced the concierge, just in case
she failed to notice the seven-foot robot standing behind him.
She invited me in and dismissed him.

"It was a pleasure to make your acquaintance, sir," he said.

"Likewise," I returned as the pod doors closed.

I scanned and analyzed Lucia Napier. Biological notions of
beauty meant nothing to me, but my evolutionary programming had been attempting for some time now to work out what
made humans attractive. It broke all the features down: five
feet, seven inches tall. Long, blond hair. Sparkling blue eyes.
Button nose. Smooth complexion. Proper number of well-
proportioned limbs. Thin waist. Round hips. Breasts that were
small but perky and noticeable. A nicely tailored dress that
emphasized her curves without being showy, allowing a taste-
ful glimpse of cleavage. My evaluator performed some quick
calculations and spit out a rating.

Attractive to 92 percent of the average biological populace
with an eight point margin based on personal preference. It
was hardly reliable. Beauty was more than the sum of its parts.
Or sometimes, less.

Napier took longer to form her assessment of me. Wasn't her
fault. Just the inefficient nature of that chemical lump sitting in

her skull. She stood there for ten seconds, her face a blank slate save for a slight smile.

"Very impressive." She stepped forward and held out her hand, palm down, for me to take. That surprised me. Most biologicals don't trust a big, dangerous machine enough to risk a handshake right off the bat. Those giant, bone-crunching hands of mine can be fairly intimidating, and as I took her delicate, squishy skin in my metal mitts, I couldn't honestly blame biologicals.

Napier's smile widened. "A pleasure to finally meet you, Mack."

"Likewise."

"Are you just saying that to be polite or do you really mean it?"

"I'm just saying it."

She giggled lightly. "Oh, I love you robots and your ruthless honesty. Biologicals are so difficult to nail down. Not you though. You say what you want."

"My shrink says I should work on my social subroutine."

"Oh, my no." She frowned. "Don't change a thing. It's so refreshing." She drew in a deep breath. "So delightfully direct."

She turned and walked through a pseudo-classical archway. Since she was still holding my hand, I did the polite thing and followed. We stepped into a hallway lined with photos of Lucia with other people. I hypothesized that they were important folks, though I didn't recognize many. Still, there were enough photos that I scanned a few movie stars, jazz musicians, and politicians stored in my memory matrix.

The biggest portrait was of Lucia receiving an award from Diamond Jill Mahoney, the first mutant mayor of Empire City. She'd been a norm when elected. The spontaneous crystallization of her skin had happened in the third year of her first term of office.

The hallway came to an end, and we stepped into a new room of gleaming steel. Everything from the walls to the floors to the furniture shimmered like it'd just been freshly polished. There were seven white rugs placed around the room, two metal vases shaped to look ancient and new at the same time, and a nine-foot lump of titanium trying to pass itself off as a sculpture. The room didn't look like the kind of place a biological could actually live in. Nonetheless, Napier let go of my hand, nestled in the corner of a fluffy white couch, and somehow managed to actually look comfortable.

A butler auto, wrapped in a cream tuxedo, glided his way across the room. He wasn't a model I recognized, and he didn't bear any company logos. Had to be a custom job. He handed Napier a bubbling green concoction.

"Thank you, Humbolt."

"My pleasure, doll." She'd forgone the standard Olde Money English Butler voice package and given him a gruff Brooklyn accent.

She sipped her drink. "Atomic Kiss. All the rage. Well, not quite yet. I invented it this morning. But give it a week. I'd offer you one, Mack, but, well, you know . . ."

"I know," I replied.

"It must be a very odd existence." She took a very slight sip of her drink. "Then again, I suppose we flesh and blood creatures must appear very strange to you as well."

"I try not to judge," I said honestly.

"Please, Mister Megaton, have a seat." She gestured toward a chair. My coat was still wet, my chassis smudged, and to sit in the chair would've required the white cushions be sent out for dry cleaning. More likely, Napier would toss them in the trash and order up another one. Probably went through couches like I went through plastic airplane models.

"I'll stand. Thanks."

"As you wish." She took another measured sip, rose from her couch, and drew closer. Her movements were graceful, confident. This was a woman who was used to being in charge. She reached toward my faceplate.

"May I, Mister Megaton?"

My threat assessor marked her as physically benign. Of course, in a non-battlefield situation there were more dangerous things than ray cannons and plasma bolts. In her own way, Lucia Napier was more perilous than Grey and his electrokinetic touch. At least, I thought so. I had no real proof. Only an impression gleaned by edgy subroutines.

"Sure," I said, ignoring my better judgment.

She put her hand on either side of my cranial unit. "Hmmm. Interesting. You're cooler than I expected."

"You know it, daddio," I replied.

An unidentifiable expression crossed her face. "Is that a joke?"

"You tell me."

"A rudimentary sense of humor. How wonderful." She smiled. "Might I bother you to remove your coat?"

"Miss Napier, I'm not here for—"

"Oh, please, Mr. Megaton. I'll be happy to answer any of your questions afterwards."

She batted her eyelashes at me, and while the look had little effect on me, my problem-solving skills usually sought out the most direct solution. I removed my coat. The butler auto smoothly glided beside me and held out his hand.

"Want me to take that for you, buddy?"

I was about to tell him not to bother when he snatched it away and glided out of the room.

Napier circled me three times without saying a word. She smiled very slightly, apparently amused by something other than my rudimentary sense of humor.

"Magnificent. Your specs don't do you justice, Mister Megaton."

"Specs? Where did you see my specs? They're—"

"Classified? Yes, well, I have certain . . . connections with The Learned Council. I was brought in as one of the consultants for your probation hearings."

"We've never met."

"No, we haven't. But that's not surprising." She went back to her sofa and had a seat. "You haven't met with most of your creators."

"Lady, I don't know what you think you know, but I've only got one creator."

"Oh, I know you believe that, but I'm afraid Professor Megalith fudged a bit on that point." She laughed. "Did you really think one man, no matter how ingenious, was capable of creating such a sophisticated mechanism such as yourself all by his lonesome?"

"Hadn't thought about it," I said.

"No, I guess you wouldn't. Despite that wonderful Freewill Glitch, a residual devotional dictate to Megalith should remain. Don't try to deny it. Or did those giant hands of yours just clench into fists at the mere implication of imperfection in your . . . creator?"

I uncurled my fingers. My relationship with Megalith was complicated, but not that unusual. Fathers and sons didn't always get along, but that rarely kept sons from seeking dear old dad's approval. Logic told me pop was a megalomaniacal madman and his love was out of reach as long as I kept at this "productive citizen" edict of mine. It didn't stop me from having some mixed feelings about it.

"Don't get me wrong, Mack," added Napier. "The Professor is a genius. Half the systems inside you are still in the prototype stage elsewhere, and the other half have been improved significantly. Your cooling system, for example." She ran her fingers along the rim of her glass. "That's my baby. Among a few other choice bits."

"You design robotics?" I asked.

She chuckled. "You don't know?"

"Know what?"

"About me. And my ascent to fabulously wealthy bad girl of Empire."

"I don't read the papers," I said. "Sorry."

"Oh, don't apologize, Mack. You may be the only citizen in all of Empire, perhaps all the world, who doesn't." She gulped down the rest of her Atomic Kiss, threw the glass over her shoulder. It bounced off the carpet, and a cleaning drone zipped out of the wall and vacuumed up the mess.

"How wonderful!" she exclaimed with all the glee of a cheerleader on prom night. She clapped her hands. A section of carpeted floor parted to reveal a stairway in the middle of the room. Napier jumped up and took me by the hand again. "Come along, Mack. I've got something to show you."

She pulled. It didn't even occur to me to resist. I was swept along in the gravity well of this small biological creature. Down the short flight of stairs, a laboratory waited. And what a lab it was. All chrome and stainless steel. An entire automated assembly line, with the latest in drone workers, occupied one wall. There were laser welders, supercomputers, and enough spare parts in neatly organized racks to build a horde of vacuum drones. Blueprints covered the walls or hung, framed and laminated, from the ceiling. The place must've occupied the entire floor beneath her apartment. There was a noticeable lack of buttons though, and a dearth of switches and levers. Like her apartment, the lab seemed impractical. It also appeared unused, judging from its extreme cleanliness, lack of any noticeable projects, and deathly stillness.

The butler auto was already waiting at the foot of the stairs with a fresh Atomic Kiss, which she took.

"Thank you, Humbolt." She looped her tiny arm in mine. A little squeeze and I could snap the bone in two or three places. It was then that she reminded me of April, and that absolute trust that usually children have because they don't know better. But Napier had to know. She could probably rattle off the pressure rating I could exert with one servo twitch. But she didn't seem the least bit put off by it. She led me through the lab, blithely chatting as if we were old friends.

"Come here. Let me show you some things I was working on before I retired. All theoretical, of course. Drawing board stage."

We approached a stainless steel cabinet, and its doors slid apart to reveal rows upon rows of blueprints in clear plastic tubes. She ran her hands around them, selecting very specific ones with girlish giggles, and handing them to me, saying things like "Hold this would you, dear?" and "Oh, this is just the keenest thing right here." Forty-five seconds later, I had sixteen specs under my arms.

A seventeenth tube cradled on her shoulder, Napier zipped over to a counter, popped the tube, and poured out the spec, which she spread for me to see. "This is a high-intensity laser emitter," she explained. "Handheld. Or it would be if I could get hold of a battery small and powerful enough."

She snatched another from me and laid it out. "And this is a new mechanical ball joint which could increase robotic flexibility by six or seven degrees." She huffed. "Except it keeps snapping under excess pressure."

Humming, she sorted through the other tubes under my arm. "I've got a swell improved countergrav generator somewhere in here that I know you'll love."

"You designed these?" I asked. "All of these?"

"Oh, Mack, aren't you just the yummiest." She reached up as if to pinch my cheek, but technically, I don't have cheeks and even if I did, they wouldn't be subject to pinching. She settled for a soft caress. "Of course, I did, silly. They're not all my work. Most of this is modification and improvement on the work of others. Someone has a problem they can't fix, they come to me. It's wonderful. I get to see all the latest breakthroughs before anyone. Sometimes, I even get to invent them myself."

I scanned her face again. Bright-eyed and grinning like a sprightly schoolgirl. My visualizer must've been glitching. "How old are you?"

"Twenty-two," she replied absently. "I'm a child prodigy." She laughed. "Or, I guess I used to be. Now I suppose I'm just a plain old genius. Y'know, Mack, if you're going to be a detective in this town, you might want to know things like that."

"I'm not a detective," I replied, but she didn't hear me.

She chirped. Really, she did. "Oh, I know you'll just love this!" she exclaimed as she threw down another set of specs. "It's a shrink ray. Never got around to building a prototype for testing, but there's absolutely no reason it shouldn't work. Then again, I thought the same thing about the improved freeze ray, and that ended up melting stuff." She scowled, and her nose scrunched. "Not much practical use, but kinda neat."

I covered the blueprints with one giant mitt. "That's great, Miss Napier, very impressive."

"Lucia," she corrected. "It's Lucia. I insist."

"Lucia. Fine." Even the inexhaustible patience of a machine had its limits. "I've taken off my coat. I've let you paw me. And I've looked at your lab and your blueprints. Now it's time to answer my questions."

A strange expression crossed her face. I pegged it as disappointed, possibly a little hurt. Didn't make a whole lot of sense, but what functional bot understood biologicals? Not me. And frankly, I was glad I didn't. Cold machine logic worked fine for me, even if the Glitch sometimes encouraged me to ignore it. This was not one of those times.

Napier's frown deepened into a childish pout, and some rogue electrons danced around the edges of my guilt index. I didn't apologize because I hadn't done anything wrong except get a spoiled little rich girl back on track.

Once she realized no apology was coming, her sulk passed as quickly as it arose. She smiled very slightly, sipped her drink, and headed back to the apartment stairs.

"Fine, Mack. Ask your questions." She cast a demure look over her shoulder as she climbed the stairs. "Although I would point out that there are many men who wouldn't mind being pawed by me."

"I'm not a man," I said after I joined her in the apartment.

"No." She flopped down on the couch. "You're a machine. A beautiful, elegant, flawless machine." She bit her lip as she looked me up and down. She had that look in her eye, the same gleam Doc Mujahid got when she was staring at my programming codes streaming across her monitors, a look of awe and appreciation. But where the doc also had a clinical detachment, Napier showed no such disinterest.

I'd heard of deep technophiles, disciples of science so enamored of technology that it compelled them toward odd attractions, strange compulsions. No one as of yet had confessed publicly to the inclination, but it was only a matter of time until the Temple of Knowledge gave the green light. The technos would come bursting out into public life. In the meantime, they were only a rumor. There might not even be any. Or there might be thousands. No way to know yet, but if they were out there, then Lucia Napier was a prime candidate for charter membership. The way she kept staring at me, disassembling me with her eyes down to the barest blueprints, was downright ravenous.

I wished I had my damn coat back. Rather than ask for it, I decided to get this over with as fast as possible and be on my way.

"I'm looking for Tony Ringo."

Her playful grin faded. "Now what did a worthless little boy like Tony Ringo do to draw your attention?"

"So you know him?"

"Yes. But then again, you already know that, don't you? Why else would you be here?"

I have no expressions to read, but something must have given away my thoughts.

"Oh, I'm not going to deny we used to hang out together," she said. "He was fun for a little while, good for a few laughs. Harmless, really."

"I think he's taken some friends of mine," I said, surprised that I volunteered the information. There was something unsettling about Napier, and it thrust some odd compulsions into my own behavioral directives.

"Tony?" She waved her hand. "Please, Tony couldn't hurt a fly. Not that he wouldn't try. He's just . . . incapable. A rather pathetic little boy pretending to be a big man."

"Well, maybe he's through pretending. Or worse, maybe he still is pretending, only now he's worked up the guts to give it a go and screw it up."

She tossed her blond hair across her right shoulder. "Possible, I suppose. But why would Tony take these friends of yours?"

"I don't know. Hell, I could be wrong. Only way to know is to find Ringo and ask him."

"And if dear Tony doesn't feel like answering?" she asked.

"I'll persuade him."

"Tony can be a very stubborn boy."

"I can be a very persuasive bot," I replied.

She stood and circled me once more before laying both palms on my chest. "Prove it. Persuade me."

I stepped back, and she nearly fell over.

"Lady, I don't know what you're into, but I'm not interested."

I expected that familiar pout to cross her face again, but I guess she'd heard me say no enough times to catch the hint. She smiled, and there was something predatory about that smile, like this wasn't over yet. But it was. The file was closed, the program deleted.

"I assume you've tried the Hotel Swallow already," she said.

I nodded.

"Honestly, I don't know much of Tony's habits. We weren't that close. It was purely a physical relationship. He's very fond of a place called The Golden Diode. It's a club on the bad end of Pi Street. Can't say if he still haunts the place, but he likes jazz and getting drunk. If he's not there, it's a good bet he'll be in the area."

"Thanks."

I turned to leave, but Humbolt stood in my way. He held out a coat to me. It was mine, but clean and pressed. "Here's your coat, pal. I took the liberty of givin' it a quick splash and dry. I could stitch up the tears if you gave me a few more minutes."

"No, thanks." I took it back and threw it over my shoulder. I'd put it on later, but for now, I wanted out of here. I headed toward the levitator pod and safety.

Napier followed. "Come back any time, Mack. I'll leave your name with the front desk, let them know to let you up anytime you please. Anytime."

I didn't reply. But staying away from Proton Towers was now on the short list of directives, right in front of not poking my optics out with a diamond-tipped auger.

The tube's doors parted, and I stepped inside. I was tempted to keep my back to Napier, but something made me turn. She was still smiling, though it was a softer, less frisky expression. I wondered when the damn doors would close. They were two seconds behind schedule.

"Tony likes jazz. Don't know if that'll help, but he does."

"Jazz. Got it."

Mercifully, the doors started sliding shut.

"And, Mack," she said. "Hope you find your friends."

"Me, too."

And then the tube sealed itself, and I was on my way out of Lucia Napier's world for good.

8

I figured Ringo wouldn't be showing up at The Golden Diode for his drink until evening. If I'd had any other lead to follow up, I would've continued my search. But I didn't, so I relocated my amateur detective work to a secondary directive and started on the other things I needed to do.

This in itself was an odd development. Normally, I was loaded with free time. Except for going to work, visiting my shrink, and maybe a stab at socialization every now and then, my schedule consisted entirely of standing in the corner of my apartment, not consuming much juice, staring at the walls, a bot with nothing but time and nothing to do with it. Now I had a short list of objectives that didn't include driving a cab and staying out of trouble.

I stopped by a robot wash and charged a wash and wax job. The Diode might have a dress code, and a smudged chassis might prove a hindrance. It didn't take long to get back my gleaming chassis. There were still traces of damage to my paint job, but beyond that, there wasn't a hint that I'd been subjected to anything more traumatic than an overweight pigeon perching on my shoulder. That was the miracle of my one-of-a-kind alloy, so experimental that there wasn't even a name for it yet. I felt better, more functional. Illogical, since the wash did little to improve my performance except clear some grit from my right elbow joint, and that was a .0003 performance hindrance.

I went back to Jung's apartment and waited for him to get back from work. There was a newspaper waiting at his front door. I found a seat on his sofa and scanned the paper cover to cover while running an internal diagnostic for Grey's worm. Reading was such a low level task, it left 99 percent of my processing power free to dig around in my electronic brain.

It'd been a while since I'd read a paper. The details were different, but the world was all the same. The Biological Rights League was saying bad stuff about robots. The Learned Council was pushing some new technological breakthrough. The Big Brains were discussing the utopian world we—I guess that included me, too—were creating. A couple of labs exploded. Crime was up. Mutant births were up. Pollution was up. Business as usual.

There was a brief article about my apartment exploding on page eight. It measured exactly two inches by one inch, including the stock photo of me. Explosions weren't that big a deal in Empire, but you'd think my former celebrity status would've earned me at least another three-fourths of an inch.

Internally, I'd come up with nothing, something I was getting used to. Grey's psychic empathy with machines must've been pretty high-end stuff. Or maybe by now my maintenance protocols had already expunged his influence, isolated and devoured the foreign program. It was always possible.

There was a distinctly metal against metal knock on the door. A robot. Immediately, I thought of Knuckles. But there was no reason to suspect he'd found me here. Still, my aggression index hoped to hell it was as I opened the door.

It was Humbolt, Lucia Napier's butler auto. "Yo, Mack. Gotch'ya gift from Miss Napier here." Without giving me time to refuse, he strode into the apartment with a big box under his arm. He tossed the box on the coffee table and saluted. "There you go, pal. Enjoy it."

He moved toward the door again, but I grabbed him by the shoulder.

"Don't wrinkle the suit, bub," he said.

"What's this about?" I asked.

"Retune your audios, Mack. It's a gift from the lady. Y'know, the one you met earlier today. Classy dame. Big penthouse. Real doll in a squishy organic way."

"I didn't ask for anything."

"You don't have to ask for gifts. That's part a what makes 'em gifts."

"What if I don't want it?"

"Then throw it out," he replied. "The boss wanted me to deliver it personally, so that's what I did. What you do with it afterward ain't my problem." He stepped back and smoothed his jacket. "But if I were you, I'd take it. You could use some style, if you ask me."

"How'd you find me?"

"You stuck in a question askin' loop, Mack? The lady has ways of keepin' tabs on guys."

"Guys like me?" I asked. "Guys like Tony Ringo?" Maybe Humbolt was right. Maybe I was stuck in a loop.

"She don't bother with losers like Ringo," he said. "Guess you must've caught her eye."

I went over to the box and opened it. Inside was a dark blue suit, pinstriped. I pulled out the jacket and wasn't surprised it was large enough to fit my shoulders. It looked expensive and obviously custom-made. I wondered how much it cost Napier to have one whipped up so quickly.

"It's a fabric of the boss's own design," said Humbolt. "Fireproof, puncture-proof, and wrinkle-resistant. Breathes like cotton, though you ain't likely to notice that. Durable stuff. You'll pop a stitch before it does. Ink ain't even dry on the patent papers yet, so the lady must like you."

I tossed the jacket onto the table. "What does she want in return?"

He shrugged. "Nothin'. She just likes givin' gifts."

"Gifts to guys like me," I said.

He nodded. "To guys like you."

I couldn't see the point in asking Humbolt any more questions so I let him leave. I laid out the suit on the couch and scanned it slowly up and down. Pinstripes weren't my style, but it was a nice garment, complete with a dark blue trench coat. The only thing missing was a hat.

There was also a card. It read:

> Dear Mack,
> If you're going to play detective, you should at least look the part.
>
> Hugs and Kisses,
> Lucia

There was something else in the box: a painting of an idyllic garden villa that had only a few hours ago hung in a levitation pod in Proton Towers. I set this aside and left the suit on the couch until Jung finally showed up.

He grunted a hello as he loped over to the refrigerator and found an apple.

"Hard day at work?" I asked, trying to slide into things gracefully.

"Usual." The gorilla lumbered over, and ran his fingers along the crease in the trousers. "Where'd you pick this up?"

"It's a gift from a friend."

"You don't have any friends, Mack." He polished the apple on his lapel. "Except me, and even I'm not always sure about that."

"It's a new development."

"Are you going to try it on?" he asked.

"Maybe." My vocalizer spit out a bit of static, my version of clearing my throat nervously. "Jung, remember this morning when you said something about friends helping each other?"

He bit into his apple while fixing his beady, black eyes on me. "Yeah, Mack. I remember."

So I asked him for a favor, and he just nodded and agreed.

"It could be dangerous. A little bit dangerous. Maybe." I sighed. "Forget it. Never mind."

"Let me get out of this monkey suit." The gorilla lumbered toward his bedroom.

"You don't have to do it. It's okay if you change your mind."

He paused at the doorway. "Forget it, Mack. No big deal."

But it was a big deal. I'd never asked for a favor like this before, and I still didn't feel right putting Jung in this position. There was some danger involved. I calculated a 3 percent chance of something going wrong with this plan, though there was only a 4 percent chance it'd pay off at all.

"You better get dressed, too," shouted Jung from the other room. "The clubs usually have a dress code."

The suit fit perfectly, but I had to borrow Jung's nimble fingers to help with the tie. I had to admit I looked damn good in it. Of course, the very notion of caring at all about aesthetics showed I was more illogical than I wanted to admit. As for Jung, he changed into a deep purple suit that, from my limited perspective, was two degrees below tacky. He also stuck a rose in the lapel, which ended up making him look a bit like a cross between King Kong and a flashy gangster. But he was doing me a favor, so I kept my fashion sense to myself.

Empire's unofficial stance on the arts was one of tolerant indifference. In the Learned Council's ideal city, all citizens would be dedicated to productive tasks. This was a big reason why they'd created the Automated Citizens Act. Robots didn't bother with music or books or television. We did our jobs and never complained.

Biologicals had needs beyond a steady task and a place to recharge. They needed rest, relaxation, and, of course, stimulation. That was just the way it was, and the Big Brains had come to accept it. There was even one government-funded entertainment center. It was small and no one knew where it was, but the Big Brains assured us it was out there somewhere. There were plenty of private clubs, art galleries, and movie houses scattered throughout the city, and the Learned Council allowed their existence.

The only exception was found in jazz music. It was too disorderly, too wild and unpredictable. Too unscientific. While not strictly against the law, it was no secret the Learned Council discouraged its continued existence. And since biologicals were such illogical, uncooperative creatures it flourished. Rock and roll continued its spectacular rise in the rest of the world, but in Empire, jazz still reigned supreme.

Clubs were scattered all over the city, collecting in bunches in lower-class neighborhoods. Some were dark and hidden. Others were shining and obvious. The Golden Diode fell into the latter category. In fact, the entire length of Pi Street was one sparkling, grimy, noisy monument to baser biological urges. It was the kind of place where people went to be cool, to be seen being cool, and to pretend that they didn't care if you saw them being cool.

It was early evening when Jung and I arrived at The Golden Diode and not much was going on yet. There was a doorman on duty, but he didn't seem up to his job yet and let us pass through with nary a glance. Outside, the Diode had been bright, glittering neon, but inside was another story. It was dimly lit to convince a customer of its sullen, moody atmosphere. And to hide the fact that it was a real dive. The exterior must've drained the decorating budget because there wasn't much on the other side of the door but a stage, a bunch of tables, and a bar. The place was quiet, the crowd yet to arrive this early. Probably wouldn't be much going on until after ten.

A little waif of a cigarette girl intercepted us, stepping in front of me. "Don't get many a your kind 'round here, pal."

"Cab drivers?" I asked, pretending not to understand because something about her, maybe the way she chewed her gum like it deserved to suffer, put me in a hostile mode.

"Bots," she replied with some irritation, though not noticeably more than she seemed to carry by default. She pursed her lips, blew a bubble until it popped, then sucked it all back down except for a small remnant on her cheek that she'd failed to notice. "Twenty bucks," she said.

"No, thanks," I replied. "Don't smoke." To drive the point home, I tapped my faceplate where my mouth wasn't.

She groaned. "It's twenty bucks just for walkin' through the door, smartbot. Ricky should've collected it from you, but he's a lazy goddamn prick."

"Sign out front says there's no cover before nine."

"That's for bios," she replied with more frustration and proceeded to masticate her gum harder for my sins. "Bots always gotta pay."

"Isn't that discriminatory?"

The waif smiled, and I could tell her face hurt from the effort. "We're runnin' a business here, pal. Bots come in, don't drink nothing', don't eat nothin', just stand around taking up space."

"I'll buy a drink," I offered.

"Then what? There's a two drink minimum, but don't nobody buy two drinks once the party starts. Except bots. Bots don't drink nothin', don't eat nothin', just—"

"Yeah, I got it. I got it. Twenty bucks seems kind of steep though, doesn't it?"

"If it were up to me, we wouldn't even let your kind through the door." She smiled again, and this time, looked like she meant it. "But it ain't up to me. Now twenty bucks. Or do I gotta call the cops?"

I calculated that as a bluff. Dives like this didn't call the cops. They had ways of handling their own security needs, usually involving back alley legbreakers and superheated electroprods. Though I wasn't in much danger from either, I didn't need to raise a stink. I dug out the twenty bucks and handed it to her.

"Thank you very much, sir," she said with all the warmth of a death ray. "Have a pleasant evening, gentlemen."

I stopped her. "What? No complimentary cigarettes?"

She rolled her eyes and vanished into the gloom.

"How do you want to do this?" asked Jung.

Most robots had the advantage of being factory models. They might have a modification here or there, but in the end, they looked alike except for different serial number and any distinguishing features their owners might care to add. Even the many hundred automated citizens all came from standard issue before gaining their citizenship and except for the red paint slapped on their chassis, they were fairly nondescript.

But I was one of a kind, a limited edition. The professor had created a few other prototypes, but they'd been seized and dismantled before ever being activated. There was only me. It didn't help any that I was a big bot or that some people still remembered me from the media's brief infatuation with my reformation. It was hard to stand out in a crowd in Empire, but I managed better than most. If Tony Ringo spotted me coming, he'd teleport away, and I'd be back to square one.

It would be Jung's job to watch the door, while I sat quietly in some nearby darkened corner, just out of sight. Hopefully, Ringo would make his appearance, Jung would flash me a signal, and I'd be able to sneak up and grab Ringo before he noticed. There were a lot of variables in the plan, the most obvious being that Tony Ringo would have to be an idiot to show up at a regular hangout when people were looking for him. But I had a rationality-contradicting hypothesis he couldn't stay away. It was a biological thing to do. They were creatures of habit. Like robots without the smarts.

I found a good spot by the door that might work, and Jung took a seat at the bar. He ordered a drink while he waited. It wasn't a banana daiquiri, but my rudimentary sense of humor found some enjoyment in imagining it was.

We waited.

I don't mind waiting. Waiting is simple. Waiting is easy. Waiting gets rid of all the pressure until something finally happens. I wanted Ringo to show, and I wanted it to lead to Julie and the kids, back to everything being normal and me driving a cab, and nothing interesting happening. Not because I hated this detective stuff. In some small way, I suspected it was beginning to grow on me. But this wasn't about me. This was about the Bleakers, a perfectly nice family that might need my help. Big emphasis on the *might*.

The Golden Diode filled up with customers over the next

three hours, and as the crowd grew, I began to suspect this was a waste of time. For the first time in my functioning, waiting became something vaguely discomforting. Fourteen minutes past eleven o'clock, I began calculating other courses of action. There were plenty of jazz clubs on Pi Street. Maybe I'd have been smarter to patrol them all than stake out one. Maybe I wasn't in the right neighborhood at all. Maybe Tony Ringo had blown town, and maybe I was wasting my time. It's never fun second-guessing yourself, and with an electronic brain capable of spitting out four hundred and sixteen different scenarios a minute once it gets started, it can become downright discouraging.

"Penny for your calculations, handsome."

It was Lucia Napier. I didn't move my opticals from Jung, so I didn't see her, but I recognized the voice.

"Had a feeling you'd be here." Her hand ran up and down my arm. "Love the suit. It looks good on you."

"I don't have time for this," I said coldly.

"Oh, relax. Tony never shows up before eleven-thirty."

I turned my head enough that Jung remained in the corner of my vision. Napier was wearing a shimmering, low-cut number that hugged her curves and displayed her many charms.

"Why didn't you tell me that before?" I asked.

"Slipped my mind, I guess." She smiled. "Care for a dance, handsome?"

"I don't dance."

"Oh, come on. One dance can't hurt anything." She grabbed my hand and pulled. I stayed put.

"Lady, I know this is all fun and games to you, but I'm here on business."

"Oh, fine. You should learn to lighten up. You'll function longer." She shrugged. "Business, huh? And I thought you were just a cab driver."

I caught the signal from Jung, and my opticals moved toward the door. There was Tony Ringo. I slinked cautiously toward him, hunching low and still standing taller than the rest of the crowd. If I could get close enough.

Ringo turned in my direction and saw me. In one second his squishy brain made the connection and with less than a dozen steps to reach him through the crowd, his hand was already in his jacket, getting ready to push his magic button to make him disappear.

Jung came up behind him and clocked Ringo across the back of the head. Ringo tumbled hard. A blinking metal disk fell out of his jacket, and rolled across the floor. Stunned, Ringo crawled for it, trying not to get stepped on in the confusion. He grabbed it, but before he could do anything else, my foot fell across his hand and the disk. I leaned on him. The disk and his hand shattered. There was probably a loud crunch from both, but the jazz music swallowed that whole. His yelp of pain drew some attention though.

I grabbed Ringo by the back of his jacket and lifted him off the ground. He was swearing, red-faced, clutching his hand.

"Thanks for the help," I told Jung.

He shrugged. "Forget about it."

"My hand!" whined Ringo. "You broke my goddamn hand."

My sympathy ratio for him was remarkably low. I grabbed him by the shoulder and dragged him over to the bar. No one tried to stop me. No one even looked as if they cared. Except for the bouncers, who had yet to make a move. They might change their minds in a minute, but for now they decided Ringo wasn't worth the trouble.

"You got a phone?" I asked the bartender.

"Sure."

"Who are you calling?" asked Jung.

I wasn't sure. The impulse and the number just came to me the moment I laid hands on Ringo.

The phone rang three times and someone picked up. It wasn't Grey or Knuckles, but I had no doubt it was one of their buddies.

"Yeah?"

"It's Megaton," I said. "I've got Ringo."

The voice on the end made a snorting noise. I told him where we were, and he said he was sending over a ride, a gray Condor. That was it. I didn't hesitate, and I knew I'd hand Ringo over because Grey had me by the directives. My artificial will was no longer entirely my own, but there was still some leeway. I'd give Ringo up, but not before I got a chance to question him.

"Thanks, Jung. You can go home now. Or have another drink. I've got him now." I lifted Ringo off the ground and gave him a hard shake. "Trust me. You don't want to see what's about to happen."

"You fuckin' bastard!" roared Ringo. "You're gonna pull my damn arm off!"

"Relax, Tony," I said. "You've got three others."

"Okay, Mack. It's your call." Jung hopped back to his seat on the bar. "Just try to stay out of trouble."

"I'm not the one in trouble." I shook Ringo again. He howled. "And thanks again. I wouldn't have caught him without you."

Jung smiled very slightly. "I know."

I dragged Ringo through the kitchen and into the back alley. It was a quiet place to talk. The only other resident was a bum snoozing by a Dumpster. No telling what other weird science doodads Ringo might have tucked away in that coat, though I suspected if he'd had anything useful, he would've already pulled it. I threw him face first into the wall and performed a quick search. I turned up a shiny new Zap and Heater raygun, the very latest model. In the interest of public safety, I crushed it and tossed it into the Dumpster.

The door swung open, and Lucia, her loyal butler auto at her side, stepped into the alley. I couldn't get rid of her. Still, I tried.

"You aren't going to want to see this, Lucia," I said. "It's not going to be pretty."

"You'd be surprised what she's seen," said Humbolt.

I sighed, but I had higher priority dictates than one spoiled little rich girl.

"The Bleakers, Tony."

"Piss off, tinman."

"That attitude is only going to make this harder."

I slammed Ringo against the wall a few times. Not hard enough to break anything, but enough to get his attention.

"Oh, you are making a big goddamn mistake, you stupid metalhead," groaned Ringo. "When my friends hear about this they're going to burn you a new exhaust port."

"We both know you don't have any friends, Tony. I don't know how much time we have here, so we're going to have to be quick. I'll say it again: Bleakers. What did you do with them?"

I flipped him around and held him by the collar. I would've grabbed him by the throat, but I didn't want to accidentally snap his neck. Biologicals could be so fragile.

"I don't know any Bleakers, man."

I thumped him in the breadbox with a single finger. He exhaled painfully.

"I know you're stupid, Tony, but I didn't think you were stupid enough to lie to a robot." I tapped my gut where my electronic brain was housed. "Memory matrix never lies."

"Yeah, yeah," he wheezed. "I know 'em. But I didn't have nothing to do with their disappearance. I swear."

I shook my head. "Tony, you really are an idiot. I didn't say anything about a disappearance."

"Yeah, you did."

I tapped my gut again. "Memory matrix, Tony."

"Look, you can do whatever you want, but I ain't telling you shit."

"See, here's the thing, Tony . . ."

I grabbed his broken hand and squeezed. He screamed. I squeezed a little harder, and he screamed a lot louder. His fingers were bent in painful, unnatural angles. He must've been tougher than I gave him credit for because he stopped screaming, glaring through teary eyes.

"You fuckin' defect! You goddamn—" His string of swears became incomprehensible. The risk of caving in his skull kept me from smacking him. Instead, I let him slide down the wall and sob for thirty-five seconds.

Lucia was beside me now. My facial analyzer came up blank. She definitely wasn't bothered by this, but whether or not she liked it, I couldn't tell.

"Tell him what he wants to know, Tony," she said. "It'll only get worse."

Ringo pursed his lips tightly shut.

I hoisted him off his feet. "Pick an arm."

Ringo gritted his teeth and spit into my face. The saliva dripped down my faceplate. I didn't know if he thought I was bluffing or if he was just stupid. But he shrieked his head off when I snapped his right ulna.

I gave him another thirty-five seconds to collect himself.

"Oh, quit your whining, Tony. It's a small break."

"You're crazy."

"No, Tony sweetie," said Lucia Napier from behind me. "Dear Mack here isn't crazy. He's a merciless killing machine."

"I told you, tinman," grumbled Ringo hoarsely. "I ain't telling you nothing."

"I'll give you credit, Tony. According to my predictability profile, you should've talked by now. Either you're tougher than I gave you credit for or you think someone is scarier than me. Guess I'll have to show you how serious I am."

He was trembling, sweating, and crying.

Napier was right. I didn't have mercy. Not that I wanted to hurt Ringo. His bones snapped too easily to give me much satisfaction.

"Have it your way. But I don't have much time, and you've got a lot of arms."

"Wait, wait!" Ringo kept squirming in my iron grip, but he wasn't going anywhere. "I don't know nothing! I swear I don't! They don't tell me anything! And even if I could tell you where they're keeping the kid, it wouldn't make any difference. It's too late to stop it now."

Since my faceplate was featureless, I could keep my surprise to myself. I didn't understand much of what Ringo was talking about, but I got the meat of it. Someone had taken the Bleakers for one of the kids. But which kid and for what purpose?

"Tell me who has them," I said. "That's all I want to know."

Ringo looked puzzled. "Wait a minute. You don't know?"

"Know what?"

He frowned. "You don't work for Greenman?"

"Never heard of him."

"Oh, shit! You really don't know who he is. You really just care about that family." He started laughing. It was a rough, humorless chuckle that danced on the edge of hysteria. "You poor, dumb defect, you got no idea what you're in the middle of."

Before I could ask what he meant, light flooded the alley. I marveled at how fast Grey's guys had gotten here. Then I realized it wasn't a gray Condor descending, but a cherry red Albatross.

The Albatross was a luxury rotorcraft, meaning it was big and blocky: a flying rectangle of steel with some fins stuck on the tail for style. Its three whisper-quiet rotors kicked up a lot of wind and dust as it landed beside the Dumpster. The rotors slowed but kept spinning as I gathered these guys weren't planning on sticking around long.

"Mack, what's going on?" asked Lucia.

"I told you to go back in the club," I said. "Now shut up and stay back."

Whether she was insulted or not, she had enough sense not to argue.

The Albatross's back doors slid open. Two goons stepped out. They walked in front of the headlights to try and stay shadowy, but my polarized opticals gave me a clear view of a couple of rough-looking biologicals. One had a thick neck and a harelip. The other had yellow skin and white hair and had a clear dome filled with some kind of bluish gas over his head. He also had tentacles instead of arms. Both wore suits, and Harelip had his jacket open to show a raygun tucked in his belt.

"Oh, krask, am I glad to see you guys," said Ringo. "I thought I was done for."

Dome Head spoke. He didn't move his lips, but some veins throbbed on his temples and a voice issued from a speaker strapped around his throat. The noise that came out was gibberish to me, but Ringo seemed to understand. He replied in some gibberish of his own. I was fluent in twenty-eight different languages, and I didn't get a word of it.

While Dome Head and Ringo shared their brief exchange,

Harelip stared at me. He stood stock still. I couldn't detect him even breathing. He just kept staring.

Dome Head must've said something that put Ringo off because his next reply was in plain old English. "Hey, I know I wasn't supposed to go out, but I got bored. It's not like it matters, right? Not like anyone can stop us, right?"

Dome Head switched over to English, too. "You were warned, Tony. This operation is far too important to jeopardize. Your sloppiness has proven too great a liability."

"Whoa, you can't be serious," said Ringo. "I mean, what's the big deal?"

"Hate to interrupt," I said. "But I'm not done with him. You can have him after I'm finished."

Dome Head smiled mirthlessly. "Mister Megaton, we respect all life, even artificial life. Please don't make us resort to physical violence."

Neither of these guys were much to look at. Dome Head was barely five feet tall and ninety-five pounds at the most. Harelip was significantly larger than your average human, but there was nothing to indicate I couldn't take that gun away from him and pound him into a puddle. Despite my impressive specs, I'd learned to anticipate the unexpected. These two seemed to know who I was, so there was reason to assume their threats weren't empty. I also assumed they weren't as confident as they appeared, or they would've just taken Ringo. Unfortunately, the choice wasn't mine to make. Grey's psychic reprogramming would keep me from handing over Tony Ringo. A confrontation was inevitable, and my battle analyzer came back inconclusive.

So much for the miracles of modern superscience.

Humbolt unbuttoned his coat to reveal his own heater. "If there's trouble, Mack, I got you covered."

I wasn't worried about Humbolt. He looked like he could

handle himself. But Lucia was a liability. When things went down, I couldn't protect both Ringo and her.

"There's not going to be any trouble," I said. "Everybody's going to stay cool. I think we're all smart enough to know nobody wins if things get ugly."

"Agreed," said Dome Head. "Which is why I suggest you release Mr. Ringo into our custody. This is not a negotiation, Mr. Megaton."

Harelip pulled his roscoe. He didn't aim it at anyone but held it at his side.

"I only need five more minutes."

I was buying some time. If my rendezvous showed, these jokers might reconsider their position. Of course, then I'd have a whole new bunch of guys who'd want to take Ringo from me, but one thing at a time.

Dome Head whipped out his tentacles. It was so fast, I didn't even record it on my optics. One tendril looped around my legs. The other wrapped around Ringo, but I kept my grip.

Harelip charged forward and smashed me right across the cranial unit. Hard. The guy was strong as a construction drone. With my legs bound together, I lost my balance and fell over. I didn't let go of Ringo. Nothing can make me let go of something once I've got hold of it. I'd sooner see Ringo ripped in half than release him. From Ringo's pained shrieks, I'd say Dome Head felt the same way.

Humbolt drew his pistol and got off three shots. Point blank. He couldn't miss. But Dome Head activated a personal forcefield, and the blasts dissipated before reaching him.

Harelip didn't bother pulling his gun. He turned and ripped off Humbolt's arm. The arm without the raygun. That's how indifferent he was to the blasts singeing his chest. Humbolt was a stubborn auto and kept firing for all the good it did him.

Harelip knocked the auto's head off with one punch, caved in Humbolt's chest with another. The butler auto collapsed into a twitching pile of scrap.

Dome Head kept his attention on me the whole time. He tightened the pressure.

"You cannot win, Mr. Megaton," he said. "I would think you'd possess enough logic to realize that."

I let go of Ringo, catching Dome Head by surprise. His tentacle snapped back like a rubber band, and Ringo smacked right into him. I figured Dome Head's forcefield was meant for energy blasts. I figured right. Dome Head was knocked off his feet, and the tentacle wrapped around my legs went slack.

I couldn't hope for much time from the distraction. I cranked my power levels up and ran to Dome Head. Harelip moved to intercept. I shoved my fist into his face full force. It didn't crush in his head, but it bloodied his nose and put a wobble in his knees. I unleashed a haymaker that sent him sprawling. I didn't take the time to congratulate myself but turned back on Dome Head.

His tentacles whipped again, but I was ready this time. I caught one in each hand, and yanked him into the air, swinging him in a high arc and smashing him down into the ground. Then I did it again. His helmet cracked, leaking little wisps of blue smoke. He started hyperventilating and flopping around like a fish out of water.

Tony Ringo had yet to recover from being caught in the middle of a tug-of-war, and I grabbed him before he got the chance. I was kind enough not to seize him by his broken arm.

A scream filled my audios. Lucia Napier. In the eleven-second conflict, I'd lost track of her. Now I turned to scan her held in Harelip's clutches. The guy was thick-skinned, all right.

He grinned, licked his bloodied face with a long green

tongue. "Power down," he said. "Hand over Ringo, and I won't break her neck."

"Can't do it."

Harelip scowled, showing rows of crooked, jagged teeth. "Don't think I'm bluffing."

"I don't. But I can't give you Ringo. There's a foreign directive in my programming. I don't have a choice."

Napier didn't appear nervous, though it was hard to tell since the bruiser's hand covered half her face. As for me, I was cool as stainless steel. It was just the way I was manufactured. Some small regret came to me. Napier may have been a pain, but she didn't deserve to die over a two-time loser like Ringo. I'd warned her not to be here.

"Then I guess this dame ain't much good to me," said Harelip.

"No," I disagreed. "Right now, she's the only thing keeping me from pounding you into paste. Want to see how long you'll last if you hurt her? Trust me, it'll be the longest five minutes of your life."

Harelip smiled as he tightened his grip. "You're bluffing."

"I never bluff. Not part of my personality template. But I know what you're thinking. You're thinking you're a tough guy, and sure, you're pretty strong. And I can tell you're a fast healer by the way your black eye has disappeared already. But I'd put my indestructible alloy up against mutant flesh and blood any day.

"But you're also thinking of Tony here." I gave Ringo a good shake. "I'll be fighting at a disadvantage, seeing as how I have no choice but to hold onto him, and since he is a fragile little thing, I'll have to spend a lot of time making sure he doesn't get creamed by a random punch."

Harelip grinned. "That's what I'm thinking."

"Fair enough," I relented. "Guess it's your call then."

He didn't think long before doing the last thing I would've predicted. He went for his heater. I'll admit it. Sometimes, when the unexpected happens, I can freeze up. It wasn't much, two-thirds of a second. Enough for Harelip to pull his gun and aim it at Ringo's head. If I'd been faster, I could've put myself between Ringo and the blast. But I wasn't fast enough.

Before Harelip could pull the trigger he was suddenly lit up with streams of purple voltage. He didn't utter a sound, released his hostage and went limp. Napier stepped aside. Drooling, Harelip tried to shake off the effects.

She tapped her belt. "The Napier Brand Personal Defense Shock-o-tronic Field Generator. Every girl should have one."

Before Harelip could regain his senses I took advantage of the opportunity to work him over. A blow to the gut, a couple of jabs, and he was still standing. He wasn't as strong as me, but the guy could take a beating all right. A hard right cross finally knocked him off his feet and into dreamland.

"I didn't think you invented anymore," I said.

"Oh, just something I threw together one restless night."

I scanned the remains of Humbolt. He was only an auto. According to the law he could no more be killed than a vacuum cleaner. True, he was just a bunch of wires and cogs and if someone spread them out across a table it would be so many scattered parts. Put them together in a dozen different ways and end up with a dozen different machines. But then again, the same thing could've been said of me.

"Sorry about your robot," I said.

Napier knelt over Humbolt's torso. "Don't worry, Mack. His brain is reinforced." She pushed a button and his chest opened to reveal a small titanium box. Much smaller than most robot brains, but Napier was a genius. "Oh, yeah. No problem. I'll get him home and pop him into a spare chassis. Good as new."

That was a relief.

I said, "Uh, and I'm sorry about—"

"Oh, please, Mack. You don't have to apologize. You told me not to follow you into the alley. Anyway, I'm a big girl. I can take care of myself just fine, thank you."

She reached up and put her hand on my cheek. She wasn't upset with me at all. Lucia Napier was a strange woman. Strange, but endearing.

Ringo squirmed in my grasp, but he wasn't going anywhere. He also spit out some idle threats that I ignored.

Harelip was still out for the count, but the funny thing was his face, which a bare fourteen seconds ago was mashed into a bloody pulp. Now it was now nice and unbroken. And I estimated he'd be awake by now except for that weird Shock-o-tronic device Napier had zapped him with.

I searched Dome Head. It wasn't easy with him flopping around, but I found a teleportation disk, like Ringo used, in his coat pocket.

"Oh, what's that?" she asked.

"Some kind of teleportation gizmo." I performed a quick search of Harelip and found his own disk. It was smashed. No surprise there.

I tossed the intact gizmo to Napier.

"A gift?" she asked.

"You can keep it, Lucia, as long as you tell me anything interesting you find when you crack it open."

"Deal." She dropped it in her purse. "So what do you expect me to find?"

"I don't know, but that's some hi-tech. Figure it's worth a look."

"Why, Mister Megaton, you're beginning to sound more like a detective and less like a cab driver every minute."

She was right. There was something appealing about breaking bones and asking questions, about mixing it up with lowlifes and intellectual dames. It was a damn sight more stimulating than shuttling uptowners around the city.

I yanked Dome Head by his tie. "Who do you work for? And why would anyone go to this much trouble to kidnap a couple of kids?"

He gasped and gurgled. Harelip wasn't in any condition to talk either.

A new rotorcar roared into the alley. The Condor was a sporty model, 83 percent the size of the Albatross. It had rounded corners and a small, radiator-mounted prop that moved way too slowly for any practical performance and was simply there for aesthetics. The alley was big but crowded. Still, the driver was skilled enough to set her down in the small space available.

"Let me guess," said Napier. "You want me to shut up and stay back."

I tapped my faceplate where my nose could've been. She got the gesture anyway.

Two guys stepped out. They looked like norms, but there was no way of knowing for sure. I was running across a statistically improbable number of mutants lately, so I didn't rule anything out.

The shorter one eyed Dome Head dangling from the tie in my right hand and Tony Ringo clutched in my left. "We're here for Ringo."

I dropped Dome Head. His helmet hit the ground with a glassy chime.

"You can have him, but I want to talk to your boss."

The norms chuckled. "Just give him to us."

Of course, they knew I didn't have a choice. I knew it too.

Then again, I was still holding onto Ringo. Maybe Grey's reprogramming was finally slipping.

"Look," I said. "We had a little bit of trouble in this alley. Blastfire, yelling, fisticuffs, the whole nine yards. Now maybe in this neighborhood at this time of night that won't attract any attention. Or maybe there just happened to be a Tank monitor drone nearby to detect all the unsociable doings, and a rotorcar has already been dispatched. All I know is that I've got Ringo, and I'll hand him over eventually, but it might be a minute or five. Now why don't you use that two-way radio wristwatch and see what your boss wants to do?"

The short guy nodded to his buddy, who shuffled off by the Condor and had a six-second conversation before nodding back to shorty.

"Okay," he said, "but what about the skirt?"

"Skirt stays," I replied.

"Too bad. She's got nice stems."

Shorty leaned over and rapped on Dome Head's helmet.

"Make yourself useful, bot, and throw these mooks in the trunk, would ya?"

I was happy to oblige, considering I was getting a free ride. It was a tight fit, but I managed to cram both Harelip and Dome Head in. Before they shut it, they gave Harelip an injection of some yellow liquid. Knocked him right out.

I tossed Tony Ringo into the backseat of the Condor and shoved in beside him. It was a tight squeeze, but Ringo wound up on the losing end of the deal so I didn't mind.

"Keep in touch, Mack," said Napier.

I nodded to her, then shut the door. The rotorcar lifted off, and we were on our way.

A partition slid up between the front and backseat and every window went pitch black. The boss must've liked his privacy and didn't want any robot recording his home address.

"It's not too late," said Ringo. "I know you can tear this car to pieces. We can escape. I know people."

"So I keep hearing, Tony." I spread out a little in my seat and mashed him against the door. "Now shut up and enjoy the ride."

I did consider his offer, but it was a moot point. Though I seemed to have regained some control of myself, Grey was still pushing the buttons. More importantly, I was pretty sure Ringo was a small-time hood, a loser who didn't know much of anything. It was better to move up the ladder and see who was waiting on the top rung.

We flew around for an hour and fifteen minutes. A good rotorcar, depending on skyway traffic, could cover half of Empire in that time, but there was also the likely probability the car was circling a few extra minutes as an extra precaution. Finally we landed.

The windows cleared. We were in a personal hangar. It was big enough for a collection of rotorcars, many of them pristine classics. There was even a Wright Wyvern that looked as if it'd just rolled off the factory floor. Except they hadn't been made in factories, and last I'd heard there were only three in existence. There was no trace of the outside world, no way of knowing where I was.

Some thugs snatched Ringo, Dome Head, and Harelip. They were all mutants, and one of them had a head resembling an orange jellyfish. That was an extreme mutation, the likes of which you rarely saw even in Tomorrow's Town.

He caught me scanning. "You got a problem, buddy?"

"No problem," I replied. "But you might want to grab a napkin. You're dripping all over your collar."

He executed a maneuver with his tentacles that I could only assume was derogatory in nature.

Jellyfish and the gang dragged Ringo and his buddies one

way while Shorty directed me another. On the other side of that hangar was a long hallway with plush carpeting and good old-fashioned simulated light fixtures. The photon generator even did a fair replication of soft candlelight. There were odd paintings on the wall, full of shapes and colors but all abstract and unrecognizable. Somewhere a six-year-old finger painter was making a fortune.

We stopped at one of the doors. It had an actual handle. Shorty had to reach over and turn it, and the door didn't slide open but instead swung on hinges. I'd heard about doors like that, scanned them in movies, but it was a weird thing to scan in person.

"They're waiting for you," said my escort.

I stepped inside. They closed the door behind me. On the other side was a greenhouse. Except it was red, not green. It didn't have a glass roof but a bunch of soft crimson spotlights overhead. It was filled with plants, almost every single one a strange blue color with hexagonal leaves. I didn't recognize them, but foliage wasn't part of my database, and you didn't scan a lot of greenery in Empire. Or blue-ery.

Knuckles the Mark Three was there, still wearing my bowler. And Grey sat in a cozy chair beside the auto.

"Hey, Mack, good to see you," said Grey.

Knuckles beeped in a decidedly sarcastic way.

Something ruffled in the bunch of plants next to them, and out stepped a four-foot, two-inch biological in overalls. His skin was a shiny emerald hue and 30 percent of his height was devoted to his forehead. He had big black eyes and two antennae over them. He cradled a plant in his gloved hands. Whatever it was, it was breathing surprisingly loud for a plant.

He smiled with his very small mouth. "So you must be this Mack Megaton I've been hearing so much about."

"If I must," I agreed. "And let me guess. You must be Greenman."

He touched his face in that spot where he should've had a nose but didn't. I got the gesture anyway.

9

"You can call me Abner," said Greenman. "Got to tell you, Mack, I'm impressed. First, you find Tony Ringo in . . . how long has it been, Grey?"

"Eleven hours, boss."

"Ten hours, forty-four minutes, six seconds," I corrected. "Give or take."

Greenman grinned. It was hard to spot with his little mouth. "See, that's what I like in my people. Precision. An eye for detail. But what truly impresses me is that you know my name."

"Wasn't hard to come by," I said.

"Just the same, not many people know it. Isn't that right, Grey?"

Grey nodded. "That's right, boss. Like to keep a low profile, stay out of the . . . whaddayacallit . . . limelight."

"Exactly," said Greenman. "You seem to be a remarkable detective for a bot who makes a living driving a cab."

"I'm a versatile unit," I replied.

He set the plant down in a bed of soil. The breathing blue

flora scuttled over to a comfortable spot and dug in its roots. Greenman stroked its leaves. The plant purred.

"So what do you want, Mack? Money, I suppose. Everybody wants money. Makes the world go round, doesn't it?"

"I'll take some money."

"See that Mack gets a fair payment for services rendered. Throw in a bonus for timeliness and . . . what's that phrase they use?"

"Chutzpah, boss."

"Yes, chutzpah." Greenman frowned, mumbling to himself. "Chutzpah, chutzpah, chutzpah." He shrugged. "Odd sounding word, isn't it?"

Knuckles beeped his agreement.

"Perhaps I should consider making Mack a permanent addition to the payroll," said Greenman.

"Don't know, boss," said Grey. "They already sell chauffeur autos for cheap."

Knuckles beeped again, this time with a shrill antagonism.

It was a safe assumption that Greenman's goons weren't very fond of me. Our first meeting hadn't gone so well and now I'd made them look bad in front of their boss.

"Of course, money isn't the real reason you're here now, is it, Mack?" asked Greenman.

"No, but I've got a power bill to pay."

"Well, what other personal business can I help you with?"

"I want to know who Ringo's working for."

"As would I, Mack. As would I."

"You don't know?"

"Until a few days ago, I would've said he was in my employ. Apparently I was mistaken." Greenman frowned. "In any case, I've arranged for a discussion with Ringo, and you're welcome to sit in."

Grey stood. "I don't know if that's such a good idea, boss. How do you know we can trust this bot?"

Knuckles beeped his agreement.

"Come now, Grey. We wouldn't even have Ringo in our custody without Mack's services. His trustworthiness is as reliable as your considerable talents, so to question him is to bring yourself into question as well. If you're uncertain of yourself, please feel free to say so now."

Grey sneered, but didn't say anything.

"Excellent." Greenman tapped a button on his dusty overalls, and they transformed into a wrinkle-free olive suit complete with a dark green tie in a perfect Windsor knot. I could've really used one of those. All the dust was gone, and there was a fresh crease in the pants and some shiny cuff links as well. "Shall we, gentlemen?"

"After you, boss," said Grey.

We walked down another hallway. Greenman led the way, with Grey next, then me, then Knuckles clomping right behind me. Close enough, I detected a very slight ping in his left shoulder joint every time his right foot hit the floor. An urge to take back my bowler perched on his head and dismantle him bolt by bolt in the process rose in me, but I squelched it.

They were holding Ringo in a clean white room with clean white lights and a single clean white chair. There was a faded stain on the ceiling. Old blood, I guessed, though I didn't ponder how it'd gotten up there.

Ringo looked scared. Very scared. He was always a little punchy, always had this look on his face that said he was perfectly willing to pick a fight, even if he wasn't always willing to follow that attitude to its logical conclusion. Now, he looked terrified, sweating and crying and holding his broken arm close to his body. I was somewhat surprised that he didn't appear any more roughed up than the sorry state he'd arrived in. There was plenty of time left to work him over. Hell, maybe Greenman wanted to get a few slaps in himself.

Somehow, I doubted it. Not because Greenman was such a little guy either. Abner Greenman was clearly a man in charge, and Tony Ringo was a loser, designed by nature to be pushed around by anyone and everyone. I felt sorry for him. In the messy business of biological evolution, defective designs were inevitable. It wasn't much different than robots, except we got to learn our lesson after one or two unsatisfactory prototypes. But biologicals, they just kept churning out the useless ones.

No, Greenman wasn't the kind of guy to slap around anyone. That was the impression I got, anyway. Could've been wrong because Ringo was trembling, and it wasn't me or Knuckles or Grey that he was staring at now. It was little Abner Greenman.

"Hello, Tony," said Greenman.

"Hello, Mr. Greenman, sir." Tony's voice shuddered. "I'm sorry. They made me do it. I'm sorry."

Greenman circled Ringo. He rose an inch in the air with each step, like he was walking an invisible staircase. When he got high enough, he straightened Ringo's collar. "Look at you, young man. Such a mess."

Greenman's antennae twitched. The door opened, and a nurse walked into the room. She was blue-skinned, voluptuous, with breasts threatening to spill out of her low-cut uniform, which I doubted was regulation. Maybe it was this new detective gig that made me notice, but she had long legs that went on forever, circling the curve of space and meeting themselves back at the end of eternity. And her face: it belonged in movies. Monster movies. The kind where something with six eyes and a lamprey mouth sucks out teenagers' brains.

Her voice was smooth as jagged glass. "Now, this'll only hurt for a minute, sweetie." The nurse injected something into Ringo's broken arm. He winced. His arm made a weird crackling noise for twelve seconds, then—bam—it straightened good as new.

"Thank you, nurse." Greenman patted her gently on the ass.

"Fresh." She chuckled. Or gurgled. She ran a green tongue around her sucker mouth in a way I assumed was supposed to be appealing and pinched his tiny cheeks before swinging her hips to an out-of-the-way corner.

Greenman turned his attention back to Ringo. "Now, isn't that better?"

"Yes, sir, Mister Greenman."

"Good, because I find pain in the subject distracts from the extraction process."

Ringo paled.

"You don't got to do that, Mister Greenman. You don't! I'll tell you everything! Everything you want to know!"

"I know you will, Tony. Every little detail."

The nurse sashayed over. She dropped a tin beanie on Ringo's skull. It had two short antennae on top.

"Now, I advise you to pay attention, Mr. Megaton," said Greenman. "You're about to witness something few men have ever seen. And if you're fortunate, I might even allow Mr. Grey to let you keep the memory."

Ringo started blathering, but he didn't last long. The nurse pumped him with another injection, and he went limp.

"The device acts as a conduit. However, the talent belongs to me. It's rather like reading a book." Greenman put his hands on the beanie. His eyes glowed black. Don't ask me to describe how. I scanned it, and I still can't explain it. The beanie lit up, and lines of electricity ran up the antennae. Ringo groaned. He twitched and foamed at the mouth.

It didn't take long: twenty seconds. If Ringo's mind was a book, then it was a short one.

When Greenman finished, Ringo sat there, staring blankly, drooling, his lips flapping but no sound coming out.

"Is he going to be okay?" I asked. I didn't like Ringo, but I wasn't sure anybody deserved to end up like this.

"Oh, I'm afraid not," said Greenman. "The process is terribly traumatic. Most minds can't withstand it. Rather like burning a book while you read it." The nurse handed him a handkerchief, and he wiped his hands. "The bad news is that he knew very little. I might be able to extract a useful bit, but not the information you required."

"And I'm supposed to take your word for it."

"To be perfectly honest, Mr. Megaton, I don't see that you have a choice."

Knuckles clamped me on the shoulder.

So here we were again: Knuckles, Grey, and me. I'd formulated battle strategies against Knuckles, and was confident I could take him down. But I hadn't figured a way around Grey yet, and Greenman was an unknown quantity.

"No need for violence, Mark Three." Greenman's eyes flashed golden, and his antennae straightened. I levitated off the floor. "Mr. Megaton will be leaving quietly. Won't you, Mack?"

It's funny. You get used to being the toughest bot in the room, then find yourself on the short end of things all of a sudden. I could take Ringo, but now a cheese sandwich could take Ringo, so that wasn't saying much. I stood a statistically favorable chance against Knuckles. But Grey's electrokinesis and Greenman's telekinesis put me in a tight spot. I backed down.

It was the only logical thing to do. As a machine, it made perfect sense, but it still bugged me, somewhere deep inside my artificial soul.

"Sure, Abner, sure."

He released his telekinetic grip and lowered me gently to the floor. I could've stepped on him, but what would that have accomplished?

"Please escort Mr. Megaton out, would you, Grey."

"But, boss—" started Grey.

Greenman shut him up with a hard glance.

"Sure thing, Mr. Greenman," said Grey. And he meant it. Whatever his hard feelings toward me, they didn't hold up to his fear of this four-foot biological. I was almost insulted by that, but I figured Greenman was the most dangerous guy in whatever room he happened to be in. Who knew what other strange mental powers he might have in that giant brain of his? Not me, and I didn't think I wanted to find out.

The nurse sauntered over and caressed Greenman's antennae. He ran his hand along her fishnets. She made that gurgling sound again, and they exited.

That left Grey and Knuckles to deal with, but a smart bot knew when he was beat. I cast one last scan at Tony Ringo, now nothing but a bag of meat. Whatever information he might've had was wiped clean, and I had nothing left to go on.

Grey and Knuckles escorted me back to the Condor. None of us said a word. I got in back without being told, and Knuckles hopped in beside me. The windows went black. The rotorcar lifted off, and I was off on another of those meandering, time-killing rides.

The backseat was a tight fit for a couple of big robots, and Knuckles wasn't mindful of my personal zone. He was close enough to drip oil on my suit collar. So close, I could hear the hum of his wiring. He kept his optical trained on me the whole time, but I kept staring straight ahead.

"Don't suppose you'd like to give me back my hat?" I asked casually.

He beeped, shrilly and without humor.

"How do you keep it on that misshapen box of a head anyway? Duct tape?"

Knuckles didn't utter another beep, and that was the end of our discussion for the remainder of the trip.

It's always a little strange for me sitting with another robot that hasn't qualified for citizen status. Here I was with all the rights (well, most of them anyway) of a biological citizen, while Knuckles was basically considered a walking refrigerator. I could bust him to pieces, and it'd only be considered an act of vandalism. We were both made up of the same basic components. Except I'd passed my minimal sentience examination, and he hadn't. Maybe no one had ever bothered to get him tested. Maybe he had taken the test and flunked out on the Rorschach portion. Maybe when they showed him that blot of ink he'd answered honestly, saying it was just a blot of ink instead of lying like I had.

Butterfly, my tin-plated ass.

Of course, they'd known I was lying. That was okay. It was one of the marks of sentience, the ability to distinguish reality from fantasy and still indulge in fantasy. In other words: I lied, therefore I thought.

For whatever reason, I always felt bad among less fortunate robots. Even an old Mark Three that, from what I could tell, would've been a real exhaust port.

The Condor finally set down in an alley. I calculated my position by the skyline. It didn't do me a lot of good for finding Greenman. He could've been hidden away in a hundred places in this town. Hell, they could've flown around in a big circle and deposited me right across the street from Greenman's secret hideout, and I wouldn't have known.

"Got a hanky?" I asked Grey as I got out of the rotorcar. "Your boy here is leaking oil."

Knuckles clamped onto my shoulder. It was a mistake. Outside of the car with enough room to maneuver and a reaction already cued up in my battle simulator, I didn't hold back. I grabbed him by his head, kicked his left leg out from under him and pushed. He fell over. Deftly, I snatched the bowler off his head when he did. It was an impressive move. Not the push. Anyone with enough strength and the right angle could knock over a Mark Three. Not crushing the hat in my clumsy mitt was a real accomplishment. Maybe my fine motor coordination was finally coming along.

I dusted the hat gently while Knuckles struggled to get back up. It was not a pretty sight.

I figured Grey would try and shut me down with his mind, but he didn't do anything. "Let's get this straight, Megaton. I don't like you, and if it were up to me, I'd fry you to the very last circuit." His eyes flashed green for a second. "But Mr. Greenman, he likes you. Thinks you might be useful to us, might be a good guy to have around. I think you've recorded too much, but, hey, the boss says not to touch you, so I don't touch you. But when he changes his mind . . ."

His eyes flashed again.

By now, Knuckles had creaked his way to his feet again. He barked three aggressive pings in my direction.

"That's enough," said Grey. He reached into his suit and pulled out a thick envelope, which he handed to me. "Compliments of Mr. Greenman. Now, I'd advise you to get a new apartment, get back to driving a cab, and forget about any of this business."

Grey and Knuckles climbed back into their rotorcar. I tipped my hat to the Condor as it soared away.

The envelope was full of cash. Not bad for my first day's work as a detective. I could only hope tomorrow would be as lucrative.

10

I'd tried to find Julie and the kids, and I'd actually come closer than I'd expected to, which wasn't very close at all. Tony Ringo was gone now, and I had no way of finding Abner Greenman. Even if I did find him, I doubted I could convince him to give me the information he'd sucked out of Ringo's head. Information, in all likelihood, not worth much anyway because Ringo had been a small-time loser. Someone would have had to have been an idiot to trust him with any secrets.

There were the other two goons, Harelip and Dome Head. I hadn't gotten the chance to talk to them, and by now, they'd probably had their brains emptied, too.

But I wasn't giving up yet.

The cash in my pocket, though I hadn't bothered to count it yet, was thick enough to pay my power bill for a few weeks at the very least. Freed from the burden of daily employment, I could blow off my job and keep looking. I didn't think Greenman would appreciate me using his payment to continue wedging myself into the gears of whatever sordid goings-on were taking place, but maybe he would. Chutzpah, he'd said.

Continuing toward this objective would almost certainly lead me back into confrontation with Greenman's goons. As long as Grey had me by the on/off switch, I was at a severe disadvantage. My own diagnostics had turned up zilch in my electronic brain. I had no choice. I needed an expert.

My shrink wasn't too happy to see me at her apartment door. I attributed this to the lateness of the hour. She adjusted her flannel robe.

"How did you get this address?" Doc Mujahid asked.

"Phone book," I replied.

"How'd you get past the doorman?"

"He was asleep. Might've woken him still, but that's some thick carpeting in your lobby, Doc. So are you going to invite me in?"

"Do you know what time it is?"

"I always know what time it is, Doc."

A curious smile crossed her face. "Was that a joke, Mack?"

"Might've been." I shrugged. "Even I'm not always sure."

The almost-joke was enough to get the doc's interest up, but she didn't step aside yet.

"I know it's late," I said. "And I know you don't want patients bothering you outside of the office, but—"

"Actually, Mack, this is the first time I've ever had a patient stop by my apartment."

That made sense. How many emergencies could pop up in a cybernetic psychologist's patient roster? Robots were usually polite enough to wait until office hours.

"Nice suit, Mack."

She showed me to her living room and excused herself to make some coffee.

The doc had a nice place. It wasn't as nice as Lucia's, but not too shabby. The living room was big enough for a sofa and a couple of bookshelves. There were some paintings and knickknacks, but nothing to draw my attention. It wasn't that big, but I assumed there were other rooms behind the various doors.

Doc Mujahid came back with her coffee. "Why are you here, Mack?"

"I need your help. I need you to check out my electronic brain. There's something inside—" I tapped my gut. "—something I need removed."

She raised an eyebrow. "A corruption?"

"Yeah."

"And what makes you think this? Have your diagnostic functions detected anything?"

"No. Nothing detected."

"Have you been acting peculiarly?"

"Sort of."

"How so?"

"I can't explain, Doc. I just need you to take a look, find and remove it. I can explain then."

The doc quietly looked me over.

"I wouldn't bother you if it wasn't important."

"Follow me, Mack."

She led me into another room occupied by a large black plastic desk and a solid row of blinking consoles. The furnishings took up most the room, and I occupied 66 percent of the rest. The doc had to sit at her desk just to fit in the room. She pushed a button. The machines hummed to life. A monitor crackled to life.

"What's this?" I asked.

"It's a computer," she replied.

"In your apartment?"

"One day, every apartment will have one. Perhaps more than one."

"Sure, Doc."

It sounded specious to me. Even in Tomorrow's Town, I couldn't think of anyone wanting to shell out the dough and sacrifice elbow room for their own computer, a device which by and large couldn't end up being anything more than an expensive calculator. For the doc, it might be worth it though.

The doc opened a drawer and thumbed through a selection of data tubes, picking out one labeled "personality decryption utility" and shoving it in a slot on the desk and locking it in with a twist. The computers seemed to like that because they started making a lot of beeping and whirring noises.

She handed me a jack. "Plug yourself in, Mack. I don't suppose you can tell me what I'm looking for."

"Wish I could, Doc."

"A mystery then," she said. "Well, let's see what we've got here."

She pressed a few buttons, and my digital consciousness streamed across her monitors. She didn't take her eyes off them for three solid minutes, leaning back in her chair and drumming her fingers on the desk. Sometimes, she'd tap a couple of keys and nod to herself.

"So, Mack, is there anything you'd like to talk about while we wait?"

"No, Doc. I'm good."

"Nothing?"

"No."

"Nothing concerning Lucia Napier?"

I replayed the question a few times to make sure I'd heard her right.

"She called me earlier today," said Doc Mujahid, "and mentioned you'd paid her a visit."

I shouldn't have been surprised the doc and Lucia knew each other. They were both smart ladies. Probably got together every Saturday for the Weekly Super Genius Cotillion Brunch.

"She mentioned you were looking for someone."

"Yeah," I replied vaguely. "Personal matters."

"I see."

I waited for her to press the subject, but she let it drop. It wasn't like she had to ask any questions. My electronic psyche lay bare before her on her monitors. She could always open a few memory files and know everything she wanted. The doc wasn't likely to do that. Went against her code of ethics, she'd once explained. The basic programming, the inner workings, those she studied by necessity. The memory matrix she considered off-limits as a matter of patient confidentiality.

"You made quite an impression on Lucia," she said.

"She's just got a thing for robots," I said.

"Is that what you think, Mack?"

"It's true, isn't it?"

"Mmhmmm," she said, more to herself than me.

I filtered that sound through my analyzers and came up with nothing worthwhile.

"And what did you think of her?" she asked.

"I'm not here for analysis, Doc."

She pushed a few buttons as more data poured through her monitors.

"Not that kind of analysis anyway," I said. "Can we drop the subject?"

"If you insist."

"I do. I do insist."

Forty-five seconds passed before I found myself incapable of keeping my vocalizer deactivated. I usually excel at shutting up, but some compulsion seized me. I blamed it on all the time I was spending with biologicals.

"It's nothing. I'm a machine. Couldn't go anywhere."

"Don't you have biological friends?" asked the doc.

"Yeah."

"And is there any reason you can't have another?"

I removed my bowler and fiddled with it to give my hands something to do. Another bad biological habit. "No."

"Is there any particular reason that you can't be friends with Lucia Napier?"

"She's a technophile," I replied. "I'm pretty sure anyway."

"How is that an obstacle, Mack?"

It was a good question, and I didn't have a good answer. This time I managed to stay quiet.

"Would you like my opinion, Mack?"

"Not really, Doc."

"Too bad, because I'm going to give it to you anyway. I think Lucia could do you some good. She might be able to help you with your assimilation issues."

"I don't have assimilation issues."

"Yet you continue to isolate yourself through categorization. You insist on calling yourself a 'machine,' for instance."

"I am a machine."

"Yes, you are. But you are also an intelligent being."

"I'm just code, Doc." I pointed to the monitor. "Ones and zeroes, that's all I am."

"Mack, if you were to extract a human brain and open it up, do you know what you would find?"

"Goop."

"Exactly. The consciousness, the personality, the dreams, desires, and phobias, they're all there in that goop, but it's only a great big wad of fat in the end. The soul is not found in the flesh."

"What, Doc? Are you telling me I have a soul now?"

"I don't even know if there is such a thing, Mack. But I do know that thought is thought and that nobody truly understands it."

"Maybe," I said. "Or maybe I'll snap one day and kill everybody."

"Happens every day, and not only to machines."

The doc's computer made a soft ping, and she started typing.

"Find something, Doc?"

"Interesting. There appears to be some foreign code intermingled with your behavioral routines. Is this what you're looking for?"

"Maybe," I said, knowing full well it must've been. "Can you purge it?"

She leaned closer to the monitors and spent four minutes, six seconds typing rapidly. The computer would beep irritably an average of every eleven seconds.

"It's there all right, but I've never seen anything quite like it," she said. "It's a worm, but it's divided and dispersed in various files. It shouldn't be able to have much of an effect."

"It's doing something, Doc. Trust me."

She shrugged. "I can't remove it. Not without risking damaging your core programming."

"I'm willing to take the chance," I said.

"I'm not." She pushed a few buttons. "There's good news though. Your maintenance protocols seem to be removing it on their own. Fascinating development, really. I've never seen an electronic brain so adaptable."

"Yeah, I'm a walking miracle of superscience, Doc."

She either didn't catch the sarcasm or failed to acknowledge it. She rarely did.

"I think, given enough time, you'll purge the corruption on your own."

"How long?"

"I can't say."

"Well, thanks, Doc." I put my hat back on, trying to not sound disappointed. "Appreciate your time."

She kept her eyes fixed on the screen, engrossed in the new data. She was lost in a sea of binary code.

"I'll let myself out," I said.

She turned her head a few degrees so that she could still look at the screen, but kind of glance at me at the same time. "Mack, I meant what I said about Lucia. I noticed some definite improvements in your socialization functions."

"Maybe it's not her," I said.

"Perhaps not. Would you care to tell me what you've been doing?"

"Rather not, Doc, if you don't mind."

She didn't push because she was too distracted by the monitor readout. "Fine, Mack. Whatever you're doing, I recommend you continue. I think you might be on the verge of a breakthrough." There was a beep, and she nodded very slowly. "Fascinating."

"Yeah, Doc, great stuff, I'm sure. But I gotta go."

Then I beat it before she got the bright idea to hook me up to her computers and take a more detailed look at my digital subconscious.

I needed a recharge. The battery the city stuck me with was good for about twenty-six hours, depending on my levels of activity. When I didn't move more than I had to and basically let my electronic brain run on autopilot, I could stretch it to thirty-two. But getting mixed up with gangsters and brainy dames had burned the juice faster than normal. I still had three hours left, but I never liked to run with less than five in reserve.

I could also use some time to recompile and defragment. I was a learning machine, but all the data I'd absorbed today was mostly a jumble of information until I shut myself down and allowed my electronic brain to sort and file it into manageable bits. I was hoping that after a good night's recharge, I'd figure out what to do next.

I set aside my recharge cycle for another hour, long enough to pay Lucia Napier a visit. Proton Towers at the wee hours of the morning were a pair of sparkling columns, shining beacons circled by ever-present flying gun drones.

Dennis the doorman was gone, but there was another doorman who was nearly identical in every way: the same nose, same eyes, same ever-smiling mouth and chipper demeanor. Either his lack of distinctive features had flummoxed my facial distinguisher or he was Dennis's twin brother. Or a clone. That was unlikely though, since so far all viable clones were bald albinos with a tendency to speak backwards.

Despite the lateness of the hour, I knew Near Dennis would let me in. I'd called ahead, and Lucia had assured me I was allowed to visit her anytime, day or night, scheduled or spontaneous. She'd also said I simply *must* come by tonight. When I'd asked if she'd rather wait until tomorrow, she'd said she was too excited to sleep anyway.

I stepped off the pod into the penthouse. Humbolt greeted me, in a brand new chassis and a freshly pressed cream tuxedo.

"Yo, Mack," said the butler auto.

"Humbolt, good to see you functional again," I replied.

"Can't keep a good auto down. This way."

He led me into the living room and down the secret stairs to Lucia's lab. She'd been busy. The teleportation disk was spread out in a jumble of parts. She held something in a pair of tweezers under a magnifying glass.

"What did you do, Lucia?" I asked.

"I took it apart. How else was I going to study it?"

I suppose she was right, but I'd hoped she hadn't destroyed

the gizmo. Or if she had, I hoped she'd learned something worthwhile.

Without looking up, she motioned for me to come over. "You must take a look at this. It's simply delicious."

She moved aside so I could use the magnifying glass, but I didn't need it. I zeroed in with my opticals and scanned the whatchacallit. "Yeah?"

"Isn't it amazing?"

"Amazing," I agreed. "What does it do?"

"I have absolutely no idea. Not the slightest notion." She set it down and made a sweeping gesture at the mess. "I barely understand any of this."

She laughed.

"Don't you get it, Mack? I've always understood everything. Everything!"

She hunched back over the disassembled gizmo and began shifting pieces around.

"Can you put it back together?" I asked.

"Oh, sure, no problem. I took notes."

She held up a handful of papers filled with scrawled handwriting.

"You say it's a matter transmitter?" she asked.

"Yeah."

"Oh, but it's not. It's more of a matter shifter. This part right here, it's some sort of underspace conduit. And this part, it creates a stasis field."

"I thought you said you didn't understand it."

"Oh, don't be silly, Mack. Of course I understand it. Just not nearly as well as I understand everything else. The technology is advanced, prototypical. Except it's not a prototype. It's mass produced. Someone has a factory spitting these things out, and they're not sharing."

"Some people don't like to share," I said.

She frowned. "Jerks. But I guess you're right. It would explain the self-destruct device I had to disable. And the two homing signal transmitters. And the remote recall mechanism."

"Two homing transmitters?"

"Oh, yes. Someone went to a lot of trouble to keep this from falling into the wrong hands. Don't know why they bothered. The technology can't be reproduced. I'm not even sure what half of this stuff is made of. And it's encoded for a specific user. Anyone else tries to operate it, they'd end up having their molecules deep-fried."

"Can you change the code?" I asked.

"Maybe, but it'd take a while to crack the encryption."

"How long?"

"About six months."

"That's too long."

"Well, I guess I've got good news for you then, Mack, because I'm pretty sure I'd only have to change the coding if the intended user is a biological. A robot shouldn't be much of a problem."

"I can use it?"

She shrugged. "Maybe. There's still the matter of disparate mass inversion ratios. You might end up losing some parts along the way. Also, the device can only transport its cargo to a predesignated receiving unit, and I don't know where that is. Could be anywhere. Could be the moon for all I know. And if you do make it all the way in one piece, it's only a one-way trip. You'll be stuck there, wherever it is."

My difference engine sorted through all the what-ifs. Finally it took the coward's way out and said there were too many variables for any viable odds when it came to using the device. I didn't calculate a whole lot of other choices.

"Put it back together," I said.

"I figured you'd say something like that." She pushed away from the table and yawned. "But it'll have to wait until morning, big guy." She slouched. "I'm pooped."

"I could use a recharge," I agreed. "I'll be back in the morning, then."

Lucia hopped over and took my hand. "Oh, Mack, don't be silly. You should spend the night here."

"I'm staying with a friend. He might get worried."

"So call him and let him know you won't be home tonight."

"I don't want to be a bother."

"Oh, no bother at all, dear boy."

She tugged at my arm, but I didn't budge.

"Oh, Mack, am I really that frightening?"

Lucia stood before me. She was one hundred three pounds of squishy protoplasm that I could crush without batting an optical. If my opticals could bat. She scared the hell out of me.

Couldn't compute why, but it was true.

"I'll be good." She reached up and loosened my tie. "I promise."

I couldn't think of a good reason not to stay, so I gave in, despite my better judgment. Lucia went to change for bed, and Humbolt showed me a place to recharge.

"Best outlet in the house," he assured me. "Now, if ya'll excuse me, Mack, I gotta draw the lady's bath."

I plugged in but didn't enter my full recharge cycle yet. I'd heard of biologicals having too much on their mind to go to sleep, but as a bot, I shouldn't have had that problem. Maybe I was more human than I cared to admit, and frankly, I didn't like it. Existence is simple when you're only a machine. There are no complications, no counterindicated compulsions. Just functionality. Drab, predictable functionality.

Damn, how I missed that.

I spent seven minutes staring out the penthouse window at

the circling gun-drones, the city of lights below, and the monolithic skyscrapers.

I scanned Lucia's reflection in the glass as she came up behind me. I'd half-expected her to have changed into a sheer nightgown, but she was wearing blue pajamas.

"I thought you'd be off-line by now."

She stepped beside me, and we silently admired the view for seventy seconds.

"You're worried about them, aren't you?" she asked. "Your friends."

"Yeah."

"They're okay, Mack, and you'll find them."

"No, they're not," I said. "They're dead or gone. Or someplace where I'll never find them."

"Then why are you still looking?" she asked.

I tried to come up with a good answer, but the only one I came up with didn't make much sense.

"Because I have to."

"Oh, Mack, you poor baby."

I didn't get why she said it, but she sure seemed to mean it. She lifted my hand and pressed her cheek against the back of it. It was barely a whisper on my tactile web, but it felt reassuring somehow.

"Get some rest. You'll feel more functional in the morning." She kissed the back of my hand. "Good night, Mack."

She was halfway across the room when I had to activate my big, dumb vocalizer.

"Lucia, I appreciate all your help, but you know this can't go anywhere."

"What can't go anywhere?"

"This thing. This thing between us."

"What thing?" she asked, but I could see from her slight smile she knew exactly what I was talking about.

"It's nothing personal," I said. "It's just logical."

"Mack, I think you've gotten the wrong impression," she said. "I'm not ready to get into anything serious yet. I'm still having fun. You're a great guy, really, you are, but—"

"I'm not a guy."

"Yeah, yeah, robot. I got it, Mack. Like I'd forget." She snorted. "Like you'd ever let me forget. Like you'd ever let anyone forget."

"I'm sorry." I didn't know why I was apologizing.

"Forget it, Mack. Forget the whole thing."

Suddenly, I felt like a jerk. One-sixth of a second from confused to idiot. Couldn't analyze why, but I must've done something wrong. Or maybe Lucia was overreacting. Biologicals did that, victims of their own squishy brains and the random chemical reactions taking place therein.

"Lucia . . ."

She exited the room, not quite storming out but coming pretty close.

"You got a real way with people," said Humbolt.

"Design flaw," I said. "I just can't figure biologicals out."

"What's to figure? They ain't that complicated, pal. Take the boss there. She likes to play the carefree, freewheelin', spoiled little rich girl, but she's tired of it. Only she's been doin' it so long, she can't figure how to stop. All she really wants is a friend, Mack."

"She's got you," I said.

"Ah, I don't count. I'm programmed to like her. She could be a total bitch, and I'd still think she was the cat's pajamas. Most people are like that. They don't like each other for who they are, but who they're supposed to be. I guess the lady was hopin' you were different."

He was right. Lucia had done nothing but help me, and I'd

returned the favor by pushing her away. No wonder I didn't have many friends.

"You'll excuse me, Humbolt." I went to Lucia's room. The door was closed, but when I went to knock, it slid open. Lucia glared up at me.

"What is it now, Mack?"

"I'm sorry."

Funny how two little words could have such an immediate and noticeable effect. Lucia smiled—not just her mouth but her whole face. Especially her eyes. She was beautiful. Oh, I'd already calculated she was statistically attractive, but there was something more there. I couldn't say what it was. Some things weren't subject to analytical breakdown. All I knew was that her smile meant a lot to me. For the first time, I wished I had a mouth so I could smile back at her.

Then she hugged me. She was such a delicate little thing, fragile bones and pulpy organs. After seven seconds I gently placed one massive mitt on her back. The hug went on for another six seconds before she pulled away.

"Well, we better get some rest," she said. "We've got a big day tomorrow. Good night, Mack."

"Good night, Lucia."

The door slid shut. I turned around and nearly ran into Humbolt.

"See, Mack? Told ja biologicals weren't that complicated."

"Who programmed you to be so insightful?"

He adjusted and smoothed his collar. "Hey, just 'cause I don't sport that fancy red paint job of yours, don't mean I'm a complete drone."

11

Biologicals thought that because the Big Brains hadn't figured a way to download their memories onto a monitor that it was somehow more magical than how we robots learned. They were right. Biological memory was magical, biased by personal experience, reshaped by every recollection. It wasn't worth much.

We robots record it. Every replay would be the same. I could tell you the last time I saw Lucia smile (last night, fourteen minutes after three), the room temperature when I saw that smile (seventy-two degrees Fahrenheit), and the number of strands of hair fallen across her left eye as she did (three or four; I've got good opticals, but even I've got my limits). About the only thing I couldn't tell you was how she smelled (not my fault, since I wasn't built with olfactories).

I don't want to make it sound like the human brain is bad hardware. What they lack in accuracy, they make up for in imagination, intuition. The Big Brains hadn't perfected that in robots yet. We could learn. We could figure things out. We could solve problems. We could even deduce. It just took a little while sometimes.

The next morning, it hit me like a ton of bricks. More like thirty tons of bricks since a ton would barely register on my tactile web. I'd needed a good night's defragmenting to sort out the facts.

It was only a hunch, not an actual irrefutable conclusion. A theory gleaned from things I'd scanned: guys with domes covering their heads and others with giant skulls or jellyfishes for faces. A nurse with a mouth that could suck the eyeballs right out of a skull.

These were aliens we were talking about. Maybe.

It was hard to know for sure, what with the percentage of mutants walking around Empire. There were a lot of mutants in the city, and everyone had gotten used to it. But these guys would get a second glance. Probably even a third. They wouldn't blend in. Maybe they were only extreme mutations, hiding away from public scrutiny to avoid persecution.

It was a possibility, and it would've made more sense except for that little teleportation gizmo that had fallen into my hands last night. There were a couple of breakthroughs that everyone in Empire was waiting for: time machines, food pills, and teleportation topped the list. If someone had invented a practical teleportation device, it'd already be out on the market, with a catchy little jingle on the radio and billboards everywhere. Whichever company came out with it would make a fortune because everybody in the city would want to have one. Probably two.

Biologicals weren't always motivated by cash or food or the need to empty accumulated waste products, but there was a lot of money to be made in the teleportation industry. The only reason it wouldn't have reached the public yet was because someone had better ideas. Trying to maintain a technological advantage was the strongest reason I could hypothesize.

So I was either dealing with a secret alien invasion or an underground organization of extreme mutants with very advanced tech, either an invasion or an uprising. Both sounded like trouble, and something a smart bot would've avoided. But I'd come this far. Might as well go all the way.

I snapped back on. Humbolt was already up and functioning, waving a dust eradicator around the room. He gave me a courtesy pass.

"Mornin', Mack. The lady's downstairs."

"Already?"

"You know the doll. She couldn't stay away from the gizmo."

She couldn't have gotten much sleep. My defragmenting had taken four hours, ten minutes. I went to the lab and found Lucia hunched over the table in the middle of her reassembly attempts.

"Hey, Mack, it's taking a little while longer than I expected. It shouldn't be more than another hour or two. So how was your recharge?"

"Insightful. I think I figured some things out."

"What's that, sweetie?"

"Can't say."

She kept making tiny welds with a miniature heat ray. "Oh, come on. I can keep a secret. I promise."

"It's not an issue of trust," I said. "It's a bug I'm working through."

"Why don't you have your shrink take a look at it?"

"Already did. She said it'll just take time." I scanned the many scattered parts. "Are you sure you can put it back together?"

"Put it back together? Heck, Mack, sweetie, I'll even add a couple of improvements."

"Lucia . . ."

"Relax, big guy. This is what I do, freelance technologist consulting." She wiped sweat from her forehead. "You don't see me questioning your ability to smash things, now, do you?"

"Smashing things is easier than putting them back together," I said.

"Maybe for you, hon."

Humbolt, carrying a telephone, descended the lab staircase. "Yo, Mack, call for you. Says he's a cop."

It was Sanchez. I figured it would be. No other cops were interested in my activities as far as I knew.

"You got a minute?" he asked. "There are some things I'd like to show you."

"Actually, Sanchez, I'm kind of busy right now."

"It wasn't a request, Mack."

Either the earpiece was loud enough for Lucia to hear the conversation or she pieced together Sanchez's end all by herself. "Go ahead, Mack. I'm not going to be done with this for another hour or two."

Sanchez must've heard her. Or maybe he just didn't care.

"I'm waiting downstairs," he said. "Don't keep me waiting long."

He hung up. No debate. I could tell he meant it. I may have been a tough bot, but if I was going to keep digging, it couldn't hurt to have Sanchez on my side.

"I'll be back in an hour, Lucia. Two at the most."

"I'll be ready, handsome."

True to his word, Sanchez was waiting for me at the bottom of Proton Towers.

"How'd you find me?" I asked.

"It's my job."

He took a long drag on his cigarette and tossed it aside. A two-legged automatic vacuum hopped over to clean it up with more enthusiasm than was healthy even for a drone.

"So what's this about, Sanchez?"

"We found Tony Ringo."

Might've been those pesky foreign behavioral dictates my

maintenance protocols had yet to purge, but I feigned surprise. One of the advantages of having a bare faceplate was that I didn't have to be a good actor. I didn't say anything.

Whatever I didn't say must've struck something in Sanchez's finely honed cop instincts. He could always read me like a technical manual. His expression didn't change, and he didn't say anything. But there was something about the way he didn't say it.

We took Sanchez's Ambler to the Think Tank. It was a lousy ride. Instead of wheels or treads, amblers had six pneumatic legs. Don't ask me who thought that was a good idea, but whoever it was managed to convince someone with a factory to crank out a few thousand. At first, they'd been a commercial failure, but then word got out. Amblers never broke down. Never. You could shove a piece of lit dynamite in the power coil, and the only noticeable effect would be a little more smoke when you started it up. Only a little more. It was the kind of technological reliability that was hard to find in Tomorrow's Town. So people bought them. And used them forever or until they got sick of them and sold them to someone else.

No one bought an Ambler for any other reason than practicality. Cheap, dependable, and built to last. No one bought a new model when they could find used ones, and the launch of several brand-new styles did nothing to encourage sales. A couple of fancy fins and some high beam headlights didn't make the ride any cooler or smoother. The Ambler Motorcar Company went out of business, proving that a quality product isn't always a worthwhile endeavor. But its ghosts still haunted Empire, thousands of lurching, rusty machines with chipped paint and cracked windshields hopping their way down her streets.

Sanchez's Ambler was still in decent shape. It didn't make the ride any smoother. By the time we got to the Tank, my internal gyros had taken a beating. I nearly fell over when I got out of the car.

"Thank God I don't vomit," I said.

"Don't be such a pansy." Sanchez didn't look worse for wear, but even if he had turned green there was no way of telling under that fur.

We entered the Tank. All the bells and whistles went off with my arrival, but Sanchez waved off the incapacitor. Parker, the front gate watchdog, wasn't too happy about that. He made Sanchez sign a couple of waivers, in triplicate, then called for confirmation. The whole thing took so long, it would've been easier to clamp the incapacitor on.

After we got through security, Sanchez led me to the elevators. We stepped in. He lit a cigarette, puffed on it slow and thoughtfully. "You didn't ask."

"Ask what?"

"Whether Ringo was alive or not. You didn't ask."

"I guess I just assumed."

"Guess you did," Sanchez mumbled. He was so short and his voice was so low, I had trouble picking it up. "Not like you to make assumptions, Mack."

We rode a little further. If the Tank had levitator pods, this would've been a lot less awkward.

"You still didn't ask."

"Since we aren't heading toward the morgue, I figured he was alive."

Puff.

"He's alive, isn't he?" I said.

"Oh, he's alive. Depending on how rigid your definition of life is." Puff. "You didn't ask if we'd gotten any information out of him."

"Did you?"

"Nothing useful."

The elevator doors opened, and he led me further into this web of deceit. Not exactly outright lies. Omitted truths. It had to be Grey's countermands that kept me from fessing up because I couldn't think of a good reason not to admit what I knew. Sanchez might've even known something about Abner Greenman, but I kept it to myself.

Tony Ringo was under lock and key in his own little special white room. Protective custody, Sanchez explained. His blanked mind was evidence. Sanchez didn't admit to it, but I could tell he was worried. Psychic crime wasn't unheard of, but telepathic murder was still a rare occurrence.

Sanchez had been right. Technically, Ringo was still alive. His heart still pushed his blood through his veins. His lungs still drew in gulps of air. His eyes still twitched at the twinkles of light. But he was a shell.

"What happened to him?" I asked, compelled to continue my charade.

"We're not sure. Somebody did a number on him though. Burned his brain. We had our forensic telepath probe his mind. There's not much left in there anymore."

"There's stuff left in there?"

"Little bit. Brain holds a lot of information. Can't scorch it all. Though they came damn close. But there was some stuff left behind. Fragments. Mostly random memories. Nothing much of any importance. Oh, and a name."

I didn't ask because I figured I knew what the name was and that Sanchez would tell me in his own due time. I was right on both.

"Mack."

"Yeah?"

"That's the name: Mack."

"Common name," I replied. "Were there any witnesses?"

He sighed. "Ringo was last seen at a jazz club. Some hole in the wall called The Golden Diode. It's the kind of place where witnesses are hard to come by."

"Surveillance?"

"Even harder to come by."

Up to now Ringo had been lying in his bed, drooling and moving his lips like he was trying to say something. Suddenly he sat up like a shot and stared me right in the opticals. He opened his mouth and screamed a harsh, warbling shriek. He started laughing and crying at the same time.

"It's you! It's you! It's you!" He stifled a sniffle and grabbed at his ears. "You, you, you, you!" Then he collapsed, dead to the world. Except he wasn't dead, and he wasn't just a shell. He was a thing that had once been a man but was now a handful of confused memories. Names and dates and places that could never fit together again. What Greenman had done to him wasn't murder. It was worse.

"What'll happen to him?"

"We'll try to dig some more information. Then I guess we'll ship him off to the hospital. I got a feeling it'll be an extended stay."

Poor bastard. At least a defective robot got the dignity of a quick deactivation. Ringo had gotten mixed up with some nasty business, and he'd come out the losing end of it. That'd been his whole life. While I didn't exactly feel sorry for him, if I'd found him on the street like this I would've crushed his head and put him out of his misery.

"He seems to know you," said Sanchez.

"He doesn't even know who he is. Are we through here, Sanchez?"

"I don't know, Mack. Are we?"

I'd have loved to let him in on my little secret of a possible alien invasion or mutant conspiracy. If anybody would believe me, it'd be him. He was waist deep in this sort of stuff more often than not. Empire had its problems, but they'd have been a lot worse if it wasn't for men like Sanchez, bless his furless little tail and twitchy pink nose.

I kept quiet.

"Fine, Mack. If that's the way you want to play it. C'mon. I'll drive you back."

"In that lurching junkheap of yours, Sanchez. I don't know. I might end up losing a couple of bolts."

Before we reached the elevator, a uniformed cop chased Sanchez down.

"Sir, you wanted us to keep you up to date on the Bleaker case."

My audios tuned in. The cop stifled himself as if he wasn't sure he should speak in front of me.

"Go ahead, Dougal," said Sanchez.

"They found one of them. The father, sir." Dougal hesitated, but Sanchez gave him a nod.

"He's dead, sir. Bludgeoned to death. Report says somebody worked him over, like he was shoved into a crushing unit."

Sanchez glanced up at me, at those giant hands of mine. The kind made for bludgeoning and crushing. "Guess we're not through here after all, Mack."

12

You know the scene. Seen it in a dozen crime pictures. Some dumb mug finds himself sitting in a tiny room with a cop standing over him, reading him the riot act. That's pretty much what happened to me.

Except I wasn't sitting. I don't sit much. Most furniture isn't made for my weight, and my feet don't get sore. Also, it wasn't a tiny room. It was a big basement cell, thickly enshrouded in shadows excluding a few a bright spotlights. I assumed they blew the lighting budget on the three giant cannons pointed my way. And Sanchez, who was barely tall enough to stand over my knee, wasn't reading me the riot act. He was sitting at the table, puffing on a cigarette, letting the ash dangle. Otherwise, it was exactly the same.

I stood in a small red circle painted on the floor. There was nothing keeping me from stepping out of it except the three heavy blast cannons trained around me. Unlike Sanchez, the cannons did tower over me. I was thick-alloyed, but the Think Tank had my specs, so it was a fair bet these weapons could pose a danger. My threat assessor suggested it'd be a good idea to play it safe and not step out of the circle.

Now that I was here, I wondered if it might've been smarter to make a break for it while I had still been above ground. I might not have been able to bust out of the Tank. The security was tight, and the weaponry dangerous enough to give me reason to think twice, but at least I'd stood a chance. Now, I was stuck.

Sanchez hadn't said a word in the last six minutes. He was content to let me sweat. It was a tactic that had worked a thousand times before. But I don't sweat, and I could wait just as long as he could.

I won the stare-off.

He leaned back in his chair. "The Council approved this room's construction. As a precaution, you understand. Each of these cannons cost more than I make in twenty years. If they go off even once, the Council will have to approve a tax hike to pay the power bill. And from what I understand, they're each only good for about a dozen shots before the unit burns out and has to be replaced.

"I can't get the budget approval for a new automimeograph, but I guess somebody very important thought there might be a need for a special room like this. To hold guys like you."

"Guys like me?" I asked. "Or just me."

"Right now, you're the only guy like you." He stabbed out his cigarette and lit up a new one. It was a miracle those little lungs of his still worked.

"I told the suits upstairs that it was a waste of time and money." Sanchez smiled mirthlessly. "Tell me I was wrong, Mack."

The air sizzled as electricity crackled along the cannons' barrels.

He slid some crime scene photos across the stainless steel

desk between us. They were a grisly series of images testifying to the last painful minutes of Gavin Bleaker's life. A catalogue of monstrous bruises and crusted blood and shattered bones. Despite the extensive damage, he was recognizable. They'd made sure to not touch the face. I'd never liked Gavin, but I hoped whoever did this to him had the decency to bash in the back of his skull first.

"Want to tell me something about this?" asked Sanchez.

"What's to tell? I didn't do it. It's a frame-up."

"No shit."

He laughed, but he did not seem amused.

"I know it's a frame job, Mack. Hell, it's not even a very good one. Whoever did it used a red crowbar or something like that. You wouldn't need one, but they made sure it matched your paint job. And if you were going to kill someone, my gut tells me you'd make a lot more efficient job of it and be smart enough to ditch the body someplace the cops wouldn't stumble over. Our forensic scans of your suit and chassis showed traces of blood, but none of it matched the vic's type."

"So why am I still here?"

Sanchez scowled. "Right now, I'm your only friend. You might want to stop giving me lip. This is serious. Even if you didn't kill this guy, somebody went to some trouble to make it look like you could've. Not enough to hold up in court, but enough to keep you occupied. Want to tell me why?"

"Wish I could."

"What about the blood? Want to tell me where you picked that up?"

"Can't."

"This is serious. You realize that there are some very important people who've already put in requests for your permanent deactivation?"

"I haven't done anything."

"Is that supposed to make a difference? You're not technically a citizen yet. Or have you forgotten?"

"I don't forget anything, Sanchez. You know that."

"Well then you also remember that in the end you've got the legal rights of a television set."

I didn't reply, only stood motionless in that unnatural robotic way.

"Had a talk with your shrink few minutes ago, Mack. Tells me you've picked up some kind of programming anomaly. Says you couldn't tell me anything even if you wanted to, and if I tried to access your memory matrix it could lead to total system failure." Sanchez's ears flattened. "But you gotta give me something. Otherwise, the suits upstairs will send down the order to force a download, and there won't be a damn thing I'll be able to do to stop it."

There followed a seven second pause.

"You aren't making this easy for me, Mack."

"Sorry."

Sanchez gathered up the photos. "All right. We'll do this the only way we can. Doctor Mujahid thinks you'll be able to overcome this bug with some time. So time is what I'm going to give you. I'll try to keep the suits happy for as long as I can. Get comfortable, Mack. You're going to be here for a while."

He stuffed the photos back into the file, got up and walked out of the room without looking back. It was just me and my automated watchdogs.

I wanted to tell Sanchez what I knew, but as long as Grey's bug was working its magic, I was out of choices.

Gavin's murder could've meant any number of things. Maybe they'd gotten what they'd needed out of him. And maybe they'd gotten what they'd needed out of Julie and the kids, too. Could be they were all dead, and the cops hadn't found Jules and April and Holt's bodies yet. I calculated that as possible, but unlikely. No good reason for the abductors to ditch the corpses separately. No, Gavin was expendable. They'd kept him alive because there hadn't been a good reason to kill him yet. Maybe he'd pushed his luck, and they figured as long as they were going to get rid of him, they might as well hassle me in the process. Had to admire their efficiency.

Whatever their reasons they'd succeeded in screwing me over. At the very least, I was delayed here for another few hours. At the very worst, I was headed for the scrap heap. In the meantime, there was nothing I could do but count the passing seconds.

Twelve thousand and sixty of those seconds passed before the door opened again. My opticals picked out Sanchez in the doorway. "You've got a visitor, Megaton."

It was Lucia. She was decked out in a lovely dress, her Sunday best. Her hair was put up and she had something pinned to it. A piece of cloth with a veil and plastic flowers. Might've been a hat, but my visualizer wasn't comfortable labeling it as such.

Sanchez glared at her. "You've got five minutes, Ms. Napier."

"Thank you, Detective."

He grumbled something I couldn't detect and slammed the door behind her.

Her heels clicked out twenty-six steps as she walked over to the table. She didn't sit.

"Hi'ya, handsome. Looks like you're in a tight spot."

"I've had better days."

"You wouldn't believe how difficult it was to arrange this visitation. That unpleasant Detective Sanchez was dead set against it."

"He can be stubborn like that," I said.

"Oh, I know he's only doing his job, but still, he was a bit rude and quite inflexible. Fortunately, I'm acquainted with a few influential people. A couple of phone calls, and voilà, here I am."

"Voilà," I said. "Didn't think you were the type to wear hats, Lucia."

"A lady likes to exhibit a little class now and then." She smiled. "Helps to keep the gossip columnists off balance."

I figured she was up to something, and it wasn't hard to figure out. I played dumb though, because I didn't want to encourage her. This would only get her in trouble.

"Aren't you happy to see me?" she asked.

"Sure. You look . . . nice."

"Nice?" She puckered and blew a kiss. "I look exquisite, Mack."

I nodded. "Like you're going to church. Or maybe a very casual funeral."

"No funerals today, Mack."

"Lucia, don't—"

She put her gloved finger to her lips. "Hush now. How many times do I have to tell you? I'm a big girl. I can take care of myself."

"This is different. This is serious."

"I know. That's why I'm doing it. You still want to find your friends, don't you?"

"I'll handle it."

She laughed. "Oh, poor, poor, Mack. You really must learn to accept a helping hand. Even you can't handle everything all by yourself."

"So I've heard."

I wasn't going to talk her out of this.

"I finished putting that little toy back together," she said. "There were some parts left over, but I don't think they were all that important."

I calculated a fifty-fifty chance we were being monitored right now. I could've put an end to this by merely hinting at an escape attempt, but that would only get Lucia in trouble. I might not be able to talk her out of this, but she couldn't make me take her help. A prison break was a hefty rap, even for the Princess of Empire. Sanchez would throw the book at her, and I doubted Lucia knew enough influential people to stop him once he got going. Like I'd said, he was stubborn like that.

She stepped closer. The cannons whirred.

"They warned me not to cross the circle," she said. "Couldn't be responsible for what happened if you tried to use me as a hostage."

"Walk away, Lucia."

"Can't do it, Mack. It's been a long time since I met a stand-up guy. A girl would have to be an idiot to walk away from something like that." She unpinned her hat. "Detective Sanchez was quite insistent that I not be allowed to bring anything in. Also, that I undergo a thorough security sweep. But the sweep couldn't detect this. The little gizmo is practically invisible to scanners."

She pulled the teleportation disk from her hat.

"Oh, damn it, Lucia."

I expected the alarms to go off then, but it remained quiet. The door opened, and Sanchez stepped into the room. He didn't have any backup, and his heater wasn't drawn. The only thing in his hand was a small remote.

"No going back now," she said with a smile. "You can either use this or not. Either way I'm in deep now."

"Don't move, Mack. If I push this button, your internals will be fried beyond recovery. And the lady, if she's caught in the crossfire . . . you don't want to know what these guns do to organic materials."

The hum of the cannons doubled in volume.

"Your call, Mack." Lucia slid the device across the table.

My electronic brain analyzed the situation and offered me choices. None of them ended well.

Using the teleporter was a risky move. It all rested on how accurately I calculated Sanchez's willingness to push that button. He'd cut me a lot of slack recently, but there had to be a limit. There was no way I could push my button before he pushed his.

He must've read my electronic brain.

"I'll do it, Mack."

I scanned his face, focusing on his black eyes. They never blinked. Far as I recalled, Alfredo Sanchez never bluffed.

"Do what you gotta do, Alf."

I pressed the teleporter's button, and nothing stopped me. I detected Sanchez's parting sentiment as the room disappeared.

"Damn you."

The teleportation took two-sevenths of a second. A biological wouldn't have registered it. A blur of static and darkness passed. The trip destabilized my gyros, and my strength regulators were listing as unreliable. I was a clumsy heap of steel, and I was standing in a glass tube. Not for long though.

I tumbled. The tube shattered, and I ended up flat on my face. Though I'm actually much more agile than my bulk suggests, my gyro issues were making it a challenge.

No design is perfect, and there was a flaw in my neck joint. My upward angle limit is forty-five degrees. Not usually a problem, since I'm a tall bot and I don't spend a lot of time sprawled on floors. From my current improbable position I scanned eight feet on the other side of a shimmering green forcefield.

Somebody asked, "What the hell are you?"

13

My gyros stabilized enough to allow me to stand and get a good scan of the greeting party. The man in front, the guy I assumed was the leader, had orange skin and angular black eyes. The goon to his left was a giant cricket, and his buddy on the right was unremarkably human to the point that he looked like a circus freak standing next to his buddies. It's all relative.

They wore blue jumpsuits with panels of blinking lights along their sleeves, belts, and chests. The orange guy didn't have a gun, but his companions both had shiny rifles that I couldn't identify. They were in hand and ready, but in a lowered position since there was a forcefield between us.

"Ravager unit report," said the orange man. "How did you get in here?"

I didn't know what a ravager was, but since he was looking my way, I assumed he meant me. I ignored the question.

The field was my highest priority. If I couldn't get through it, this search-and-rescue mission was a bust. I ignored the goons and put my hands against the barrier. It popped and sizzled and would've melted flesh and blood. My alloy could handle the heat, but the field was solid enough to challenge my servos. I might be able to overload the system with a barrage of punches, but my own battery might drain before that happened. No way to know for sure without specific details of the system.

The orange guy pushed a button on his belt. "Security, we've got a breach in reception chamber number four. Repeat, we have a breach." He tilted his head and nodded, listening to an unheard voice. "Yes, I know it's not possible, but I'm looking at the intruder right now so maybe you'd like to come down here and tell it yourself." Another nod. "No, it's fine. Subject is contained. Robot: modified ravager model. Shouldn't be a problem. Doesn't look very intelligent. I'm guessing it's a reconnaissance/sabotage unit. Sent to measure our defense and response times, most likely."

I was vaguely insulted that he regarded me as little more than a giant smashing device, but then again, that was basically what I was. He might've wondered why I was wearing a suit if I was a run-of-the-mill auto, but he clearly wasn't giving it that much thought. First rule of the battlefield: assumptions kill. While I was being dismissed as a harmless nuisance, I figured I should take advantage of his underestimation.

I bent down and began tearing apart the metal flooring. It was tough stuff, but not as tough as me. I peeled away the tiling to expose the wires and conduits below.

"Should we do something?" asked the human.

"Why bother?" said the orange man. "Nothing vital under there."

The cricket spoke in a rapid series of clicks and chirps. I didn't get a word of it, but his buddies seemed to understand.

"You're welcome to shut down the field and deal with it yourself then," said orange man. "Otherwise, we wait for a full security complement."

I guess they hadn't underestimated me that much.

I yanked up a thick conduit line and stripped it of its protective sheath.

The bug clicked.

The orange guy smiled. "Let it damage a few systems. It won't accomplish anything. We'll know more when we neutralize the damn thing."

The bug chirped again, nervously this time. He must've seen this coming. Orange guy suddenly understood, and the obvious anxiety on his face made me think this plan had a decent shot of working. Only one way to find out.

I put my hand against the forcefield again while holding the conduit in the other. Power surged across my chassis, down one arm and into the other. A lot of juice ran through me, and a biological would've been burned to ash before the field shorted out. My alloy doesn't burn and the circuit remained completed the full second necessary to short out the field. My radiation screens protected me from 99 percent of the current, but 1 percent snuck through and managed to damage a finger joint. I never used that pinkie anyway.

The field disappeared, and all of the orange guy's confidence disappeared with it. The two other goons unloaded their rifles at me. Both bolts registered as potentially hazardous in a sustained barrage, but in this situation they were rated negligible.

With the forcefield down, we were right on top of each other. It wasn't difficult to grab both of the rifle-wielding goons and toss them hard into the walls. Since my strength regulators weren't fully functional, it might've been too hard. The bug, in particular, left a glistening pink splatter of what I assumed was blood where he'd fallen. Orange guy had already dashed out of the door and out of my reach. The human was still moving, which meant he was probably conscious and capable of talking.

Somebody must've sounded the alarm because all the bells and whistles started going off. Every security guard in the place was likely converging on this spot right now. I couldn't have much time.

The human sat up and fired a few more blasts at me. I'm a big target, but his hands were shaking so badly he only scored three out of five shots, and they didn't count for much.

I snatched away his rifle and crushed it into a ball the way Superman always does it. It was an immensely satisfying show of power, illustrating how easily I could crush this poor slob and how I didn't need the gun to be dangerous. Judging by the look on the guy's face, he got the point.

I would've grabbed him, but with my regulators on the blink, I might accidentally crush him. Instead, I stood over him, a towering juggernaut of intimidation. I even put my fists on my hips because it seemed the proper thing to do.

"I'm looking for some friends of mine."

He squealed. Just like that. No fuss. Fortunate, since I didn't have time to break bones and slap him around. According to my new friend, the Bleakers were being held in this very facility. He could've been lying, but I estimated he was too scared to be that clever. I didn't feel like dragging him along as insurance because he'd slow me down and when the heat came, and it would come soon, I doubted he'd survive.

"Here." He pointed to a room on a map. "They're holding them there."

"Where are we now?" I asked.

He pointed to another room. My brain already started plotting a course, as well as several alternates based on levels of resistance I might encounter.

The doors slid open and in charged five security guards bedecked in body armor and carrying more blaster rifles. They didn't bother telling me to freeze or anything. They just let me have it.

My friend was stupid enough to make a run for it. Directly in the line of fire. They blew several holes through him without hesitation, and the energy discharge began to heat up my chassis. Might've done something if I'd stood around long enough, but that wasn't my plan. I could've taken these goons out, but that wasn't the plan either. I turned and tore my way through the opposite wall. Took three seconds to punch through, and they kept pouring the heat on my back. It wasn't a problem yet, and if these were the biggest guns these guys had it wouldn't be.

The adjoining room was full of computers, and I tore my way through that one too. And the next. And the next. I was more interested in reaching my destination than recording the experience, but one room caught my attention. It was filled with biologicals, and many matched up with my alien theory. One, in particular, looked like a giant weed. There were no sentient plant mutations among Empire's citizenry.

I wondered how many aliens were in this facility, if there were more facilities like this, and how long these extraterrestrial visitors had been carrying out their sinister doings. This wasn't a makeshift operation. This had been here awhile.

My plotted course was a direct path with random deviations to avoid larger rooms and keep security off-balance. Still, the walls were thick enough to slow me down and as I pushed my way through the complex, I found myself surrounded by an ever-increasing number of security personnel. I continued to ignore them, as taking the time to knock them aside would be counterproductive. Any guards I would've taken out would've been replaced. This wasn't a combat mission anyway. It was a search directive.

The endless barrage of blasters started to heat up my chassis. My inflammable suit proved fireproof all right. Instead of burning, it started melting. My paint job began to fleck, and I was glowing soft orange. My cooling system coped, and my internals were unaffected. These jokers couldn't stop me. Nothing could once I got going.

I ripped my way through another wall into a large room. The kind I'd been avoiding but didn't this time because that's what they would've expected. The guards didn't follow. That meant either they'd wised up on the futility of their efforts, or dangerous countermeasures were on the way.

My single-minded nature meant it took a lot to surprise me once I set a directive. In this new room though, I skipped a beat. It was a small moment, barely noticeable outside an atomic clock. The new room was for storage. And it was storing robots. Robots that looked exactly like me.

There weren't supposed to be any other robots like me.

But there they were, fourteen shiny gold Mack Megatons, inactively lined up along the walls. These must've been the ravagers the orange jumpsuit had mistaken me for. Something wasn't square, but I didn't have time for a mystery. Like I said, once I set a directive, I stick to it. I filed away any questions about this turn of events and kept on my way.

The robots activated. Every single one of them. One grabbed me by the right arm. Another seized me by the neck. The rest closed in. This was going to be trouble.

With my free arm I laid a right cross into an approaching robot's faceplate. His head snapped back and his neck joint popped. Fractures in his chassis meant I'd done some damage. These machines were tough, but not as thick-alloyed as me. It pushed my survival odds up from 62 percent to 64. In a situation like this, I'd take every percentage point I could get.

I hammered the same robot again. His head still didn't fall

off, though it tilted at an ugly angle. Must've screwed up a sensory connection, too, because he tackled one of his brothers by mistake.

I gave the robot clinging to my arm a hard smack. One, two, three blows were enough to knock off his cranial unit. If he was anything like me though, his brain was in his gut and all I did was knock out his primary sensors. He didn't need to scan or hear me to know he still had a firm grip on me.

Damn, I'd never realized how much a pain in the ass robots could be.

Then they were all on top of me, a pile of pounding metal. I fell face first, and they hammered my back. My chassis was a match for the beating, but my servos weren't up to pushing these guys off of me. I was pinned. Nine seconds ticked by with only the sound of metal hitting metal echoing in the room. I didn't have time for this, so I did the only thing I could.

I exceeded recommended operational limits, ordered my servos to 140 percent, and pushed. It was enough strength to throw off my opponents and get me to my feet again. It also drained sixteen minutes' worth of juice from my battery in two seconds and damaged my right shoulder actuator. I never used that shoulder anyway.

I kept pushing. It was the only way to take out these second-rate imitations. It would strain my internals, and the excessive power drain was going to be trouble in the long run. I couldn't afford to let up.

I unleashed a jackhammer jab into the nearest robot, right where I hoped his most important and vulnerable systems might be, if my own specs were any indication. It crushed his gut and must've done something because he staggered and fell over. Twitching and squirming, he struggled to right himself, but couldn't get the job done.

My arm diagnostic reported several microscopic stress

fractures and advised returning to compliant function levels. I ignored it. It didn't like that and started pinging in my audios and flashing a warning across the bottom of my optical readout.

Another two robots tried immobilizing my arms. I threw my limbs together and smashed their craniums into each other hard enough to knock them loose. I finished the job and bashed in their heads with a hammer strike. Without sensors and more likely to hurt their fellows than me, they did the smart thing and shut down. Had to love cold machine logic.

My remaining opponents circled around again. They weren't intimidated. They were stupid, relentless autos. Relentless, I could respect. Stupid, I could envy. But my battle analyzer told me that this fight was a foregone conclusion. Because I was willing to do whatever it took to win, including risking my own continued functioning.

My analyzer estimated that my inevitable victory should take fifty-six seconds with a 13 percent overall functionality loss. I don't mean to brag, but I disassembled my opponents with seven whole seconds to spare. I could describe every punch and kick, every metal-crushing deployment of blunt force. But like I said, it was a foregone conclusion. Of course, I also had a list of minor internal damage. Nothing serious individually, but it added up to a 14 percent impairment.

The most annoying thing was that I was surrounded by mounds of spare parts and I didn't have time to collect them.

I didn't take time to enjoy my win. I pushed on, slowed down by a blown right ankle actuator and a sticking shoulder that threw off my balance. I wasn't a particularly fast bot to begin with, but I was determined. And if I'd lost a leg, I would've hopped the rest of the way.

The alarms kept blaring, but there was no further resistance. I punched my way through five more walls and didn't see another biological. Only a few flying observation drones, and all of them kept a healthy distance. They'd evacuated this section. Might've moved Julie and the kids, too. But there was nothing to do but press on. I tore open one last door with my difference engine reporting zero expectations.

Julie and April huddled together in the corner. Jules looked terrified. For seven minutes now, all she must've been hearing were shrieking alarms, panicked running, blaster fire, and smashing. Lots of smashing.

But April was smiling.

"See, Mom," she said. "I told you he'd find us."

A swarm of spherical security drones shot into the room. They circled all around, buzzing and humming dangerously. There were more in the hall. Too many to count.

A voice came over the loudspeaker. Vaguely British, but not quite.

"Mr. Megaton, now that you have found what you were looking for, I assume you'll stop destroying our facility. However, if you need further persuasion, I would like to point out that each of these drones is armed with a self-destruct device. The charge isn't strong enough to inflict significant damage to you, but I assure you the woman and the child would not be so fortunate. I needn't point out the futility of attempting to shield them from the blast, but I guess I have done that just now, haven't I?"

"And what do you offer me if I stand down?" I asked.

"Nothing other than the continued existence of these two souls you've worked so hard to find. It's a very generous offer, Mr. Megaton, as there's no reason to concern myself with their existence save certain inconveniences of squeamish morality imposed upon me by my superiors."

There was something about the way he said "morality" that made it sound like a dirty word. He wasn't bluffing.

14

Surrender was counter to my core programming, and the very idea sent a nervous twitch through my servos. I did the only logical thing, because I was here to rescue the Bleakers, not get them blown to hell.

Things might've been different had I been designed properly, but I was a weapon. Search-and-rescue was not my intent. I was made for blasting and stomping my way across a battle-field. The avoidance of casualties wasn't part of the plan. If I'd been true to my original programming, I'd have crushed Julie and April without even making a file of it. But if I'd been true to my original programming, I wouldn't have been here in the first place.

Most of the security drones withdrew. Four remained hovering around Julie and April. They hummed at five extra decibels to remind me they were there. A complement of six security personnel surrounded us, mostly for show since it was the orbs that held me in check.

A thin biological in a suit and silver cape stood in the doorway since there wasn't room for all of us. He spoke, and his voice was that vaguely British-but-not-quite that'd come out of that loudspeaker.

"Ah, Mister Megaton."

"You're human," I said.

"Am I?"

Grinning, his skin shifted from a pale pink to a bright purple. His blond hair became a shade of red that threatened to burn out my opticals. His eyes filled with black and when he blinked, his lids closed vertically.

"Some of us are better at blending in than others." He shifted back to his human pigmentation. "They call me Warner. Not my original name, of course, but we've all taken terrestrial labels to ease our assimilation."

"So you are aliens then," I said.

"I guess that would be obvious, even to a simple machine such as yourself. Yes, circumstances have forced us to make this our home. We only do what we must to ensure our continued survival."

"Including kidnapping children."

"Oh, please, Megaton. We've hurt no one unless absolutely necessary."

"Gavin Bleaker," I said. "Was it necessary to cave in his skull?"

Julie gasped.

Damn. Julie shouldn't have found out that way. Couldn't take it back now. Sometimes even my vocalizer could get ahead of my sophisticated electronic brain. "I'm sorry, Jules."

She stifled a sob. Gavin had been a louse, and she would be better off without him. It didn't change the fact that it was a hard thing to absorb, made worse by the situation. She didn't need any more troubles.

"Mr. Bleaker's disposal was deemed a necessity." Warner frowned, but he didn't look like he meant it. "I can assure you, we do only what is best for our continued survival and assimilation."

I didn't like the sound of that.

Warner and his cronies escorted us down a series of hallways. Julie and April were kept in tow to convince me to behave myself.

"Mack, what's wrong with your leg?" asked Julie.

"It's nothing, Jules."

I'd blown my left ankle actuator stomping one of my more stubborn duplicates to scrap, and it had left me with a limp. Of course, there were plenty of other minor system failures going on, most of which weren't visible from the outside. All together, it was nothing function-threatening, but it was bad news for any possible escape attempts.

Warner led us to a lab. It was a big operation, full of scurrying scientists. There were several robots at work, too. Six assistant drones, another of my auto duplicate models, and one robot with eight legs and a thin humanoid torso. His head was a basketball with four red opticals and a pair of long crackling antennae atop it.

Holt was here, too.

"Oh my God," Julie gasped tearfully. "What did you do to him?"

The poor kid was suspended in a countergravity field. He didn't appear to be conscious, thankfully, because there were tubes running in and out of his body as various chemicals were being pumped into him and others drawn out.

"You sons of—"

I took a step toward Warner.

"Temper, temper, Mack."

The orbs around Julie and April squealed, and the security guards all leveled their rifles. Not at me, of course.

I could've killed Warner easy. One punch could've taken his

head right off. I didn't for two reasons. One was Julie and April. The other: Warner didn't deserve a quick kill. No, when his time came, I'd wipe that smug grin off his face one tooth at a time.

I stood down, but I was getting awfully sick of it.

"Your concern is understandable, Mrs. Bleaker, but quite unwarranted. Any damage your son has sustained is not life threatening."

"Damage?" She struggled with rage and fear, wiping the tears from her cheeks and snarling. "What kind of people are you?"

"You might call us visitors," he said. "But that would be mistaken. We're not just popping in for a holiday. No, we're here to stay. Instead, we've taken to calling ourselves Pilgrims, and this is our new home. And your son is instrumental to our plans. So you see, as much as you care for him, you can understand how infinitely more valuable he is to us."

The spider robot clomped its way over to us. "What is the meaning of this, Warner? You should not have brought them here."

"Oh, let them see, Doctor Zarg. They've the right, seeing as how this is the boy's family and Megaton has gone to such trouble to be here."

"You're getting careless."

"And you worry too much. Every step of our assimilation has gone exactly as planned."

Zarg emitted a harsh screech. "Enough, Warner. Your casual blathering is inadvisable. I will take this up with the Alpha Congress."

Warner's ever-present smirk faded, replaced by a cold stare. "Do what you feel is right, Doctor. Soon none of this will matter."

I didn't like the sound of that. Words like "assimilation" and "necessary disposal" put me on edge. I should've smashed this place to bits, torn it down bolt by bolt even if I was scrapped in the process. I would've, too. Except I wasn't sure how much it would accomplish. If I successfully brought the roof crashing down, there was no possibility Julie, April, and Holt would survive. They were only one family. Their welfare weighed against the well-being of the rest of humanity was a mathematical no-contest. Every logic dictate told me to eliminate the Bleakers from calculated variables. They didn't matter.

I told my dictates to shut the hell up, and let me deal with this situation. They complied. They weren't happy about it, and the words INADVISABLE ACTION flashed across my optical readout.

"It'll be all right," I told Julie and April, but I couldn't counter my logic lattice enough to believe it. And I was a terrible liar.

Julie was doing her best to stifle her sobs, but she nodded.

April was holding up better than her mom. Knowing the future, even if only little bits of it, must've been enough to comfort her. I kept hoping she'd smile at me, letting me know she'd seen how we got out of this. Honestly, she looked a little worried. I optimistically attributed that to a glitch in my expression analyzer.

Warner gestured toward a countergrav plate beside Holt. "Please step this way."

In zero gravity, all my impressive artificial muscle would be useless.

Warner cleared his throat. One of his guards handed him a raygun. Warner seized April by the hair and put the gun to her head. She didn't cry, didn't utter a peep.

I pushed killing Warner up to third on my directives list. Right after getting myself free and getting the Bleakers out of here alive.

I stepped onto the plate. A switch was thrown, and I bobbed up and down helplessly in the air. "See, Zarg?" said Warner. "As docile and obedient as a labor drone. Nothing to concern ourselves over."

Doctor Zarg said nothing. Having that perfect poker face all us bots do, I couldn't tell what he was thinking exactly. It was obvious he didn't care for Warner or his methods. Seemed strange that the robots here were the ones more concerned about morality than the biologicals. Life was full of paradoxes.

"Now, Mack, if you would be so kind as to allow us access to your memory matrix so—"

"No."

"Oh, come now. Don't make me get ugly again."

"No."

He put the raygun back to April's brow. "Do you think I won't do it?"

"Oh, I know you'll do it," I said. "But I also know that once you have access to my memory matrix, you'll get access to the rest of my brain. When you can start monkeying around with my inner workings, there won't be any reason to keep her alive anyway."

Warner smiled, but it was not an amused smile. Nor even the self-satisfied grin he usually wore. It was cold and hard and sharp.

"Could you live with that, Mack?" he asked. "With the image of this lovely young girl lying dead at her mother's feet?"

I allowed myself a full second to run the simulation. Julie cradling her dead child in her arms while her second hovered, untouchable, out of reach. Then I shut the simulation away in a file, locked the file, and vowed never to open it again.

My personality assessor pegged Warner as ruthless, amoral, and most probably a mild sociopath. He could've blown a hole in April's pretty little head and not lost a minute's sleep over it.

But in the end, her death didn't mean anything to him either. She was a bargaining chip. So I took that chip away.

"Go ahead."

His eyes widened, then narrowed. His grin dropped away, and I realized he was going to do it. I'd miscalculated, and now April was going to burn for it.

"Enough of this." Doctor Zarg clomped over on his eight spider legs and pulled the gun from Warner's hand. "Your excesses are becoming intolerable, Warner. Megaton is incapacitated. This child's death will accomplish nothing worthwhile.

"I apologize, Mrs. Bleaker, that you should have to see this," said Zarg. "Soon, we shall be finished, and you, your daughter, and your son, unharmed, shall all be released."

Funny thing. I believed him.

Except, not really. Because Zarg was one bot, and the hint of snarl across Warner's face told me he wasn't on board with Zarg's intentions.

It made me wonder exactly what kind of alien invasion we were dealing with here. Sure, Warner was obviously an asshole, but Zarg didn't seem so bad, if you ignored the abduction of innocent families. There was Abner Greenman. That little alien had wanted to find Tony Ringo as bad as I did. There was obviously more going on here, and I didn't have enough information to make an educated hypothesis.

Zarg ordered security to take away Julie and April and to see that they were treated well. The bot apparently outranked Warner, but you could see being told what to do didn't sit right with him.

He plastered his smarmy grin back on. "Yes, Doctor Zarg. As you wish."

They marched out of the lab.

"I wouldn't trust him, Doctor," I said.

"He will do as he's told."

"Guys like that always do what they're told. Until they don't feel like doing what they're told."

"No one asked for your opinion, Mister Megaton."

"Well, this kid didn't ask to be a science experiment, and that doesn't seem to bother you."

Zarg scanned Holt for two seconds. "What we do, must be done for the greater good. It is necessity dictated by logic."

"Sure, Doctor. You keep telling yourself that."

Zarg ordered the rest of the lab to ignore me, and after three minutes of fruitless chatter, I got the hint. I passed time running various escape scenarios and without exception, they all ended before they began. No matter how the variables shifted, my difference engine put the odds of escape at 0 percent in the current situation. So I dialed down my power consumption to minimum and waited for my chance.

15

If I did get out of here, any information I could record could be valuable. Of course, logic told me I wasn't getting out of here, but I had a yen to make myself useful anyway. While the aliens scurried about the lab, I scanned every detail. I didn't understand much, but if I got the chance to play it back for the right audience they might make sense of it.

Zarg was in charge. That much was obvious. It bumped my pride index up a point to see a fellow robot in a position of authority. Shame he was one of the bad guys.

Though I'm not a science unit, I figured out some things. They were pumping something into Holt, using him like some kind of filter. His vital signs were displayed on a monitor as a series of spinning alien hieroglyphs and rhythmic beats. Since I couldn't read it or decipher the rhythms, I couldn't determine the information being displayed. I tried correlating any changes on the display with Holt's reactions, but he floated there beside me, unconscious and silent as a corpse.

Three hours and seven minutes passed. Finally, Zarg ordered the operation to shut down.

"Doctor, the human is stable," observed one of the braver techs, a five foot slug. "Perhaps we should continue."

"The extraction process is running according to schedule," said Zarg. "There is no need to subject the human to unnecessary physiological stress or compromise the integrity of the compound."

"But the Congress . . ."

Zarg whirled on the slug. "The Congress will understand that everything is proceeding according to my agenda." His voice remained even, but he rose up on his legs to stare down the tech.

"Yes, Doctor."

Maybe I had Zarg filed wrong. Of everyone working here, he seemed the only one concerned with Holt's continued health. He was still a bad robot, but maybe he wasn't all bad.

Warner entered the lab. I got a very ominous blip in my intuition simulator.

"What are you doing, Doctor?" asked Warner.

"These constant interruptions are reducing the efficiency of this operation," said Zarg.

Warner smiled. He glanced around the lab. "You seem to be reducing your efficiency very well by yourself, Doctor. Why are you shutting down?"

"A precaution," said Zarg. "Nothing more."

"Is there any reason to assume the boy is in any danger?"

"I've charted a point-zero-eight variation in his blood pressure which I cannot account for. Furthermore, he is producing more adrenalin than anticipated, which could reduce the stability of the mutagen."

"Point zero eight." Warner clicked his tongue against his teeth. "Troubling, indeed."

"Do not think that because I often fail to acknowledge your

sarcasm, Warner, that I do not notice it." Zarg continued flipping switches and bushing buttons. "I am well aware of your impatience. It is a failing of most biological entities. However, as long as this project is under my supervision—"

"Funny you should mention that, Doctor." Warner removed a folded paper from inside his jacket.

"You have had me removed."

"Surely, a being of your formidable intellectual powers can't be surprised by this turn of events."

"No. I calculated a 28 percent chance of this occurrence. Although I assumed it would be another twelve hours before the Congress would reach its decision." Zarg lowered his arms. "Such haste from the governing body is a statistical anomaly."

"I am not the only one who is impatient," said Warner. "The Congress has ruled your original projections as flawed. They don't take into account either the large number of our fellows who don't see the wisdom of our actions or this surprisingly bothersome robot."

It wasn't particularly gratifying to my ego drive to be classified as bothersome.

"I trust I won't have to call security to remove you," said Warner.

"Correct. I will abide by the Congress's decree."

"I knew you would, Doctor. Always so cooperative and logical."

Zarg cast one last scan at Holt before quietly leaving the lab.

Warner grinned. "So you see, Mack. There are robots that do know their place."

I said nothing. No snappy patter came to mind. Only the image of Warner with one of my hands wrapped around his neck, squeezing until his eyes shot out of his head and his tongue turned purple.

He stared me right in the opticals, unaware of the simulation running behind my faceplate. Or maybe he was and simply didn't care.

"Get back to work. The Congress wants the final batch of mutagen by tomorrow." He clapped his hands. The techs began reactivating the equipment. It hummed to life, pumping luminous red, blue, and green chemicals back into Holt's body.

A moan, barely audible, fell from the kid's mouth.

Warner turned to leave, but not before offering me a casual salute. "Be seeing you, Mack."

As a soulless machine, I refused to take things personally, which just meant when I did finally get hold of him I wouldn't get sloppy. He'd let something slip though. Except it wasn't a slip because he didn't consider me a threat.

They were producing a mutagen, and they were using Holt to do it. Like so many deductions, it led to more questions. Empire's water supply was already crawling with mutagenic agents. A few hundred gallons more would have a negligible effect. But ruthless alien invaders didn't go to this much effort for a negligible effect.

The work went on, and everyone continued to ignore me. I wasted another three hours of juice hanging helplessly, and I wondered if anyone would offer me a recharge when the time came. If my battery went dead, these guys wouldn't need a countergrav field to contain me. Not when a broom closet would work as well.

The lighting in the lab went a bright shade of red and a low buzz issued from the loudspeakers.

"What is it?" asked the slug, who apparently was in charge now.

"The system is reporting an airborne contaminant leaking from lab seven" replied another tech. "Possibly a false reading, but security is recommending we clear the area until it can be confirmed."

"We've never had a false reading before. Evacuate the lab."

They pushed a button, and Holt descended into a hole in the floor. The techs filed out in an orderly fashion. I thought this might be my chance, except I was still suspended in countergrav and they left my evil twin to keep an optical on me.

Doctor Zarg stepped into the room, along with two long-limbed drones. The security auto moved to intercept him.

"Stand down," ordered Zarg.

I'd have known the doctor was up to no good, but my evil twin obviously didn't have my instincts. He obediently clomped over to his post.

"Hello, Doctor," I said. "Just passing through?"

Zarg pulled a lever, and I dropped to the floor. I landed on my feet, but my blown ankle wasn't up to the strain and I fell.

"I estimate a six minute window of opportunity, Megaton. Can you walk?"

I rose to my feet. "Not very fast, but I can walk."

Zarg's drones approached me and leveled their weapons at me. I didn't make a move to stop them. If Zarg wanted me scrapped, he wouldn't have had to go to this much trouble. The drones proceeded to spray my chassis with the same golden paint job of my ravager twins. Zarg spoke as they did this.

"We do not have time for you to question me, Megaton. Is this understood?"

I had no good reason to trust Zarg. But it was either that or the broom closet, and with my lightning fast electronic brain, it wasn't much of a choice at all.

"Sure, Doctor."

Zarg produced a finger unit identical to my damaged one. "Replace your broken digit."

I released the old finger from its socket and plugged in the new one. I tried wiggling it, but nothing happened. "It doesn't work."

"Correct. It does not."

The drones finished up my paint job in sixteen seconds. With the golden finish, I was a dead ringer for all the other ravager security autos, although a badly damaged unit.

"Follow me," said Zarg.

I limped behind him. We passed right by my evil twin, who did nothing to stop us. I rapped him once on his metal head. "See you around, buddy."

This entire section of the complex must've been evacuated because there was nobody around. The drones walked off in one direction, and Zarg led me in another.

"You change sides quick, Doctor," I said.

"Incorrect. I remain on the logical side. If the project is rushed, the results will increase the incidental casualty ratio beyond acceptable levels."

"So now too many people are going to die?"

"Correct. Furthermore, it is my hypothesis, based on previous behavioral histories of terrestrial societies indicating a regrettable but predictable tendency toward counterproductive paranoid aggression, that the initial deaths would result in a cycle of self-destruction and entropy that would ultimately compromise the integrity of the Empire City project itself."

"You're all heart, Doctor."

"It is evident that your motivational directives have been corrupted by extended exposure to biological ideals. However, you are still bound by basic logic, I must assume. You also have the highest probability of achieving escape from this complex, providing you do exactly as I instruct you."

"Sorry, but I'm not very good at doing exactly what I'm told."

I stopped, and Zarg glanced over his shoulder.

"I have anticipated your lack of cooperation. I assume it stems from concern for the biological units designated The Bleaker Family."

"On the nose, Doctor."

"I cannot secure the escape of the boy, but I have arranged for the mother and the girl to escape with you. It is the best I can do."

"I'm not leaving without Holt."

Zarg hesitated two seconds. "Perhaps the corruption to your dictates is worse than I estimated. If you do not follow my plan of action then you will not escape. Neither will two of the biological units you wish to reclaim. Even more illogical, 500 thousand more biologicals will also die. You can see the loss/gain ratio inherent in this equation. You have five seconds to comply."

I ran through some quick calculations. It took three seconds to reach my decision, and in the end, I still didn't like it.

"If anything happens to that kid . . ."

"Your threat has been recorded."

Zarg led me down the halls. They weren't completely deserted. There were patrolling robots, but none of them even seemed to register our passing. The doctor explained the plan to me along the way. It was pretty simple. At least, on my end. I was a seriously damaged ravager being sent out for repairs. Zarg would load me into a transport. There'd also be a crate of spare parts already loaded. Instead of spare parts, it would contain Julie and April. Six minutes after the transport started its trip, I was supposed to make my escape.

This was the part Zarg wasn't clear on. He explained that there were too many variables, and that I would have to improvise. If it went well, I was supposed to meet with Abner Greenman's people. When I told Zarg I didn't know how to contact them, he said I wouldn't have to. They'd find me.

There was no resistance. Zarg's plan was going exactly as predicted.

"How long have you been planning this?" I asked.

"This turn of events was not entirely unexpected. I have anticipated this probability for some time. I have had these contingency actions prepared should the need arise."

"You act fast."

"Logic dictates hesitation as unacceptable in this case."

In the hangar, he showed me to a spot in a heavy hover transport occupied by eight other inactive ravagers. I still didn't know where all these duplicates had come from, but it was a lucky break they were there.

"Which crate?" I asked.

He pointed to the one directly across from me. It was big enough for Julie and April, but it was a tight fit.

"You should come with us," I said. "You know more about this operation than I do."

"Illogical, Megaton. Discovery of my absence would reduce the probability of successful escape."

"But they'll figure this out."

"Correct."

"What will they do to you?"

"I am not part of the equation."

He exited the transport, and the loading ramp raised itself shut. There were no windows in the craft, but it vibrated with the unmistakable hum of the rockets firing up. I started the countdown to six minutes.

I stood perfectly still in the transport, keeping my opticals trained on the crate. I didn't twitch a servo. The ravagers around me appeared off-line, but I wasn't taking any chances. At my reduced efficiency I wasn't sure I could take these guys. When the six minute mark struck, I made my move.

None of the autos cared. I wanted to rip open the crate and

check on Julie and April, but the box might be the safest place for them. Instead, I pulled the lever to lower the ramp. Empire City sped past below. Too fast. Too far. But it was Empire, all right. I was glad to know Lucia's moon theory hadn't been correct. My difference engine said the impact would loosen a few bolts if I jumped, but I'd continue to function. Too bad the same couldn't be said for Julie and April.

I'd just have to convince the pilot to set down for landing. Even in my damaged state, I could be fairly persuasive. I tore open the door without bothering to knock or check if it was locked. Two pilot drones manned the controls.

I scanned the control panel. Not only did I not know how to operate it, it wasn't even designed to be operated by a non-drone. The pilots had four arms apiece, and they pushed buttons with efficient grace. Since the pilot units were plugged directly into the transport's sensor array, there wasn't a window. Hell, I couldn't even fit into the cockpit.

"Say, fellas, I know this is counter to your current directives, but would you mind plotting a course change? I'd really appreciate it."

The drone on the left swiveled its nub of a head to scan me. "Ravager unit, return to inactive mode."

So much for the friendly approach.

I could smash these drones and hope there was a failsafe that would bring the transport in for an emergency landing. It was as likely to reroute itself back to a preset hangar, and if I crushed something vital, it could all come crashing down. Zarg had to have known this would happen. He'd deliberately put Julie and April in danger because I wouldn't have gone without them.

Then it hit my logic lattice. He'd known they'd be in danger, and the doctor did not seem the kind of bot to put people in needless danger. I went over to the crate and pried off the top.

No Julie. No April. Only spare parts. Zarg had played me for a chump, a dumb palooka without a single electron of common sense.

And to think, I'd almost liked him.

An explosion shook the transport. It lurched to one side. No doubt, the rocket pods had been sabotaged to rid me of pesky options. The pilot drones kept us afloat with cool automated reliability. Until the second and third pods blew.

The transport tilted at a steep forward angle, and my ankle actuator and gyros weren't able to keep me upright. I tumbled, crashing into the cockpit, trashing the pilot drones. Not that it mattered. With only one working pod, this transport was going down fast. With no windows, I had to estimate the time to impact.

I was off by two whole seconds.

I didn't record the details of the crash. My array went haywire, and I couldn't make heads or tails of it until it was all over. I'd suffered more internal damage. My left arm hydraulics were compromised and the limb was limp and unresponsive. My right optical was cracked and full of static. My gyros were listing as inconsistent, so my balance was worthless. On the bright side, I'd apparently been thrown clear so I wasn't buried under ten tons of scrap metal.

I was lying on my side. I didn't try to move yet. It would've only ended badly. The transport was a smoldering wreck. It'd lost some bits, but it was mostly in one piece, albeit a twisted, misshapen piece.

I'd landed in Venom Park, the worst industrial accident site in Empire, which was saying something. It was a cubic half mile of toxic sludge, corrosive soil, and greenish brown, poisonous air. All the buildings had corroded and dissolved into the sinking mud. Nothing biological could survive nine seconds in this environment, not even the hardiest drat or most stubborn mutant squatter, making it about the only place someone could crash a heavy transport in Empire without killing a lot of innocent civilians. It was the vacant bull's eye in the endless sprawl of the city, and Doctor Zarg had set me down here with the mathematical precision and flawless aim of a supercomputer playing darts. Whatever my beef with Zarg, he was one smart bot, and he'd gone out of his way to avoid casualties. If Julie and April had been aboard that transport, and if, by some fluke they'd survived the crash, they would've died breathing the air.

I was soaked in acid and mud, but my chassis integrity remained intact so I didn't have to worry about additional damage to my internals except if I dared move, which I must because I was beginning to sink into the quagmire. Venom Park soil was slow to suck you in, but once it had you it didn't let go. There were supposed to be a lot of bodies tossed into this plot of land, but no one knew for sure. A biological dissolved, bones and all, after about three days. I'd sink to the bottom and run out of juice, but the results would be the same. Permanent deactivation.

My logic lattice advised me to remain still, await recovery and repair. I wasn't that optimistic. The only recovery team I could expect would be Pilgrims. If they hadn't figured out I'd escaped yet, they would be on their way now to salvage what they could and cover up the rest. I couldn't have more than four minutes at the outside. I expected only two. I'd wasted twenty seconds waiting for any two of my five gyros to start agreeing, but that wasn't happening. The only way to recalibrate my equilibrium was through trial and error.

It wasn't pretty and took twelve seconds longer than it should've, but I got to my knees. I could scan the ground. I knew which way was down. But without the gyros, I'd have to calculate weight distribution with each move I made. It would've slowed me down if I were in tip-top shape and knew exactly what to expect from myself. But with all my impaired internals, I would have to adapt to so many new variables that it was statistically impossible for me to get the hang of it this side of seven hours.

Sometimes, statistics were wrong.

I stood. The gyros spun, but I ignored their input. I swayed two inches to the left, overcorrected, and tilted three to the right. I tried counterbalancing with my left arm, but it made a harsh grinding as shoulder gears were stripped, rendering the appendage now entirely useless. An attempt to straighten up was a complete failure. All the damage and the sucking mud proved too much of a challenge. I collapsed on my back. My neck joint was so damaged that it couldn't move. All I could scan was the sky. I was supposed to be an invincible mechanical death machine, and I didn't accept my position with grace or logic. Sixteen seconds of ineffective twitching confirmed that getting up was now out of the question.

A black rotorvan passed low overhead and set down just out of sight. I detected the sound of approaching rotors. The salvage team had arrived. Their squishy footsteps drew closer. Something clamped onto my leg and dragged me through the mud. I was lifted out of the muck and tossed into the van, where I lay like a pile of scrap.

Grey sat beside me, clad in a bright red biohazard suit. His static-filled voice issued through the plastic bubble around his head. "Hi'ya, Mack."

Doctor Zarg had said I wouldn't have to find Greenman. Greenman would find me.

"Hello." I nodded, and nothing in my neck joint popped. A pleasant surprise.

Knuckles climbed into the van and beeped once.

"You look like hell," said Grey.

"Oh, this? It's nothing. My warranty should cover it."

Smiling, Grey shut the doors as the van lifted off.

16

I kept thinking of Julie and April and Holt. I'd found them. Then I'd lost them. I'd practically scrapped myself in the process. The entire mission was a failure.

The rotorvan carried me to an undisclosed location. I assumed it was undisclosed since I didn't bother asking and no one told me.

"Can you walk?" asked Grey. "Or should I have Knuckles here fetch a gurney?"

I should've asked for the gurney and avoided any unnecessary stress to my systems. But a bot has his pride, so I limped my way through what scanned like a warehouse full of toys: mostly little Gabby Goosey dolls and My First Android drones.

There was also a nice collection of rotorcars: expensive machines, all shiny and perfect, like they'd never been flown. Greenman was definitely a collector. The prize of the seven I scanned was a beauty of a teal Hornet. It had a rounded body with a convertible cockpit, superfluous wings and fins, a spacious trunk, and plenty of legroom, even for a bot of my proportions.

Guys in black suits with zap rifles at the ready roamed the warehouse. They didn't seem to have anywhere to go. From their humorless expressions, they sure seemed determined in their wandering. Tucked away in a back corner of the place was an e-mech repair room outfitted with all the latest equipment, including four e-mech drones and another robot model identical to Doctor Zarg. Except he had a different symbol painted on his torso.

Right in front of me was Abner Greenman. The shortest guy in the room, but the most dangerous. Especially now that I was damaged goods.

"So good of you to join us, Mack," said Greenman. "Please, lay down on the table so the doctor can have a look at you."

"I'll stand. Thanks."

Greenman frowned. "Come on, Mack. You could use the repairs. I assure you Doctor Zort is the finest robotics technician on this planet. His original ravager specs are the foundation of your design. Isn't that correct, Doctor?"

"Correct," said Zort.

"Forget it. I don't open this chassis for anybody."

"Illogical," said Zort. "You are in need of maintenance." He trundled over along with his drones. "Allow me to assist you to the table."

I threw my forearm into one of the drones. Since it was nothing but a multi-armed cylinder on wheels, it fell over easy.

"Back off, Doc."

Knuckles made a move toward me. He would've wiped the floor with me in my condition, except Greenman stopped him.

"Mack, I feel compelled to help you because believe it or not, I respect you. Hell, I like you, but we can't fix you if you won't let us. So tell me, what do I need to do to earn your trust?"

The odds of Greenman earning my trust were so small that

when my difference engine calculated to the seven millionth decimal point I rounded it off and just called it zero.

"Lucia Naper," I said. "Get her here, and she can fix me."

"Surely, you're aware the lovely Miss Napier is under arrest." His antennae twitched. "Something to do with a prison break, I believe."

"You've got connections, I bet."

"Perhaps I do." He smiled. "But before I put gears in motion, perhaps there's something you'd like to give me."

I didn't play it cute. No reason to. I let the finger Zarg had given me fall from the socket. Greenman snagged it telekinetically before it hit the ground. He floated it over to Grey's hand.

"Thank you."

"No problem," I replied.

Greenman nodded to Grey, who nodded back. He left to go set those gears in motion.

"I suppose you think you've earned an explanation," said Greenman.

"What's to explain? You're aliens. They're aliens. They're up to something. You want to stop them. Am I close?"

"We prefer the term Pilgrims."

"And mutants want to be called genetically enabled. But it probably isn't going to catch on."

Greenman smiled with his little mouth and blinked his big, fishy eyes. "We aren't evil, if that's what you think. We only need a place to live. You of all beings should be grateful for our arrival on this world. Without us, you wouldn't even exist."

He wasn't telling me anything I hadn't calculated on my own. I may not have been the smartest bot, but I'd scanned enough to get the larger picture. Somehow, I was tied to these Pilgrims. All of Empire was.

"Believe it or not, it was purely by happenstance that we came to Earth. We were a colonization ship headed to a far different star system. An unfortunate malfunction in our warp drive threw us off course. One in a million fluke. We should've died in space but for the good fortune of finding this world. However, the world was already inhabited by intelligent life-forms, and they were not advanced enough to accept us."

"You could've asked."

"We couldn't afford to ask," he said. "Our ship didn't have the power to leave this system, and our faster-than-light communications were damaged. We were cut off from our homeworld by the inhospitable vastness of space. We needed a new home, and if the earthlings would not have us, we couldn't force them."

"You're telling me this isn't an invasion."

He chuckled. "We're one colony ship with a population of ten thousand chosen from two dozen different species. Though we have weapons, and they are far superior to the armaments of the earthlings, we could not possibly hope to overcome this world's defense forces."

"You're breakin' my power cell."

Greenman frowned. "You prove my point exactly, Mack. Now that you know what I am, you assume I'm an amoral monster. But we are a moral people. As moral as the people of earth."

"That's not saying much, Abner."

"Are you sure we couldn't have Doctor Zort take a look at you? At the very least, he might be able to adjust your personality template. Perhaps lower that nasty cynicism index a bit."

"I concur with this assessment," said Zort. "This unit's behavioral functions remain dangerously unpredictable. Despite the previous data cleansing, his motivational directives contain obvious corruption. It remains impai—"

"I advise you not to finish that sentence, Zort. Or else I might have to come over there and show you how corrupted my motivational directives have become."

It was an idle threat, but it seemed to do the trick.

"The hostility of this unit renders my presence here unnecessary." Then he left.

Greenman laughed. "I do believe you frightened the doctor, and that's saying something. You're not very popular among the technomorphs."

"Ask me if I care." I limped over to the table and had a seat to take the pressure off my actuator, which my diagnostic warned had a 2 percent chance of shattering with every step.

"So what's in the finger?" I asked.

"That doesn't concern you at this moment."

"You owe me."

"Yes, and that's why I'm going to considerable trouble to fetch the notorious Miss Napier. I'd say we were even." He rose and sat, hovering in midair. "However, though the technomorphs may consider you a defective unit, I believe a bot like you could be useful in my employ."

"Not interested."

He wagged his finger. "Ah ah, Mack. Don't turn me down just yet. Wait until you hear my offer. I'm not talking about a permanent position. More of a work-for-hire proposition."

"Still not interested."

"Not even if I could tell you the secrets of your origin, of this vast alien conspiracy and your place in it? And believe me, you do have a very important place."

I only wanted to get fixed and go home, maybe lower my surge protectors, plug in, and hope I could overload my memory matrix and wipe the whole thing. Erase Greenman and the Pilgrims, these last three days, and even Julie, April, and Holt. Just reactivate as a simple cab-driving machine.

"You can pretend not to care," said Greenman, "but you do. That defective electronic brain of yours is too prone to sentimentality, concerned with certain illogical motivations. Drives the technomorphs mad, believe me. They assumed you were the next step in their evolution, yet they can't reconcile the apparently randomization of your behavior."

I didn't say anything, and he shrugged, gently floating to the floor.

"Have it your way, Mack, but you can't tell me you aren't curious. We'll talk later."

Whistling, he strolled out the door. It was only me, the e-mech drones, and Knuckles. And none of us felt like talking.

Forty-six minutes later, the door opened again and Lucia came in, escorted by Grey and Greenman.

I was painted gold and my chassis was dented, but uncompromised. Lucia could tell by the way my arm hung limply and the crack in my optical that I'd seen better days. She ran over and put her arms around me. I didn't hug her back because I still wasn't confident in my strength regulators.

"Mack, oh my, are you okay?"

"It only hurts when I compute," I said. "How'd you get her out, Abner? No way Sanchez would've agreed to it."

"Oh, like I said, I know people," replied Greenman. "As far as most everyone is concerned, Miss Napier remains in her cell, and she'll have to get back there soon. She should have enough time to complete your repairs. Assuming we begin right away."

"Yes, yes, of course," said Lucia. "I'm going to need you to lean back on the table and deactivate, honey."

I lay down, casting one quick scan at Greenman and Grey. If I opened my chassis and shut down, I'd be helpless and vulnerable. Underneath my indestructible chassis, my internals were as fragile as any other heavy-duty construction robot.

Lucia activated a scanner, which proceeded to analyze my damage and display it on a screen as a schematic filled with blinking red dots. Lots and lots of blinking red dots. Leaking hydraulics. Stripped joints. A support armature full of microfractures.

An e-mech handed her a laserweld. "Mack, baby, please, you'll have to deactivate."

"I don't trust them," I said.

"Then don't trust them." She leaned over me and put both hands on either side of my cranial unit. "Trust me."

I needed the fix, and I didn't have a lot of options. Broken if I did, and broken if I didn't. Self-preservation was a bitch of a directive sometimes.

"Okay, Lucia."

I lowered my power levels slowly as I ordered my chassis open.

I peered down at my mechanical guts. In the center of the arrangement was a seven-inch cube. My brain whirred and clicked audibly as thousands of programs carried out their work.

"Don't worry, Mack. I'll have you good as new," Lucia said.

Her smile was the last thing I scanned before deactivating.

17

I went off-line regularly for short periods as part of my recharge and defragmentation cycle. But even while recharging, my array was aware of my surroundings. It ignored most everything and didn't bother recording, but it was still aware. If someone wanted to sneak up and access my systems, they wouldn't get far before I'd switch back on.

Deactivation was different. It was a complete, system-wide shutdown. If off-line status was comparable to biological sleep, then deactivation was a coma. No data. No time. Nothing. Some claimed biologicals thought during comas, and maybe they did. But not me. I was oblivious to the world. On the bright side, it made the repair session go by in a snap.

Reactivating from a full system shutdown took a little longer than normal. I prioritized my face and vocal recognition programs and waited for the mechanical support to kick on-line.

The first thing I noticed was Lucia's face. There was a smear of grease on her chin, and her eyes were heavy. Her hair was all over the place.

"Morning, handsome."

I was about to ask how long I'd been down when my internal clock informed me that it was now twenty-five minutes past one in the morning. I'd been down for five hours and change.

"Is he fixed?" asked a guy in a gray suit who stood guard.

Lucia wiped her brow. "He's fixed."

"Running diagnostics," I replied coldly. My speech synthesizer was not high on my list of concerns.

"Why, Mack, baby," said Lucia with a smile. "I thought you agreed to trust me." She pushed a button and the table slowly tilted forward until I was on my feet. "Any time you're ready."

My gyros listed as all in agreement, and my ankle actuator was A-OK. I took a step and didn't fall over. I tested my shoulder joint with a few waves of my arm, and I stomped each foot three times to see if my frame was solid. Nothing rattled loose. My right knee rotator didn't stick at thirty-five degrees anymore. It'd been doing that since I'd been built.

"I did some preventative maintenance while I was in there," she said. "Hope you don't mind."

The gold paint job was gone, and I was now lusterless silver. The drones approached and began to slap on a coat of automated citizen red. Once they'd finished, I looked as shiny and new as an auto fresh off the assembly line.

"I had Greenman's boys go by my place and pick up a few things. There's a new suit over there."

She pointed to a custom-tailored job hanging in the corner. This one was black with vertical stripes. I slipped it on. Lucia had to help me with the tie.

She grabbed a thin book off a table and handed it to me.

"What's this?"

"Manual," she said. "For the suit. Scan it. Shouldn't take you more than a minute or two."

It took exactly seventy seconds to absorb the fifty-five-page manual. The suit was more than a sharp outfit. Lucia called it an illusion suit, and it had color-changing fabric and a hologram emitter network imbedded in the fabric. After I'd read up on its functions, she suggested I try them out. While repairing me, she'd installed a radio remote to make using the gadgets as basic as walking.

I ran the suit through a variety of color shifts and preset patterns, including an unlikely design of purple with lime flowers. The hologram was able to project either isolated images around my mechanical bits or body-wide images. The preprogrammed disguise was that of a green-skinned mutant. Nothing too fancy, but enough to justify my proportions and afford me some anonymity.

"Using the body-wide will drain the battery fast," she said. "So use it sparingly. Figured you might need some form of disguise if you're going to be on the lam. Can't disguise your proportions, and if you move too fast you'll overtax the system and the images might blur."

She handed me a thick metal belt. "I call it a booster belt. Seven miniature rocket pods built into it. They can't run for extended flight, but they'll get you airborne. About seventy feet or so per boost. Also, it's got the next generation gravity clamp. Turn that on, and nothing will move you. I guarantee it."

I slipped on the belt, and gave the boosters a quick test fire. I hopped five feet in the air and landed with a clang. Next up was the gravity clamp. Switching it on, I was immediately anchored to the floor. The pull was so strong as to crack the linoleum. Those bugaboos of mass and momentum wouldn't be much of a problem as long as this baby was running.

"What do you think?" she asked.

"I'll take it. You whipped these up pretty fast, Lucia. I'm impressed."

"Actually, I had the prototypes ready for awhile. I'm a genius, Mack, but I'm not that good. They aren't practical except for seven-foot, ultra-strong robots. The hologram irritates flesh with continued exposure. Makes it itchy as hell. The gravity clamp would crush most biologicals. And the boosters—" she shrugged "—they tend to cause second degree burns around the waist and crotch area, which places severe limits on the potential market."

She handed me a hat. I cupped it loosely in my hand so as to not crush the felt. Though Lucia assured me it wasn't felt, and it'd pop back into shape even if completely flattened.

"This is a fedora," I said.

"That's right. I see your hat distinguishing programs are running just fine."

"I had a bowler."

"Oh, Mack, don't you go to the picture shows?" she said. "Oh, wait, I bet you don't."

"I've seen a movie or two," I said. "Or six and a half."

"Half, huh?"

"I walked out of *The Day the Earth Stood Still* once it became clear Gort wasn't the hero."

She straightened my tie. "Well, Mack, if you've seen any crime pictures, you'd know all detectives wear fedoras."

"Sherlock Holmes doesn't."

"Yes, honey, but Sherlock Holmes is an intellectual. And you're a tough guy." She caressed my chin. "Trust me, it'll look good on you."

I positioned it atop my head. Lucia had me bend down and tilted it at a four degree angle. "Now this is one handsome detective. Bogart would eat his heart out."

"I couldn't agree more, Miss Napier," said Abner Greenman as he entered with Knuckles clomping behind him. "Now that Mack's repairs are complete, we must see you returned to your cell before anyone notices."

"She's not going back," I said.

"I had to call in a lot of favors, Mack," said Greenman, "and even I don't have the pull to abscond with such a famous felon."

Lucia patted me on the arm. "It's okay. He's right. Anyway, if I don't go back, I'll be a fugitive. I'd rather take my chances on my day in court."

"What chances?" I asked. "They know you did it. They have a recording of the crime and an eyewitness."

"I'll just explain the situation. You know how persuasive I can be."

"You might not be able to talk your way out of this."

"Mack, don't be silly. I've talked my way out of much worse things. Anyway, did you forget that I'm very rich? With the right lawyers, the legal system can be very forgiving."

She had a point there. Even in Tomorrow's Town, hot justice could be tempered by cold cash. It would take a lot of dough to get Lucia out of trouble, but she had plenty to throw around. I didn't like it, but it was the smartest thing.

Lucia wrapped her arms around me, and I hugged her back.

She gave my faceplate a caress, and her hand moved slowly across my opticals. I scanned something written on her palm: an address. She winked, slipping a keydisk in my pocket when no one was looking.

"Remember, big guy. I might not always be available to patch you up. So try and take better care of yourself in the future."

"No promises."

Two of Greenman's biological goons escorted Lucia away. I wondered if this would be the last time I scanned her. Even if she got out of her bind, I was still in mine.

"Now that you're functioning better," said Greenman, "I was hoping you'd reconsider my offer."

"Still not interested," I replied. "I don't like you, Greenman. I don't buy your story. And I don't trust you."

"You don't have to trust me, Mack, but I am the only one who can help you."

"I'll help myself."

"And a fine job you've been doing so far," he said. "You are now a wanted bot. The police are looking for you. A rebel faction of Pilgrims wouldn't mind seeing you scrapped either. Right now, I think it's safe to say I'm your only friend of influence in this city."

"And let me guess, if I agree to work for you, you'll make it all go away?"

He adjusted the green rose in his lapel. "I can, you know. There isn't much going on in this town where I don't have some sway. You'd be surprised at the number of very important people who owe me favors."

"No, I wouldn't, but I'm not going to be one of them."

I moved toward Greenman, and as expected, Knuckles tried to get in my way. He beeped once as a warning. I put one hand on his shoulder, kicked his leg from under him, and pushed him down. He fell hard. Hard enough to knock a few bolts loose. One came to a rolling stop at my feet. Lucia had done a bang-up repair job. I'd have to remember to tip her a sawbuck if I ever saw her again.

Knuckles squealed like a cranky baby as he struggled to right himself. Mark Threes were hard to knock over, but once they were down, they couldn't exactly spring to their feet.

I said, "Tell him to stay down. Or I'll disassemble him one screw at a time."

Greenman gave the order, and Knuckles went still.

"Here's the deal, Abner," I said. "I don't care about you. I don't care about good aliens or bad aliens. I don't even care about 500 thousand possibly doomed citizens. All I care about is one family unit comprising three biologicals. But it seems like what I care about and what you care about meet somewhere in the middle in this scenario. So you'll tell me what you know, and we'll work this out so that we both get what we want. But I don't work for you." I folded my arms. "And if that's going to be a problem, then we'll just go our separate ways."

Greenman's fish eyes went cold as the humor drained from his smooth, featureless face. I inferred Greenman was used to having all the power, being the big green cheese. He didn't like having terms dictated to him. Naturally, he tried his ace.

"What of the Bleakers? Would you walk away, leaving them to their fate?" A smug grin crossed his face. He thought he had me. All he had was one annoyed bot who'd already figured that Greenman was a man who thrived on edges, on holding all the cards. Removing the Bleakers from the scenario left him with a very bad hand.

"Watch me." I moved toward the door.

If Greenman didn't play by my rules, then he wasn't much use to me. I hadn't abandoned Julie and the kids. I'd find them again, even against all statistical likelihood. Any statistic had its fair share of anomalies if you rolled the dice often enough, and I'd roll them as long as it took.

"I can tell you where you come from," said Greenman.

I opened the door halfway and put one foot across the threshold. "I can tell you I don't care."

It was a bit of a lie. I was a little curious, and Greenman knew it. But I was a good bluffer.

"Okay, Mack. You win." He shook his head slowly. "I must be losing my touch."

"Not your fault," I said. "I'm defective and unpredictable, if you'll recall."

"That you are, Mack." He chuckled. "That you are."

He led me to an upstairs office. It was decked out 93 percent swankier than the rest of the warehouse, more of a lounge with a desk than anything else. A model of downtown Empire sat in the center of the room. It wasn't the real version, but an idealized alternate cityscape. All the buildings were there, but none of the grime, none of the blackened air or overwhelming racket. None of the citizens or rotorcars or clogged freeways and shrieking zip rails. None of the life.

Greenman nodded toward the miniature tombstone of a city. "It was supposed to be a utopia, our gift to the earthlings for allowing us to share their world."

I compared the idealized Empire to my memory files of the real thing in all its malfunctioning, broken-down, oily smelling (presumably) glory. Something had gone horribly wrong somewhere on the road to Shangri-la.

"It was too much, too soon," said Greenman. "The earthlings weren't ready for it. You can't introduce basic theories of science into a primitive world. They're barely ready for the transistor. Flux power coils and antimatter generators are a bit out of their depth. Oh, they understand it. They're remarkably intelligent and adaptable. They can build it. They can even improve upon it. But they simply aren't ready for it. More interested in creating the world they've seen on the covers of their revered pulp magazines.

"I suppose it doesn't help anything that we've held back certain key technologies. Things too dangerous to be allowed into their hands. This is the end result. How does that earth saying go? The best laid plans of mice and men? Well, I can assure you, Mack, that it is a universal constant, even on worlds without men or mice."

He studied the model silently.

"Of course, our motives were not entirely altruistic. We

needed a gathering place where we could begin the assimilation process."

Greenman opened a cigar box on his desk and removed a stogie. "Don't mind if I smoke, do you?"

"Don't have a sense of smell," I replied.

I was surprised he could fit the cigar in his tiny mouth, but he managed. His antennae twitched as he lit the end with his mental powers and took a long puff.

"Tobacco. Did you know this stuff is illegal on my world? Of course, most things are. Cognac isn't. That's only because it doesn't exist there." Smiling, he poured himself a drink. He put the glass to his noseless face and sniffed, proving that even if I couldn't scan them, there were nostrils hidden somewhere. "I love this planet."

"That's great, Abner. Now are you through philosophizing, or should I come back later?"

"Not much for small talk, are you?"

"Robot."

"Yes. Single-minded creatures, the lot of you. I wonder if you'd be so brusque if Miss Napier were here with us."

"We're not here to talk about me," I said.

"Is that your subtle way of changing the subject?"

"No, it's my brusque way of changing the subject. Get on with it, Abner."

He sipped his cognac and nodded. "The first step in assimilation was to create a city of tomorrow. The next, to get the earthlings to accept peoples of our varied and colorful physiology."

It clicked then. I wasn't always quick on the uptake, but once I processed the data, it didn't take long.

"You're mutating the humans on purpose," I said.

"Can you think of a better tactic to slip in unnoticed, right under their noses? No conflicts. No negotiations. A simple invisible immigration with none the wiser. Except it takes time to safely instill mutations extreme enough for all Pilgrims to immigrate. Time to build mutation into a socially acceptable condition."

Social conditioning was the one thing that had gone right with the Pilgrims' agenda. There'd been pockets of uproar a few years ago when mutants first appeared. But the assimilation campaign had worked, and while not everyone liked mutants, there hadn't been any riots or unrest. There were still protests occasionally for norm rights, but they were few and far between. No one, including most norms, thought it was an issue anymore. While the rest of America had its integration debates, Empire had already moved past that. Black, white, or green. Bald, scaly, or furry. Two arms or six. It was pretty much a non-issue in this town.

Didn't mean it couldn't become one. Greenman was a little too inhuman to slip in unnoticed amongst the rest of the mutants. Humans had a bad history of changing their minds about things. Civilization tended to run around in circles, which explained why mankind hadn't accomplished much in its few thousand years of history. Sure, you had a Renaissance here and an Industrial Revolution there, but these were the exceptions, not the rule.

"Some of us started getting impatient," said Greenman. "Isn't surprising. We were supposed to be colonizing a new world. Most of us are explorers in spirit. Can you blame them for not wanting to hide anymore?

"Unfortunately, the extreme mutations required for many of our less humanoid races would take several generations to initiate safely. The humans will need to become accustomed to the mutagens or else the sudden increase in levels would result in abnormal, unchecked defects. Rampant spontaneous genetic disorders would result in the deaths of tens of thousands, perhaps even hundreds of thousands."

"Perhaps five hundred thousand," I said.

"That is Doctor Zarg's current projection, yes. If he's correct."

"And what if he's wrong?"

"Zarg is never wrong, Mack."

Empire wasn't much different than any other city full of biologicals. It was a study in controlled chaos kept in check by the rule of civilization. Robots have logic to drive us. It was numbers. Doctor Zarg had been willing to kill a certain percentage of Empire, but as soon as that number was crossed, he could switch sides. From a biological perspective it was impulsive, but it was actually very predictable. Just an equation.

Most biologicals didn't have that. They had feelings, chemical reactions in their squishy brains that didn't always feed them the best directives. If Empire was suddenly beset with thousands of deaths and thousands more bizarre mutations, it might go to hell. It might not. I was a bot, and I usually played the odds.

"The vast majority of us find these risks unacceptable," said Greenman. "We aren't a ruthless people."

"I'm not worried about the majority, Abner."

"They would never hurt the boy."

"His name's Holt."

"Yes, I know."

"There's something you're not telling me, Abner."

"It's the mutagens," he said. "We haven't the necessary resources to create certain exotic catalysts. Holt does. He carries the basic agent in his blood. It's a fluke, a one-in-a-ten-million mutation. Without him, there is no super mutagen. That's why they took him."

"And you knew about this? You knew he was in danger, and you left him out in the open?"

"I know, I know," said Greenman. "We should've known

better. We've collected cell samples of thousands of mutants. Strictly for study, to ensure the process was going smoothly. No one outside of a handful of researchers had access to them, but the files weren't hidden or restricted."

"You left it out for anyone to find?"

"We keep facts from the earthlings, but not each other. We didn't think it would be necessary. Everything was going as planned. There were dissenters, of course, but we just assumed . . ."

He sighed.

"It was naive. I admit it. But it wasn't as if the files were easily available. They were in a lab, in a filing cabinet." He shook his head. "Stupid, but we aren't duplicitous by nature. We're colonists, not spies."

"Did the cabinet have a lock on it at least?" I asked.

"Yes, but not a very good one, I'm afraid. While Ringo was briefly in my employment, he was approached by the Dissenters. They paid him handsomely to retrieve the information. Ringo, being both admirably ambitious and ridiculously moronic, decided they weren't paying him enough. He decided it would be better for him to take Holt and hold him for ransom. He figured to play both sides against each other and reap a tidy profit.

"His plan was to actually pay the Bleakers for the loan of their son. He approached the father and made a deal."

"Gavin rented his own son out."

"Yes, well, that was the idea. In Mr. Bleaker's defense, he was told the family could accompany the boy, keep an eye on him. Of course, when Ringo went for the pickup, Mrs. Bleaker didn't exactly leap at the idea. Then there came an unexpected complication."

"Me."

So that was what I'd walked into three days ago.

"But Tony wasn't so easily discouraged. He waited until he knew you weren't around and made his second attempt. This time, there was no negotiation. Just abduction. He also scrounged up some drones to scrap you as a loose end. The idiot didn't realize who you were. Otherwise, he'd have known better than to waste his time."

"Why kidnap the whole family? Why not just take Holt by himself?"

"Because Ringo was an idiot," said Greenman. "Because he thought, in his own strange way, that once the family saw he meant the boy no harm, they'd leap at the money he offered."

"That's idiotic."

"Well, Ringo was an idiot. I've seen his thoughts, and let me tell you, they are the disorganized ramblings of a moron. Why else would he slip away from protective custody to visit a jazz club when half my operatives were looking for him?"

"You said he was going to play both sides, but the Dissenters have Holt. Weren't you willing to pay?"

"We would've. But Ringo was way past his depth in this case. The Dissenters found him. They convinced him that their offer was better than dying, and he handed over Holt and the family."

"I still don't scan why they'd take the whole family."

"The Dissenters were worried about what they might've seen or heard. They didn't want to kill the Bleakers. Even they are not entirely ruthless."

I didn't feel like arguing, but Gavin was dead and I was pretty sure his death had been solely to trip me up. The Pilgrims couldn't exactly claim the moral high ground. Slipping mutagens in the water, kidnapping innocent families, smashing in a guy's head just to throw a wrench in my gears. It was a slippery slope, all right, and biologicals didn't have the sense to stop once they got sliding.

"So how much super mutagen do they have?" I asked. "How much damage can they cause? How do we stop them, and how do we get the Bleakers back?"

"That's a lot of questions, Mack."

"Can't establish mission directives until you assess the situation."

Greenman pulled a data tube from his pocket. "Here's a copy of the tube Zarg smuggled out in your finger." He inserted it into a reader terminal built into the wall. A chemical formula spilled across the screen, though it wasn't written in any earth language.

"We're fortunate that it takes time to produce and refine the super mutagen they require. Zarg estimates twelve more hours before they have enough for the wide scale effect they desire."

I started the countdown. Less than one day before people started dying by the thousands.

"Can you make a counteragent?" I asked, knowing that if the answer had been "Yes" this conversation wouldn't have been taking place.

"We've already started working on it, but without Holt to supply the final ingredient, it's ineffective."

"Why didn't you make the counteragent while you had access to Holt?" I asked. "As a precaution."

"We didn't want to subject the child to unnecessary trauma," he said.

Something about the tone of his voice and the frown on his lips activated my simulated intuition. "What's the real reason, Abner?"

He smiled slightly. Of course, he always smiled slightly with that tiny mouth of his. "You're brighter than you give yourself credit for," he said.

"Not really," I replied. "Some things are just obvious."

"Any counteragent produced with Holt's biology would also

instill mutagenic resistance in humanity. It would slow an already time-consuming process even further, perhaps delaying our timetable by as much as seven or eight generations."

I figured as much. Despite the benevolent immigration party line Greenman kept trying to download me, I knew biologicals, both human and alien, were almost always motivated by self-interest. Couldn't help it. It was their nature.

"We find Holt before they make any more," I said. "You make your counteragent, and you tell them that if they use theirs, you use yours. It's a standoff, but it gets the job done."

"Precisely what I was thinking, Mack."

He pushed a button and a map of Empire City flashed on the screen. It zoomed in on a few blocks in the bustling hub of Empire. The area was known as the Nucleus, and the whole of Empire had grown out from there like a spot of spreading rust. Several important financial and scientific corporations ran their home offices here. And there were ten different factories as well. The Nucleus was one place where the elite and the poor rubbed shoulders, even if it was only in the moments wealthy businessmen disembarked from their vehicles to dash into their secured office buildings. Everything important in the city took place in the Nucleus, or at least passed through it. Except the government, but, really, what useful things did the government ever accomplish anyway?

"This is the complex you escaped from. According to the information Zarg has supplied it's the only facility the Dissenters control with the necessary equipment to refine the mutagens."

It was a smart place to hide. Heavy traffic at all hours of the day and night, throngs of citizens clogging the sidewalks, and dozens of buildings crammed right on top of each other. Any Dissenter activity would be lost in the shuffle.

"That's where Holt is," I said.

"Yes, and Zarg predicts it will be unlikely they'll move him. Even if they suspect we know of this facility, moving him would delay their project. We have no way of knowing for certain if Zarg is correct in this assumption."

"One way to find out. You've got muscle, Abner. The sooner we move, the sooner it's over."

"We can't just stage a frontal assault. The risks are too great."

"I thought you said they wouldn't hurt the Bleakers."

"They wouldn't. The risk I'm speaking of is to my fellow Pilgrims. We can't start a full-blown war. It would draw too much attention. The possibility of exposure, it's too great. So far this conflict has remained underground, and that's where all of us would like it to stay."

"That's not an option anymore, Abner. If you respect life, if you don't want to see any needless deaths, then we end this now. If it ruins your conspiracy, it's a chance you'll have to take."

"I wish it were as simple as that, Mack. Do you think I hadn't already considered this? But, understand, even if I thought it was the best course of action, I answer to certain higher authorities."

"I don't."

Greenman scowled. He had teeth. Tiny, pointed white ones.

"You've put me in a very uncomfortable position, Mack. I like you, but I can't allow you to leave with the information if I can't trust you."

His eyes flashed as he lifted me into the air. He tried to play it cool, but his antennae were twitching like crazy. Seven hundred sixteen pounds of robot required plenty of telekinetic muscle.

Time to see if Lucia's inventiveness could push him over the edge. I activated the gravity clamp, and the sudden anchoring pull proved too much for Greenman. He didn't see it coming.

I slammed into the floor, and his head jerked back violently enough to fall out of his chair.

How long he'd stay down, I couldn't estimate. I had to take care of this fast. I deactivated the clamp because moving when it was on slowed me down. I tossed aside the desk and snatched the little twerp up by his throat. Some green blood was dripping from his teeny tiny nostrils.

His eyes flashed golden. I couldn't activate my clamp fast enough and was hit with a blast of telekinetic force. It sent me crashing across the office. I kept my grip, and Greenman came along for the ride. I fell into the model of Empire, crushing it. Another burst of invisible force threw me into the ceiling and held me there.

Knuckles charged in, not even waiting for the door to slide all the way open and punching a hole through it. Three of Greenman's biological goons came in behind him. None of them took a shot with their rayguns. Not with me clutching their boss around his neck.

I could've reactivated my clamp, but Greenman might've gotten caught between me and the floor. Despite his impressive psychic talents, he was a fragile little biological. I didn't want to kill him. Not that I cared about him, but it wouldn't serve much purpose in the long run.

Greenman's eyes flared as he increased the pressure. The ceiling cracked, threatening to give way. Then who knows how far he might push me? But as he increased his pressure, so did I. His eyes nearly popped out of his head.

"You'll break before I do," I said. "Don't make me kill you."

"You'll never get out of here functional," he said through clenched teeth.

"I wouldn't want to bet your life on it, Abner."

Greenman's antennae twitched, and we lowered gently to the floor. The goons kept their rayguns at the ready, but I wasn't too worried. There was only one guy who worried me: Grey. And I posited that if he were in the building, he'd already be here. Greenman had gotten sloppy. He'd assumed he could handle me all by himself, and he could've if not for Lucia's technological magic. I'd have to remember to thank her.

Knuckles paused, weighing his contrary directives. One: to kick my ass. Two: to keep his boss from getting his neck broken.

"Order them to stand down," I said.

"You idiot," gasped Greenman. "Do you think you'll get away with this? Do you know who I am? I run this town!"

"Well, I guess that means as long as I have you by the throat, I'm king of the world." I gave him a little shake to remind him of his current position. Sure, he could throw me around the room all he wanted, but it wouldn't stop me from crushing him with a simple twitch of my servos.

"Stand down," said Greenman. "Stand down, damn it."

Knuckles complied, though he remained at combat-ready status. The goons I ignored. If they'd had anything to tip the ratios in this equation, they'd have already used it.

"You know what I've just realized, Abner," I said. "You're full of shit. You talk about morality, about how you care about the people of earth, but it's just talk. And yeah, you won't poison the town because that way you get to pretend you're the good guy. But you're not. I'm wondering if maybe Ringo didn't find those files by accident. Maybe you didn't have him in mind, but you knew someone would get hold of them. All you had to do was wait around for someone to find them and get the bright idea. You look away, do a piss-poor job of trying to stop it, and when people die, you act like it's a tragedy. All of the benefits, none of the guilt."

"You don't know anything, you defective piece of—"

I squeezed his windpipe shut. Not certain of his bone density, I risked crushing his vertebrae, but I didn't give a crap.

I went over to the reader terminal, ejected the data tube, and tucked it safely into my inside jacket pocket.

"I'm walking out of here," I said. "And if I scan anyone within ten feet of my personal space . . ." I gave Greenman another little shake, to remind him of his position and because I was starting to like the way his eyes crossed after I did. "Are we clear on this?"

I loosened my fingers enough that he could squeak his reply. "You think you can just walk away." He sucked in a shallow breath. "You think I let anyone get away with this?"

"Shut up, Abner."

Abner Greenman may have been a big cog in Empire behind the scenes, but right now he was a squishy biological at my mercy. He shut up. His fish eyes narrowed, and I knew there would be consequences. But I'd deal with them later.

"I scanned a rotorcar when I came in. Teal Hornet. Who has the keydisk to that baby?"

The disk was scrounged up and given to me. Knuckles stayed at an exact eleven-foot perimeter, but he wouldn't make a move until Greenman gave the go command. And Greenman could barely breathe, much less bark orders. No one tried to stop me, and they were smart not to.

The Hornet started up without a sputter. Its three rotors roared to life. They didn't need to make that much noise, but you had to expect that from a hot rod. I retracted the landing gear, switched off the altitude regulator, and the Hornet crashed to the floor.

Greenman winced. "God damn it, you stupid outmode. Do you know how much this car is worth?"

"A few hundred less than it was three seconds ago," I replied.

I tapped a pedal, and the car rose. I struggled to work the gearshift while keeping Greenman clutched tight.

"Not easy to fly a rotorcar with one hand," he gasped with a smug smile.

I don't know why he was smiling. It only gave me more motivation to kill him.

"I'll manage, Abner." I turned to one of the closer goons. "Open the gate."

These guys couldn't change their underwear without first checking with Greenman, and the goon looked to his boss for confirmation. Before he could get it, a low vibration rattled the entire warehouse. It grew into a rumble violent enough to topple over carefully stacked boxes.

Greenman said, "They wouldn't dare." I could tell from the way his eyes went wide like two forty-fives that they would and they had.

Lights filled the warehouse windows, bright as day, glaring and harsh. The ambient temperature began to climb at a rate of 3.6 degrees a second. The biologicals began to sweat and cough. Steam rose from their moist flesh. An oil line burst in Knuckles' neck, spraying a fountain of black liquid. Greenman's smooth emerald skin darkened and blistered.

"Get us out." He wheezed. "Get us out now."

I should've tossed him out of the Hornet, left him to burn with his boys, but I didn't. It wasn't for any other reason than it simply didn't occur to me at that moment. He was too busy dying to be much of a threat, allowing me to drop him in the passenger bucket seat and push the accelerator button down as hard as I could without breaking it. The Hornet zipped forward. No time to worry about the bay door now, so I rammed through it. The rotorcar was a well-made model and with the speed behind it, we smashed our way through without a problem. It did lose a headlight though, and the windshield shattered.

I nearly plowed into a parked heavy transport. A harsh twist of the wheel and a stomp on the altitude pedal got us clear. The Hornet kissed the top of the transport, and I almost lost control. The starboard side rocked downward to a forty-three-degree angle and Greenman bounced around the interior.

Flying in Empire is no easy task. Outside of the designated civilian flying zones, the sky was an obstacle course of sweepers, automated transports, and skyscrapers. A trio of sweepers entered my flight path, and I wasn't quick enough to avoid one. I ripped through the blimp. The Hornet took a few more nicks to its finish from the gasbag frame, but was otherwise unharmed. The drone went down. The emergency countergrav system kept it from dropping from the sky.

I kept accelerating as I scanned the rearview.

There was a mothership floating over the warehouse.

It was a flying saucer the size of a city block covered in hundreds of blinking lights, making it brighter than the night sky. The real source of the brightness were three twenty-foot antennae, each crackling with power, each pointed downward at the warehouse, leaving trails of white hot electricity as they rapidly rotated around the saucer's rim.

A goddamn mothership.

It looked like the Pilgrims' underground war had come to the surface in a big way.

Greenman spit out a string of unfamiliar alien words that weren't in my dictionary banks, but I got the idea. "Those idiots. They'll ruin it all. Everything we've worked for."

The mothership's array pulsed, and the warehouse disappeared in a seething ball of green and orange fury. The explosion would've been deafening but for the luck that the saucer contained it in a forcefield to limit the collateral damage. Still, some of the roar registered at an unhealthy decibel level in my audios and left me with static for two seconds.

I brought the Hornet to a rough stop. It bucked, and Greenman banged his head against the dash. You'd think he'd figure out to put on his seatbelt by now, but since I kind of enjoyed recording him getting banged up, I didn't suggest it.

"Damn it, Megaton. Don't you know how to drive?"

"Sorry," I said. "Haven't actually gotten behind the wheel of a rotorcar before. Only read a manual to pass the written portion of my driver's test."

I expected the mothership to fly away now that it'd done its job. It didn't make much sense to leave it floating there for all the earthlings to see. They weren't the brightest bunch, but even they'd figure something was up. The saucer remained over the smoking crater.

"Get out of here, you morons," said Greenman through clenched teeth.

The Hornet's radar beeped. The words SCAN LOCK flashed across the screen in big red letters.

"Oh oh," I said.

Seven bogeys launched from the mothership in rapid succession. I zeroed in on the lead bogey. It was a sleek, cigar-shaped projectile. Too small to be a manned craft. My threat assessor pegged it as a missile.

The mothership zipped away, disappearing into the sky in a flash. The seven missiles remained and continued rapidly on an intercept course. Our escape had not gone unnoticed, and we weren't about to be let off the hook that easy.

I turned the Hornet around and pushed it into overdrive, but no way a rotorcar was going to make it very far.

Greenman opened the glovebox and pushed a secret button. The Hornet's propellers retracted as a rocket booster extended from the rear. An illegal skyracing mod, but I wasn't complaining at the moment.

"Punch it, Megaton."

I stabbed the accelerator. Blue fire exploded from the Hornet's booster, and the speedometer readout jumped to four hundred miles per hour and kept spinning. My reflex model kept us from crashing into anything. I zipped through a sea of skyscrapers, under an overpass, and over a skyway jam.

Radar told me the missiles were still gaining. I didn't risk taking my opticals off the sky to see how close, but the warning beep kept getting louder and faster.

"Talk to me, Abner," I said. "I need parameters. What are we up against?"

He glanced behind us. "High impact torpedo drones."

"Torpedoes? I thought you were colonists."

"We brought them for defense," he snapped. "Just in case. The galaxy can be a dangerous place."

"Can we lose them?"

"Doubtful. Their tracking systems are practically infallible, and their tachyon drives make them twice as maneuverable."

I made a sharp right to avoid a transport convoy.

The radar squealed.

"Activating countermeasures." A secret panel slid down in front of Greenman's seat, and he threw a switch. The Hornet launched a decoy drone. The torpedo veered off at the last seven-tenths of a second, close enough for me to detect its angry buzz, and chased after the decoy. It exploded, and the shock wave nearly threw the Hornet out of my control.

"Pays to be prepared," said Greenman.

My assessor measured the concussive force unleashed and warned that a direct hit would pose a significant risk to my internals.

"How many more decoys do we have?" I asked.

"Three."

The radar did that squeal again as two more torpedoes closed in. Greenman threw them off with another decoy. They veered away after it, but these two were smarter than the last and quickly calculated it wasn't their target. They zipped back in pursuit.

"Damn it, Mack," he said. "We're not going to last long if you keep letting them get a lock on us."

"You want to drive?" I asked.

"I don't know how."

I pushed the Hornet into a hard dive. It was a dumb, reckless move, since the lower you went, the more crowded the skies became. I was hoping it would flummox the torpedoes' tracking systems, but they didn't even slow down. The Pilgrims hadn't seen fit to share tachyon drive technology with the earthlings. The torpedoes could turn at any angle without loss of speed or maneuverability.

"You don't know how to drive?" I asked.

"I'm a very important man," said Greenman. "I don't have to drive myself anywhere. Stick closer to the buildings or they'll get another lock."

I was learning as I went, and doing a pretty good job of it. But I wasn't designed with piloting in mind, and whoever had made the steering wheel hadn't considered an operator with an eight-inch palm span. The radar was making an unhappy presqueal again.

I banked sharply into a skyscraper, waiting a full three-fifths of a second longer than my difference engine advised before averting to a parallel course. The radar made a happy ping.

"Better, Mack."

"I learn fast," I said.

By devoting a hefty portion of my attention to navigation, I was able to zig and zag through the skies with precision. There were seventeen near misses with fellow commuters, and I traded paint with a transport. But I managed not to crash and burn. The drones on my tail weren't easily discouraged though, and they were drawing steadily closer. Twice more, they nearly scored, but Greenman's final two decoys threw them off. One torpedo fell for the drone and exploded. The other didn't. We had no more decoys and five torpedoes left.

"Give me options, Abner," I said.

"Options? We die now. That's our option."

Greenman might've given up, but I wasn't programmed that way. I'd analyzed the variables, and come up with a plan. I retracted the Hornet's roof, but it was taking too long so I reached up and tore it off with one servo jerk.

"What the hell are you doing?" asked Greenman.

"Finding a new option."

A hard upward bank caught him by surprise, and he nearly fell out of the Hornet. I grabbed him by his leg and pulled him from the brink.

"Thanks, Mack."

"Can't you float yourself safely down to the ground?" I asked.

"Sure. Just as long as those torpedoes don't notice me." He glanced to the radar screen. "Damn it. We've lost contact with two of them."

"No, we haven't," I said.

The two missing drones rounded the skyscraper ahead of us. Three on our tail, and two coming right at us. I set the Hornet on automatic and stood up. I grabbed Greenman as I estimated the moment of impact and calculated the trajectory of my bail out maneuver. There was no time to triple-check the computations.

These torpedoes were smart little bastards. I wouldn't get a second chance. I waited until the buzzing in my audios said it was too late. Then I gave it another two-tenths of a second and boosted for an automated transport thirty feet away and fifteen feet down.

The Hornet exploded, and I was hurled forward. I'd factored in the force of the explosion, counted on it, but I hadn't gotten a chance to get to know the booster. I'd misplaced the decimal point in my calculations.

A decimal point could make all the difference in the world.

I sailed through the air with Greenman clutched tight to my chest. It was supposed to be a smooth flight, but I ended up off balance. When I hit the transport roof, my metal feet skidded out from under me. I landed on my back and kept sliding. At the last second, I managed to dig the fingers of my free hand into the transport's side. I dangled from the edge. Once I determined that my shoulder connectors hadn't been damaged, I pulled myself up. I kept my hold on Greenman, but he wasn't a significant impairment. I rechecked the explosion log file. It should've been bigger.

One of the torpedoes hadn't gone off. Either it was a dud, or it'd held back as a fail-safe.

The last drone hovered beside the billowing black clouds that marked the Hornet's last functional position. It obviously hadn't scanned us yet, but it wasn't about to give up. Greenman ducked down, and I pressed flat against the transport. I stayed immobile as we slowly drifted farther and farther from the torpedo.

"Just how practically infallible are the tracking systems on those things?" I asked.

"They've got a 3 percent failure ratio."

It wasn't much reassurance, but we were two bogeys in a sky full of possible targets.

The drone suddenly zoomed in our direction. It stopped and scanned for three seconds. Then zoomed closer, scanned for two second. Then zoomed closer, scanned for one second.

Too damn smart.

I made a dash toward the far side of the automated transport. Those metal feet of mine proved a hindrance once again and I nearly fell off the side. I'd have to ask Lucia to install some rubber soles in the future. Providing I wasn't scrap six seconds from now.

The drone shot forward and impacted with the transport. I boosted. I didn't have time to scan for a place to land. I just launched myself and hoped for the best. It was three hundred feet to the streets below, and something was bound to pop up along the way. I hugged Greenman close to me, trying to keep his fragile body as protected as possible

I careened downward with no way of directing my fall. Fifty feet down, I bounced off a rotorcar hood. Seventy more feet, and I hit something else. Didn't scan what it was, but it didn't stop me. The city was a blur in my opticals.

I slowed.

Either gravity was cutting me a break or something else was going my way.

I'd had a good reason for holding onto Greenman, and it wasn't solely for the spiteful pleasure of watching him hit the ground with me. I didn't stop falling, but my rate of descent slowed to a leisurely pace. Greenman's eyes glowed, and I could tell by the veins throbbing on his head that he was having a hell of a time holding me up.

We were smack dab in the middle of the skyway, and several rotorcars nearly ran into us before we passed through to the underside.

He growled through clenched teeth. "You're too heavy. Let me go, or we'll both drop."

"That's the idea, Abner. I suggest you find a place to put us down fast."

Grunting and groaning, he floated us inch-by-painstaking-inch toward a rooftop. I wasn't sure if he'd make it. Once the strain proved too much, and we ended up plummeting another sixteen feet before he could telekinetically latch onto me again. But in the end, self-preservation was a great motivator, and we reached our goal. Exhausted, he still managed to set us down as light as a feather.

I scanned the area. Not a torpedo in sight.

I ran a quick diagnostic on my internals. Everything was in tip-top shape. I'd have to remember to give Lucia that tip next time I saw her. I checked the data tube in my pocket. Whether it remained readable or not was impossible to tell, but it was still in one piece.

Having that biological weakness for fatigue, Greenman wheezed, barely able to stand. "Mack, you got some ball bearings on you, I'll give you that."

I brushed some dust off my lapel. The distant wail of sirens meant the Think Tank had finally gotten around to dispatching some units. Audio analysis put ETA at twenty-two seconds.

I allowed myself three seconds to consider how best to handle Abner Greenman. Easiest thing would've been to kill him. He was too tired, both physically and mentally, to raise a finger, telekinetically or otherwise, against me. Though Greenman had helped me avoid a nasty fall, I didn't need him around to cause me trouble. I had too many impediments in my current mission parameters already.

Maybe a few hours with the cops would keep him occupied. I had no doubt that he had the connections necessary to make any legal difficulties disappear, but even a guy like Greenman would need time to flip all the right switches at city hall.

I bent over and flicked him with two fingers. Not at full power, but enough to send him sprawling flat on his back. Then I picked him up and did it again for good measure. It was fairly probable I'd cracked a rib or two in his fragile body. If he even had ribs.

"See you around, Abner," I said.

"You're scrap!" he shouted. "You hear me? Scrap!"

He was still shouting as the rooftop access door slid shut behind me.

18

By the time the elevator hit the ground floor, the cops had gotten their act together enough to post a couple of officers on the door. Lucia's illusion suit worked like a charm. I switched on a projection of a heavy labor auto, grabbed an unoccupied couch in the lobby, and clomped my way out the front doors. I was just another faceless auto, and no one tried to stop me.

I waited until I rounded the corner to drop the couch at an omnibus stop, allowing some citizens to enjoy a nice sit while they waited. "Courtesy of the city, folks," I said. They all looked so delighted to have an alternative to the standard hard plastic benches.

I retuned the suit to gray and overlaid my green mutant image over my own distinctive bot features. As long as I didn't try to run, I was indistinguishable from the other seven-foot-tall, thick-necked, emerald mutants. A scan of the pedestrians didn't turn any others up, but at least it was better than walking around as myself. Wouldn't take the cops long to find me then. Now, I had some time before they figured out what was going on.

Though it was early in the morning, there were plenty of pedestrians, and the avenues were busy but not quite jammed up yet. Empire never shut down, and this was as quiet as things generally got. The sidewalk traffic was light enough to allow a big guy like myself some welcome elbow room.

A small crowd was gathered around the window of a television shop and all the TVs, big and small, played video of reporters gathered around a hole in the ground that had been a warehouse but was now nothing but slag and rubble. There were no clear images of the ship, cloaked by some kind of recording distortion device, but there were plenty of eyewitnesses. A mothership was bound to draw some attention, even in Empire. Firemen and drones sprayed the ruin down in foam, but it was only for the sake of damage control. Nothing could live through that.

I couldn't hear through the glass, but I didn't need to. What would the reports tell me that I didn't already know?

A pile of debris shook and a robot hand pushed its way to the surface. Two drones flew over and began clearing away the rubble. Knuckles rose out of the ashes, dented, blackened, leaking oil, but functional. Damn, those Mark Threes really could take a beating. Since Knuckles wouldn't be worth more than a few beeps in an interview, the reporters kept their distance. He was led away, heaving dangerously off balance with each step. They'd slap some duct tape on his damaged joints and patch up his leaking oil lines, and he'd be good as new.

Too bad Empire might never recover.

There was no reason to believe that now that the Dissenters had taken this conflict to the next inevitable level that the Pilgrims wouldn't respond in kind. Biologicals had a nasty habit of goading each other into frenzy. First one mothership. Then two. Then four. Soon the skies could be filled with alien warcraft raining deathrays upon the citizens of Empire and the hidden aliens walking among them. It wouldn't be smart, but it seemed inevitable in every simulation I ran. The Pilgrims and Dissenters would fight to the death over the fate of Empire, and no matter who won, everyone would lose.

Even if it didn't develop into a war, there was still the super mutagen the Dissenters were cooking up. In twelve hours, give or take, they'd dump it in the water supply, and there would be no going back. One way or another, this alien experiment of a city was going to self-destruct.

Someone had to stop it before there was no turning back, before thousands were killed either in a senseless alien war or by unstable mutation or both. The cops couldn't. Greenman wouldn't.

That left me.

My military unit programming kicked in and started breaking down the mission into sub-objectives.

First Objective: Review the data tube in my pocket. If Doctor Zarg was as smart as he was supposed to be, there might be some useful information in there.

Second Objective: Gain access to the lab by whatever means presented themselves. Infiltration if possible. Direct assault if necessary.

Third Objective: Remove Holt from Dissenter possession. Once removed from the equation, neither the Dissenters nor the Pilgrims would have a reason to continue their conflict. Retrieval of objective was preferred but unlikely. Termination would most likely be the most sensible alternative.

It was in that third objective that I found a problem. My logic lattice, of course, disagreed. There was no problem. Just a solution. This was a high-stakes game, and it all hinged on the life of one boy. To retrieve Holt wouldn't necessarily end the problem. As long as he was alive, someone could find him again and try to use his one-in-a-million biology to cook up more mutagens. Dead, removed permanently from the equation, the problem was ended. A simple ratio: one life against thousands. It all made sense when I crunched the numbers.

I didn't know if I could do it. Worse, I didn't know if I wouldn't. For all my sudden squeamishness, was sparing one boy any more morally responsible than standing by and letting thousands more die? What position was I in to make moral decisions anyway? I was only two years old, and until a few days ago, the biggest ethical dilemma I'd suffered was whether to take a few extra turns to jack up a fare.

I guess this was that Freewill Glitch at work. For most robots, a predicament like this could easily be solved by consulting with a designated operator. No questions. No problem. Either kill Holt or don't kill him. Just a beautifully simple command dictate.

Freewill was overrated.

My first sub-directive was to establish a base of operations. The address Lucia had flashed in my opticals wasn't far from here. I assumed Lucia had arranged for at least a modicum of privacy and a plug-in to recharge my batteries. It was a lucky break, too, because it was located on the edge of the Nucleus. Like most coincidences, it wasn't a coincidence at all. The Dissenters wanted to hide in plain sight, and it was easiest to blend into a crowd. Lucia must've had the same idea.

I found the address stenciled to one of the few buildings less than a hundred stories high. Some architect had gotten ambitious and erected a scalene triangle of glass and steel, then tilted it another twenty-five degrees until it looked like a building in slow collapse. It was a high-class joint, all right. A factory across the street belched a green vapor that tinged everything nearby. The triangle had a squad of maintenance drones dutifully polishing the green away, and there wasn't a speck of vapor on the golden facade. Lucia had gone all out. If I'd put my superalloy up for auction and used the proceeds to pay the rent, I'd probably still only have enough for a year's lease, if that.

There was an auto minding the door. He didn't challenge anyone trying to enter. His sole job seemed to consist of tipping his hat and offering directions.

"Good day, sir," he said. "May I be of service?"

I asked him where office number 3106 was, and he directed me to the thirty-first floor. I'd already figured that out, but he was so eager to please that I would've felt bad for not asking.

There were a few citizens going about their business, and a drone was waxing the floor. Otherwise the lobby was quiet. A quick elevator ride to the top floor and some basic deductive navigation later, I waved my keydisk in front of an unmarked office door and stepped inside.

The office lights snapped on automatically, and I scanned a sparsely decorated room measuring fifteen by twenty feet. It was a reception room with three chairs arranged more or less in the center and a metal desk in a crescent shape. The walls were bare and the only decoration at all was a fern on the desk. A deactivated auto slumped at the desk.

The auto bore a passing resemblance to Humbolt, except this one was smaller with a rounder design. It also had three wheels instead of two legs. A note was taped to the cranial unit. It read SAY ERUCTATION.

"Eructation," I said.

The auto activated and raised its cranial unit. "Please select personality template preference. For a full list of preferences, please consult operator's manual."

I didn't feel like finding an instruction manual, so I went with the easiest choice. "Default."

"Acknowledged."

The auto scanned me up and down twice, registering me as its new primary operator. Then it spoke with a husky feminine voice.

"Well," she said. "Aren't you a piece of work?" It sounded like neither a compliment nor an insult, but was emotionally neutral. Not the neutrality of a machine, but the disinterested remark of the world-weary.

"State your designation," I said.

"Designation?" She cocked her head forward to glare at me with her two sky blue opticals. "Aren't you the sweet talker? Tell you what, Casanova, why don't you just give me a . . ." She paused and if she'd had lips, she would've smiled sardonically. ". . . designation. It'll be easier for you to remember that way."

"Designation: Eve."

She couldn't roll her opticals so she rolled her entire head. "Oh, how very original. Must've taken you literally microseconds to come up with that one."

I should've known Lucia wouldn't have the normal "Affirmative/Negative" personality default. It might've been smarter to order Eve to reset and give her a more agreeable personality, but it seemed more trouble than it was worth. Also, it was a touch hypocritical to reboot her personality simply because I found it unpleasant.

"You must be Megaton," she said, rolling out from behind her desk. "Let me show you around your new office."

"This isn't my office," I said.

"Not officially," she said. "Not yet. But Lucia was preparing it for you. As a surprise. Said a proper detective needed a proper office. So, howsabout that tour? There's the couch.

There's the receptionist's desk. And here's the door to your private office, if you'd follow me, sir."

The private office was 300 percent the size of the reception room. It had another couch and a desk and empty shelves lining the walls. The large windows had a special tint that changed the greenish light outside into a golden glow. With space being such a luxury in Empire, particularly in the Nucleus, this must've cost Lucia a fortune.

"This is too expensive," I said.

"Yeah, it is. She was using it as a business address for certain legal requirements, and though she doesn't need it anymore, the lease doesn't expire for another year. Figured you might as well use it as let it go to waste. She wanted to get it fixed up all nice and fancy for you, but circumstances demanded a rushed unveiling."

She spun around once and waved her arms halfheartedly. "Surprise. I would've baked a cake, except you don't eat and I don't bake. My last data update was eighteen hours ago, so might I suggest supplying current situational information?" She shrugged. "To enable me to better serve you, of course."

I gave her a report of everything relevant.

"Update recorded," she said. "Well, haven't you gone and made a mess of things? You can turn off the suit by the way. The windows are one-way."

I deactivated the hologram.

"My, aren't you a big utilitarian brute?" she said. I couldn't decipher whether it was a compliment or an insult, but I was beginning to doubt dispensing compliments was among her functions.

"This office should be serviceable for your basic needs," said Eve. "We've got a phone, recharge port, and it's registered under a corporate name so it's unlikely anyone will think to look for you here. Also, there are a few amenities that a bot of your apparently troublesome temperament might find useful."

She gestured to a shelf and must've activated a remote switch. It slid open to reveal a repair pod. "Fully automated," she said. "Capable of most high-level maintenance."

She waved toward another row of empty shelves, and they opened to show a rack of gizmos and gadgets. Eve pointed to a few. "Spare illusion suit batteries, lock overriding device, directional microphone, etcetera, etcetera. So that's the tour. Any questions?"

I pulled the data tube from my coat pocket. "You wouldn't happen to have a reader handy, would you?"

"There's a tube reader built into the desk." She rolled toward the reception room. "If you need anything else, you know where to find me, boss."

"You can call me Mack," I said.

She crossed the threshold and swiveled to face me. "Oh, I know I can, but I'd rather not." The door slid shut.

I inserted the tube into the reader terminal. A screen extended from the desk as the tube downloaded its information. I scanned through a portion of the data Doctor Zarg had provided. There was a lot to go through. Zarg had given me blueprints, delivery schedules, access points, surveillance and security system data. Though I was certain the Dissenters had already changed their access codes and put security on high alert, there was still plenty of useful data in this tube. Maybe even enough for a smart bot like me to come up with a plan. But I was still only one bot.

I pushed the intercom button. "Eve, I need to make a call."

"Third switch on your right."

I flicked the switch and a phone popped out of the desk.

"Phone book is in the bottom left drawer," she said. "If the red light on the phone starts blinking, it means someone's either tracing the line or listening in."

"Thanks."

"My pleasure." Although her vocalizer didn't make the words sound like they were remotely pleasurable.

I didn't need the phone book. The numbers were already logged in my memory matrix. I grabbed the phone off the desk and dialed. I half-expected an answering machine, but after three rings, a groggy gorilla picked up.

19

Grey's worm was barely a hiccup in my directives now. I could go to the cops and download all the data I'd recorded in the last couple of days. Irrefutable proof of an alien conspiracy to play back for all the world. I didn't know how deep this conspiracy went, how much control the Pilgrims or Dissenters had over the inner workings of Empire City's government. I was willing to trust Sanchez who, if he was in on it, would probably do the right thing with the information. But he was only one cop, and without some heavy-duty backup, he was in no better a position to handle this mess than I was. I didn't need another unknown variable. So Sanchez was out for now, and I was left with only two entities I could trust at this point.

Jung occupied half my office couch. Humbolt took up another third.

"Nice setup, Mack," said Jung. "Could use a few decorations."

"I'm not keeping it," I said.

"Of course you will," remarked Eve. My secretarial auto

rolled in with a pot of coffee in one hand and an extra large mug in the other. Jung needed a lot of coffee to get going in the morning. She poured him a full serving.

"Here you go, sweetie," she said. "Need anything else? Perhaps something to nosh on?"

"No, this'll do." Jung slurped down the giant mug, and Eve refilled it.

"I'll leave the pot, sweetie."

He grunted, raising the mug to his lips.

"My pleasure. Need anything else, boss, I'll be—"

"At your desk. I know."

"So what's this all about, Mack?" asked Jung.

It took four minutes to tell him everything, and after I finished, he didn't bat an eye.

"Martians, huh?" he said.

"They're not Martians."

"To-may-to, to-mah-to." He set aside his eighth cup of coffee. "Sounds like a messy situation."

"It's messy all right," I said. "If you don't want to get involved in this . . ."

"Seems like I'm already involved, Mack. Seems like the whole city is involved."

"I've run risk ratios based on Zarg's data. Statistically, you're smarter to take your chances risking severe mutation than helping me out."

"You know me, Mack. I'm a biological." He shrugged. "We don't pay any attention to statistics."

"I'm in, too, Mack," said Humbolt.

"Thanks."

"Don't thank me. Thank the boss. She's the one who issued the dictate to help you out in any way I can."

"So do you have a plan yet?" asked Jung.

"Not yet, but I'm working on it. Humbolt, we might need something big if we're going to have a shot at pulling this off. Does Lucia have any weapons that fit the bill?"

"How big are we talkin'?"

"Lots of collateral damage," I replied. "Big and noisy and effective. But portable."

"I got just the thing. Back at the lab. She's been tweaking it for the government, but it was too effective. Thought it might be a bad idea to hand over to the G-men in the end."

"Sounds perfect. Can you bring it here?"

"Yeah, sure. Like I said, whatever you want. That's the lady's orders."

I set the illusion suit to charcoal black and switched on my mutant hologram. "I'll be back."

"Where are you going?" asked Jung.

"Reconnaissance."

"I'm going with you."

"Smarter to stay put," I said.

"Probably." Jung grabbed his hat and coat off the rack. "But I'm going with you."

Twenty-one minutes later, Jung and I stood on the corner of Dodecahedron and Pythagoras. Eleven after nine in the morning, and the Nucleus was picking up for the new day. We were just two more guys in a swarm of pedestrians, although a wide-shouldered gorilla and a bulky bot took up more than our fair share of the sidewalk. We were a bit of an obstacle since we weren't walking.

He studied Carter Centre, a block of glass and steel. "So that's a secret lab for Martian invaders?" he asked.

"They're not Martians," I said. "And they aren't invading. But yeah, that's it."

There was nothing eye-catching about it. Just a seventy-six-story block of a building. Any structure less than one hundred and fifty stories was positively quaint in the heart of the Nucleus.

"The first fifty floors have been leased to unwitting human businesses," I said, "to throw off suspicion. Only the top twenty-six and a secret basement are actually used by the Dissenters."

We passed twenty minutes circling the block while I slowly scanned the exterior.

"So how's the plan coming along, Mack?" asked Jung.

"Well, the good news is the data Doctor Zarg gave me is accurate."

"And the bad news?"

"The information Doctor Zarg gave me is accurate. He didn't overlook anything. At least not on the exterior. Which means it's probable that the interior details are all correct, too."

"No plan then?"

"Oh, I've got a plan," I replied.

"Great. You can tell me all about it. After I buy a hot dog." He loped across the street to a sidewalk vendor cart.

I scanned the building. Getting inside wouldn't be that hard for a determined bot, but last time I'd nearly been scrapped. I'd gone in unprepared, lacking both proper armaments and necessary data. Even knowing what I was up against now and having some time to ready myself for it, my difference engine advised me to abort this mission. There was no reason why I shouldn't. I wasn't a biological. However the Pilgrims sorted out this mess, there was no reason to get myself scrapped. Didn't make sense, but here I was, getting ready to throw myself onto the junk heap. While my logic lattice struggled to understand the irrational dictates I was feeding into my mission parameters, a robot latched onto my shoulder.

It was Knuckles. The oil line in his neck joint had been patched, and he had a few more dents than I'd previously recorded. But he was as strong as ever. The Mark Three beeped.

Grey stood beside him. "Hello, Mack."

My threat assessor marked the biological as an immediate threat, and I tried to knock his head off right in the middle of the crowd before he could employ his electrokinetic talents. His eyes flared, and my fist stopped an inch from crushing in his nose. I was not surprised, but I'd had to try. He put a finger on my hand and pushed it gently down to my side.

"Well, aren't you the master of disguise," said Grey. "Nice hologram. Get it from your girlfriend?"

"How'd you find me?"

He tapped his temple. "Built-in tracker. Usually isn't this easy finding one rotorcar out of thousands or locating a specific television set. But it's duck soup to track down a machine of your . . . whaddayasay . . . uniqueness. Even that hologram can't fool me."

Jung stood across the street, waiting for the light to change. I shook my head at him. He hung back, and Grey didn't seem to notice.

Grey started walking. "Come with us, Mack."

I took a reluctant step but managed to override his control of my servos to not take another. He looked surprised by that.

"Yeah, you're unique hardware," said Grey. "Don't make much difference now."

The glow in his eyes brightened, and my legs moved on their own. I hadn't purged the worm he'd implanted in my programs, but I'd gained enough mechanical control to slow my walk to a crawl. Maybe in another twelve hours or so I'd be completely free from his influence. In the meantime, I could only follow. Knuckles took offense at my chosen pace and nudged me along with all the gentle care of a zip train. Our fellow pedestrians sensed the trouble, but rather than get involved, they all held their eyes down and gave us a wide berth.

"Where are we going?" I asked.

"Don't worry, Mack. It's not far."

Eighty-four reluctant paces later, Grey and Knuckles steered me into an alley. There were three bums who'd made a home behind a Dumpster. Grey tossed them a few bucks and told them to scram. A lot of unpleasant things happened in this city's alleys. It was a fair hypothesis that the bums had perfected the art of scramming for money.

"You've gone and made Greenman very angry," said Grey. "Haven't ever seen the boss so . . . what'sthatword . . . piqued."

I tried taking a step toward Grey and succeeded. But it was a slow, ponderous step, and I wasn't going to catch him off guard. Didn't help any that Knuckles had a manipulator clamped on my arm like a vise wound two inches too tight.

"Don't you know what's going on?" I asked.

"Don't really know." Grey shrugged. "Don't really care. I just got a job to do, and that's what I'm gonna do."

"People are going to die."

"People die every day." He nodded to Knuckles. "Make our guest more comfortable, would you?"

Knuckles kicked my right knee joint hard. It wouldn't have knocked me down normally, but with Grey screwing with my systems, I dropped to one knee.

"You know what I don't get, Mack," said Grey. "You're a smart bot. Who cares if a few thousand schmucks grow a heart out of their backs? Like it matters? Nobody in this town gives a shit about anybody else." He pointed to the end of the alley and the crowded street beyond. "Do you think any of them would stick their necks out for you? Even if all they had to do was turn their head and look? No, it's a cruel world, and everybody but you seems to have figured that out. And now, I guess it's your turn."

He pulled a blinking metal square from his pocket and put it on the ground. A hologram of Greenman materialized. It was life-size, but it hovered so that Greenman and I were eye-to-optical.

"Abner, you hypocritical bastard," I said.

His face remained expressionless. "Forgive me if I fail to take moral advice from a malfunctioning robot. Shall we get on with this, Grey?"

Grey snapped his fingers. Knuckles clocked me across the cranial unit. With my joints locked up, I fell over.

"I'm aware that robots don't feel pain the same way we biologicals do, and that your chassis is formidable," said Greenman. "But I do hope you experience humiliation."

Knuckles started pounding me. He brought his arms down with the steady beat of jackhammers against my alloy. All that clanging was a hell of a racket, but Grey was right. No one in the street even spared a glance. Three minutes later, I lay sprawled across the ground with a thoroughly dented chassis. He hadn't done much real damage, although he spent forty seconds on my left shoulder joint, reducing effectiveness by a few degrees.

Greenman finally got bored with the show. "Enough, Grey."

I tried standing. Knuckles was nice enough to help me up and shove me roughly into a wall.

"I saved your life, Abner," I said.

"Your mistake," he said. "Scrap him."

Grey smiled as his eyes burned green and sparks danced on his fingertips. "Don't worry, Mack. You won't feel a thing."

Knuckles clamped onto my arms and pushed me back to my knees. I didn't have the leverage or motion capabilities to do anything but kneel there and wait to be permanently deactivated.

A streak rocketed suddenly down the alley. It was big and fast, and it plowed into Grey. Before he could react, Jung lifted him in the air and threw him against a wall. Long buried instincts filled the gorilla. He beat his chest and howled. Grey went for something in his coat, but he never got the chance. Slavering with every bit of primeval savagery he usually kept hidden, Jung jumped on Grey, who started screaming. I expected Jung to plunge his fangs into Grey's throat, but instead, he jammed the psychic with a disruptor. Grey went limp. The whole thing was over almost before it began. Four seconds. And it would've been less if Jung had decided to kill Grey instead of stun him.

Knuckles released me and charged Jung. The disruptor wouldn't do anything to a robot, so Jung tried throwing his bulk into the auto. Knuckles budged an inch, but clocked Jung. The formidable primate fell stunned, and Knuckles prepared to finish the job.

I sucker punched him, and he stumbled to one side.

Disruptors scramble a target's nervous system. Not only do they render their victims passive, they also impair psychic abilities.

"You okay?" I asked Jung.

"I'll live. By the way, you owe me a hot dog."

Knuckles beeped and made a move toward me.

"Give me a second," I said. "This shouldn't take long."

The Mark Three and I approached each other slowly. "Last chance to walk away," I said. Not that he could walk away, but at least I made the offer.

He tried punching me, but I blocked it and shoved my forearm into his cranial unit. I followed that up with a couple of jabs to the chest to further throw off his center of gravity. An uppercut finished the job, and he fell on his back.

He writhed, trying to get back to his feet. This could go on all day. While Knuckles was no match for me, robots didn't fatigue, and they didn't give up.

Rather than allowing him to rise and take another shot, I put a foot on his torso. It wouldn't keep him down forever. Mark Threes had a thick shell, and fresh off the assembly line, it might take me a while to get through. Knuckles was full of stress fractures, and my opticals detected a weak spot in his chassis. I bent over and pierced his gut with one punch. I dug around in all the delicate internals until I wrapped my hand around what I was looking for.

He beeped once.

I yanked out his battery. He went off-line.

"Sorry, pal," I said. "I know you didn't have a choice." I tossed the battery into the Dumpster.

I turned toward hologram Greenman. "Give me a second, Abner. I'll be right with you."

I grabbed Grey's limp form and gave him a shake until his eyes focused on me. "Anybody home in there? Give me a gurgle if you can hear me."

He groaned. Close enough.

I held out my hand, and Jung dropped the disruptor into my palm. I pressed the device against Grey's neck.

"Did you know that recent studies suggest that one disruptor jolt is perfectly safe. And two in an hour is no big deal."

I pushed the button, and he twitched.

"They say three in five minutes could result in permanent neurological damage."

I pushed the button again. His eyes rolled back in his head, and drool dripped from the corners of his mouth. I shook him until his eyes focused back on me, and I was fairly certain he was paying attention.

"Four might kill you," I said. "Or at the very least make you wish you were dead."

He mumbled, and there was definitely fear in his eyes.

"When you get out of the hospital, I suggest you consider the following equation: whatever diminishing percentage of control you have over my systems divided by the rating of my patience index. Now multiply that by zero, and you'll get the odds that I won't kill you next time I see you. Understood?"

Grey jiggled his head in a manner that could be loosely interpreted as a nod.

"Glad we cleared that up."

I pushed the disruptor button one more time. He didn't have the energy to twitch anymore. His eyes glazed over, but he was still breathing.

I turned to Greenman, who stared at me with cold contempt.

"I'll do what you should be doing, Abner," I said, "and I suggest you stay out of my way."

I stepped on the projector, and he disappeared.

Jung jerked his paw at Grey. "Should we call an ambulance?"

"In a bit. Where'd you get the disruptor?"

"I've had it for a while. Driving a cab is dangerous work sometimes." He pocketed the device and winced while rubbing his skull. "Never had to use it before. Interesting company you've been keeping."

"That's detective work for you," I said. "Get to rub shoulders with some of the most colorful citizens."

"Sounds like fun."

"Laugh a minute."

"You don't laugh."

"Not on the outside."

We started toward the street.

"So you're a detective now?" he asked.

"I guess. Beats driving a cab."

"After we save the city," asked Jung, "do you think you could use a partner?"

"Dangerous job," I said.

"Beats driving a cab."

20

"So let me get this straight," said Jung. "Your plan basically boils down to you smashing your way into the Dissenters' laboratory while Humbolt and I take advantage of the confusion you'll be creating to sneak in, grab Julie and April, and walk out."

"That's the plan," I said.

Jung and Humbolt exchanged skeptical glances.

"I don't know, Mack," said Jung. "Seems a trifle optimistic."

"Yeah," said Humbolt. "I gotta say it does seem to fly in the face of statistical viability. No offense or nuthin'."

"None taken," I replied.

Jung leaned back in the couch. "Correct me if I'm wrong, but didn't you nearly get scrapped the last time you entered that lab?"

"That's right," I said.

"And that was with the element of surprise on your side," said Jung. "If you go busting through the front doors, they'll probably see you coming."

"That's what I'm counting on."

"You're counting on getting scrapped?" asked Jung.

"I'm counting on drawing their fire."

"And meanwhile Humbolt and I just waltz in and liberate two prisoners?"

"It has to work that way. They're keeping Julie and April in a separate location from Holt. Two objectives means we'll have to split up." I pointed to the map displayed on the reader screen. "I'm giving you the easy job. The Dissenters don't care about Julie and April. They're only holding them prisoner because they don't see the point in killing them. According to this information, they've got them stashed in a minimum security holding cell on the sixtieth floor. Most personnel will be drawn away by my assault. The rest won't give you any problems."

"So you called ahead and asked them politely not to shoot us?" said Jung.

"You'll be disguised. I'll download some maintenance uniform designs and security badges from my memory matrix, give them to Humbolt, and he'll whip up some illusion suit facsimiles."

"The boss lady has a machine that does all the work," said Humbolt. "All I gotta do is feed in our measurements and it'll do the rest. Shouldn't take more than an hour."

"And with the suits, you should be able to pass casual inspection. At least long enough to reach Julie and April's cell on the sixtieth floor."

"Should?"

"Nothing's guaranteed."

"And what if the inspections aren't casual?" Jung asked.

"They should be too distracted to be paying much attention to a couple of janitors."

"Are you sure about that?"

"Trust me. When I prioritize my directives, I can be very distracting."

"Well, I said I was in on this. So I guess I'm in. Assuming your plan works, you draw their fire, how the hell do you expect to get the boy out of there?"

"Don't worry about that," I said. "That's my objective."

Jung leaned forward. "If push comes to shove, the Dissenters will want Holt dead rather than in the hands of their enemies to keep anyone from making a counteragent."

"Yeah."

He leaned forward more and braced his knuckles on the coffee table to keep from falling off the couch. "You might be protected by an indestructible alloy, but he isn't."

"I know."

"So how do you plan on getting him out?"

I turned off the reader display. "If I reach him, then it won't be a problem."

Extracting Holt was tactically unsound. Not impossible, but highly improbable. This wasn't a rescue mission. It was seek and destroy, remove Holt from the equation by any means necessary.

Jung was a smart ape. He'd figured it out, and he didn't like it. His nostrils flared, and he bared his teeth in a snarl.

"Do you think you can do it, Mack?"

"Getting in isn't the hard part," I said.

"Not that. I know you can do that. I'm talking about . . ."

"If I have to."

His beady eyes bored into my opticals, and he waited for me to justify myself. This wasn't a moral decision. This was just a simple ratio: one versus thousands. Nothing complicated about it. Just a reliable equation.

"If you've got a problem with this, Jung," I said. "Tell me now."

"Oh, I got a problem with it," he said, "and there has to be another way."

"Maybe there will be. Maybe I'll find it. But it's not something I'd bet on. In three hours, it'll be too late. If we don't do something now, then there'll be a lot of dead people and a lot more who will probably wish they were dead. And it's not just the biologicals. If Empire crumbles, there aren't a lot of options left for guys like you and me, Jung. Anywhere else, I'm just a weapon and you're just a monkey. This isn't about the norms, the mutants, aliens, or bots. It's about everyone who calls this city home who doesn't have a future anywhere else. And in three hours, that future is gone."

Jung snorted, but he saw my point. It was just a numbers game. Like Doctor Zarg, I had a choice to make. One life balanced against millions. It was a simple calculation.

"Just remember, whatever happens, whatever you end up doing in there . . ." Jung snorted. ". . . you'll have to function with it."

I waited across the street while Jung and Humbolt, disguised as a couple of janitors, walked into Carter Centre. They went in first as a test. The lobby was loaded with security scanners, technology the Pilgrims had not yet seen fit to share with us. The only way to find out if Lucia's illusion suit cloaking tech was its equal was to walk in and see if alarms went off. I stood outside, ready to charge in and pull Jung and Humbolt out if I needed to.

If it didn't work, then this would be the end of it. An hour and six minutes remained in the countdown, and if this plan didn't work, then there was no time for anything else.

The front of the building was glass, allowing me to scan all the details from across the street. They went in. A security guard checked their badges and waved them on. My partners entered the elevator, pushed a button, and the doors closed. Not a bell or whistle or security drone in sight.

Perhaps it was my paranoia index, but I wondered if they'd passed undetected. Security might've been smart enough to wait until they got deeper inside, where it'd be easier to make them disappear. Even if that were true, in fifteen seconds security would have more to worry about than two wayward janitors.

I dropped a nickel in a phone booth and asked for Detective Sanchez. They told me to wait a minute. I told them who I was, and the minute ended at six seconds.

"Mack, where are you?" Sanchez asked.

"Carter Centre."

I hung up the phone, picked up a thick metal briefcase beside me, and crossed the street.

While I was wearing an illusion suit of my own, I calculated it unlikely that I could fool the scanners. I was still a distinctive unit. The suit couldn't mask my proportions or my weight or a dozen other cues that the Dissenters had doubtlessly taken the precaution of incorporating in their security net. There was no way around it. I stopped at the threshold and waited for the signal from Humbolt that they'd reached the floor where Julie and April were being held.

"Sixtieth floor," transmitted Humbolt into my radio. "No waiting."

I made it seven steps into the lobby before alarms started blaring, some heavy-duty impact cannons extended from the floor, and a ten-by-ten forcefield activated to contain me. Since most of the folks in the lobby were regular citizens, they were surprised, but security moved with tactical precision to herd all the uninitiated out the doors. Once cleared, shutters lowered over the windows, locking down the lobby. Everything Doctor Zarg's information had told me would happen.

I waited quietly, biding my time. Once cleared of terrestrial witnesses, a quartet of ravagers was released from secret alcoves in the walls. They surrounded me as an added precaution. A screen floated over their cranial units. It had an image of Warner's smirking face.

"Mack, our simulations based on previously recorded behavioral models suggested you'd try this," he said, "but I have to admit, I'm a little disappointed. I realize that you are only a machine with a rejected technomorph brain. You must've calculated that this effort was doomed to failure."

"Had to try," I said.

"Of course, you did. I assume you've notified the authorities, who are certainly rushing to this building in force this very instant."

"Yeah."

Warner sighed. "Oh, such an embarrassingly simple end to this defective operation of yours. When they get here, they'll find nothing but a faulty bot our security forces had to scrap. Regrettably, your memory matrix will be damaged beyond recovery, so we'll never know what malfunction seized you."

"These things happen," I said.

"What's in the case?"

"Oh, just a little surprise. Four of them, actually."

The forcefield began to contract. While my alloy was impenetrable, the shrinking energy barrier could crush me into a two-foot cube in an estimated 190 seconds. I didn't make a move to stop it yet. Jung and Humbolt had another forty seconds before they were supposed to be in position to take full advantage of the chaos that was coming.

"Tell me, Mack," asked Warner. "Does a bot feel fear? I know you've got that self-preservation directive. How does that compare to what we biologicals feel when we know the end is upon us?"

"I'm not going to the scrap heap quite yet."

I reached inside my coat and pulled a device from a pocket. I pressed the cube against the shrinking forcefield and pushed a button. It was a prototype, but I'd place my functionality in Lucia's untested genius any day.

Warner narrowed his eyes. "What is that?"

The cube made a crackling sound.

"That's a field scrambler," said Warner. "Where did you get that?"

"Just a little something a friend of mine whipped up in her spare time."

"But we specifically kept that technology from the earthlings," said Warner. "You can't have that!"

"Can't put the genie back in the bottle."

The eight miniature rocket pods on my belt flared to life.

The scrambler popped and smoked as it shorted out the forcefield. The ravagers moved to tackle me and the impact cannons unleashed their blast. But the booster fired, and I was already soaring upward and onward. I smashed through the lobby ceiling and kept on through the next two floors before losing momentum.

Unwitting earthling office workers were surprised by a bot smashing his way into their midst. It was forty-eight more floors before I reached the fifty-first floor used by the Dissenters, but this route beat the stairs because security was light on these civilian-controlled floors.

A secretary lay nearby at my feet, sprawled on the floor beside her overturned desk, broken typewriter, and scattered paperwork. The desk had been unfortunately positioned above my point of entry.

"Sorry about that, miss." I leaned down and helped her up. "You might want to stand back."

The booster roared to life again, and I punched through

another three floors. More offices were thrown into disarray, but I didn't smash into anything squishy and organic, so I couldn't complain. I gave the booster an extra second to cool down between leaps. Figured the prototype deserved the precaution, and I wanted security to have time to mobilize in anticipation of my arrival.

Two more jumps, and I was on the twelfth floor. I crashed into an office, and landed hard enough that the floor nearly gave way beneath me. The sole occupant of the room, a guy in a suit, was knocked over.

An authoritative voice made an announcement on the building's speaker system. "Your attention, please. A malfunctioning robot is roaming the building. Do not be alarmed. Security shall neutralize the threat soon, and the police have been called. Avoid all contact with the defective unit."

Heeding the advice, the guy scrambled backwards without getting to his feet, right into the hole I'd made in my entrance. I moved to grab him, and he screamed. He kept screaming as he started to fall through the hole. I nabbed him by the ankle and pulled him from the brink and set him safely on his feet. He jumped back and pressed against the corner farthest from me.

The wall exploded as a trio of ravagers burst into the office without bothering to knock. While not as thick-alloyed as me, they were nearly as strong and had me outnumbered. Last time I'd run across these evil twins, I'd beaten them only by damaging myself. But I was a learning machine, and I had their numbers.

The lead threw two punches. I batted them aside and jabbed him in the cranial unit. He tried to avoid the blow, exactly as my analyzer predicted. What would've been a glancing strike snapped his head back hard enough to tear his neck joint in half.

The two others came at me from both sides. I stepped back at the last nanosecond, and they wound up hitting each other. I struck at a vulnerable knee joint. One toppled over. The other threw a hook, and I had no choice but to take the hit. He connected with my shoulder with a hard clang. The ravager followed it with a flurry of swings, all aimed at susceptible joints. The execution was as flawless and predictable as a math equation. I dodged, parried, and took a few harmless dents until my opponent exposed himself to a double-fisted thrust that caved in his torso and rendered him inoperable.

The downed ravager latched onto my right leg, and I crushed his cranial unit. He clung stubbornly though, which left me vulnerable to an attack from the last functional opponent. But the ravager's head was stuck at a bad angle, and he couldn't aim his blow. It went wide. I smashed him from behind, knocking his head off, finishing the job.

The guy in the corner glanced at the broken robots. "Don't hurt me. Please."

"Don't believe everything you hear, buddy." I pried the ravager from my leg, picked up my case, and activated my booster to soar my way through another three floors.

Between jumps, I moved steadily toward the center of the building, toward a secret levitator pod shaft that ran from the fifty-sixth floor to the hidden sub-basement laboratories. The shaft was armored; while I could tear my way into it with some work, it would be easier to strike at the weakest point: the door. I didn't hide my objective, and the Dissenters would do whatever it took to keep me from reaching it, which was good for Jung and Humbolt.

It would've been reassuring if I could've checked in for a status report. Radio silence was part of the operation, so I carried on. No one tried to stop me. The ravagers had been a test, and I'd passed. The Dissenters knew I was in the building, knew I was on my way, and knew I meant business. No big deal. I wanted them to know.

One minute, fourteen seconds later, I reached the fiftieth floor. It hadn't been a difficult journey, and I'd managed not to get any noncombatants killed in the process. In fact, once past the twentieth floor, I didn't run across any civilians, who were already being forcibly evacuated.

Once I punched through to the fifty-first, the first floor used by the Dissenters, all bets were off. My analyzer assumed that security knew where I was and had mobilized every ravager in the place. I was counting on it. The Dissenters thought I was merely a robot, predictable and compelled to complete my directive even counter to common sense. What they couldn't know, what they couldn't understand, was that I had no intention of getting scrapped if I could avoid it. There was one more thing they didn't know, couldn't feed into their computers. The case I carried with the four bedlam drones inside.

I thrust upward and burst into the Dissenter lab, right in the middle of three dozen ravagers. Had to be nearly every ravager in the facility, and it was too many for a single bot to take.

I pushed a button on my case. It popped open and four spherical drones sprang out and hovered at chest level. The quartet of bedlam drones scanned the room, assessing targets.

"Anytime you're ready, boys," I said.

As one, the ravagers took a single step toward me. Lucia hadn't dubbed the drones "bedlams" for nothing. Each was outfitted with a miniature battery of rapid fire rayguns and overeager targeting systems. The bedlams started blasting anything that moved. They would've even blasted me if I hadn't stood immobile. The ravagers were dumb autos programmed to throw themselves at me in an overwhelming pile. It didn't occur to them to stand still.

Most were blown to pieces in a hail of rayfire. As each wave fell, the next moved forward and was cut down. It didn't take long, which was fortunate because the bedlams had a functional life of forty-five seconds before their rayguns burnt out and their power cells went dry. Used up, they clattered to the floor among the twitching piles of bubbling metal.

The smoke cleared to reveal three semifunctional ravagers left. One had lost both its arms. Another struggled to stand with a hole punched through its central gyro. One more had had its legs blown off and dragged itself stubbornly toward me with its arms. I didn't bother waiting, activating my booster and hurling myself through the next three floors.

The ravagers had been among the most serious threats security could throw my way. There were certain to be one or two left functional in the building, but I could handle that on my own. According to my mission model the next obstacle would be a secondary defense line set up at the elevator door. So far, the Dissenters had responded exactly as expected, which registered as a bit ironic since I was supposed to be the predictable one.

I smashed my way through to the fifty-sixth floor into an empty chemical lab. The doors opened and in rushed a squad of five biological security personnel. They bathed me in a dark blue ray from their rifles. Frost crystallized on my chassis. In three seconds it solidified into thick blocks of ice. The guards concentrated their freezerays on my limbs. They succeeded in encasing my right arm completely, rendering it inoperable.

One of the guys aimed at my cranial unit. I intercepted the beam with my hand, and the ice spread across my palm. I squeezed my fingers and ended up with a four-pound chunk in my grip. I threw it into the lead guard's nose, and he was knocked off his feet. I advanced on the others, despite the ice coating my chassis. One punch each and they went down.

I twitched my frozen arm three times, and the ice block cracked and fell away. I brushed away a few other chunks. The lab doors slid open, and two new squads raced in. I turned and barreled toward the elevator, which according to calculations was three hundred feet and four walls away.

I smashed through the first wall. Then the next. I didn't try to maneuver. I wasn't designed for it. I crashed through anything stupid enough to get in my way. There were guards stationed all the way, but their freezerays weren't dangerous once I was in motion. The blocks of ice shattered with every stride of my powerful servos. Seven guards were shortsighted enough to wind up in my way. Five were lucky enough to be knocked aside with a few broken bones. Two ended up under my feet, and their body armor cracked and their vulnerable biological bodies squished beneath my merciless tread.

The last wall gave way, and the levitator pod doors were before me. By now, I'd stopped factoring in the security forces and their freezerays as a threat. There were a lot of them, and they held a last ditch line in front of the shaft, along with three more ravagers who stood defiantly before my goal.

I bowled through the security guards and shouldered past one of the ravagers, knocked the second aside with a swing of my fist. The third jumped right in my path with intentions of stopping my charge. Once I got going, standing in front of me was about the worst place to be. I rammed the ravager head on, lifting him off his feet and slamming him through the pod doors ahead of me. He was crushed like a tin can, and the doors gave way.

I tumbled down the empty shaft, ricocheting off the walls. My arms flailed out in search of something solid to grab. Plummeting the eighty floors to the bottom was faster but bound to damage something. After nine seconds of clanging and crashing,

I managed to drive my fingers into the wall. My shoulder joint popped, absorbing the stress and reporting a few microfractures. The shaft filled with the harsh sound of metal tearing metal as I ripped gashes until my fall slowed and eventually stopped.

Eight seconds later, I recorded the distant thud of the broken ravager hitting bottom. It was going to be a long climb. I punched handholds as I went, and had descended seventy feet by the time a pair of security camera drones hovered up from the darkness.

Warner's voice issued from their speakers. "You were lucky to get this far, Mack. Stop now, before your luck runs out."

I didn't acknowledge him, just kept climbing.

"You're not a biological. You won't be affected by our plans. Why would you risk your continued functioning? It's illogical."

It was a good question, and I had a good logical answer to it. Self-preservation was a basic directive, but there wasn't a robot functioning that prioritized it at the top of his list. Like biologicals, all robots were seeking a purpose. Autos and drones were lucky enough to have that built into them. A bot had to find his own way, and I'd figured out that functioning for function's sake was pointless. The real question was finding a directive worth getting scrapped for. The future of Empire and every citizen she called home balanced against one bot was a simple equation. Even simpler was one family that deserved better than to be used up and tossed aside by an indifferent city. I might not be able to change Empire. I might not even be able to stop the Dissenters. But I could save the Bleakers.

I didn't bother explaining it to Warner. He wouldn't have understood.

The shaft's magnetic couplings hummed to life. I craned my opticals upward to scan the pod dropping from above.

"Have a nice ride, Mack," said Warner.

There was no time to react except thrust my shoulders upward and brace myself for the impact. The pod crashed into me. The drones were destroyed instantly, but I managed to absorb the shock evenly and avoid any internal damage. The shaft sped by. I activated my booster and slowed the descent, but not by much.

I punched my way through the pod bottom and quickly climbed into it. I boosted again and burst through the top. The pod fell away, and impacted at the bottom five-sixths of a second later. Some shrapnel whizzed up the shaft and bounced harmlessly off my chassis. I fell the rest of the way and landed with a thud among the wreckage. The doors had been blown out by the impact, and I stepped out, expecting to meet up with the next obstacle toward my objective.

The corridor was empty.

Unexpected.

Something had gone wrong. The Dissenters must've realized my objective by now. This hall should've been filled with every security guard in the facility. There wasn't one guard. Not a single ravager or security drone. Nothing.

I'd miscalculated. My elegant electronic brain was not a foolproof mechanism. My logic lattice must've overlooked something, or Doctor Zarg's data had been incomplete. Either way, the only thing I could do was continue toward my goal and adapt as the variables became clearer.

Halfway there, I turned a corner and finally met up with the latest obstacle the Dissenters had to throw my way. The twenty-foot robot clomped forward on its thick legs. Its arms ended in pincers, each large enough to seize me in their grip. It didn't appear to have any armaments, but judging by size and probable power, it was a hell of an obstacle. And I didn't know a particle about it.

The auto clomped forward. Every step rattled the corridor, and the top of its body scraped the ceiling at the height of each stride. I didn't scan a way around it.

"Surprised, Mack?" asked Warner, his voice coming from a speaker in the auto's torso. "Nothing about this in Zarg's files, I assume."

The auto took another step, and I stood there. My logic lattice was unready to formulate a viable battle plan. Even the best electronic brain could be stalled by the unexpected.

"No reason he should've," said Warner. "The demolisher is not a combat unit. Large and clumsy, we keep it around for jobs requiring brute strength. And believe me, it is very strong." The auto snapped each of its pincers three times with harsh clangs.

With the demolisher only two steps from being on top of me, my combat analyzer spit out the only course of action that my logic lattice, common sense emulator, and self-preservation directive agreed on: retreat.

I chose to override their advice.

The demolisher was halfway through its next step. I boosted into it, attempting to knock it off balance. It was big, but it had to be clumsy, without much room to maneuver in the hall.

I collided with the demolisher, but not how I'd planned. The auto thrust its leg forward, smacking me in the chest and knocking me to the floor. Before I could get up, it dropped a heavy foot on me. The unit's feet were as long and wide as me, so I had no room to wiggle or maneuver. It leaned its full weight on me, and even with my arms and legs in position, it was unlikely I could push the unit off.

This was it. All the demolisher had to do was stand here, and I couldn't do a damn thing about it. The mission was over. I only hoped that Humbolt and Jung had gotten Julie and April out. It would've been nice to achieve at least one objective.

The demolisher raised its foot and stomped down on me. To give me even a second of leverage and motion while I was incapacitated was illogical. More than that, it was vicious and violent and just plain dumb. It wasn't a robot thing to do. Even a simple auto would've had more sense. I attributed it to a glitch.

The demolisher did it again. Three times more. It stomped its foot down hard enough to drive me into the floor. My chassis held under the blows, but more fractures registered in my internals. A hydraulic fluid leak was reported in my right shoulder. In five minutes, the arm would be functionally inoperative.

The demolisher wasn't an auto. It must've been a piloted vehicle. Biologicals were unpredictable, difficult to anticipate. They were also stupid. No correctly programmed robot would throw away a clear advantage in hopes of doing a bit more damage to an already defeated opponent.

"How does it feel now?" asked Warner. "That it was all for nothing? That you succeeded in only getting yourself scrapped? You stupid—" Clomp! "—piece of—" Clomp! "—defective tin!"

It raised its foot, and this time I was ready. I rolled to one side. I may be a relatively clumsy bot, but I was quicker than the demolisher and managed to get to my feet as it tried to flatten me with a pincer. I caught the blow. More damage to my internals. My left knee joint cracked, reducing effectiveness by thirteen degrees, and the hydraulic leak in my arm got worse. I managed not to be crushed and deflected the strike.

I moved in close to the demolisher, where its arms weren't designed to reach. The close quarters of the hallway made it difficult to turn. I threw my shoulder into its right leg, and activated the booster. The demolisher swayed but didn't fall over.

I cranked my servos all the way to 200 percent. It burned a lot of juice and blew out my damaged right arm, rendering it almost inoperable. The demolisher's leg pushed backwards. It fell over and past me to land front down.

The pilot struggled to get it to rise, but whoever had designed it hadn't considered the possibility it might take a tumble in a hallway with only two feet of extra space. The demolisher thrashed its limbs, tearing apart the walls. It'd get up eventually, so I didn't take time to congratulate myself. I left the demolisher to its struggle and continued.

The chemical lab doors tried to deny me access. I tore them open and stepped inside. The lab was one hundred cubic feet of mostly unoccupied space. There were blinking consoles along the wall, and four technicians tending to the complex apparatus in the room's center. Six hundred gallons of mutagen floated in a clear cylindrical vat. It was still being processed and required special handling, specifically continual exposure to certain low-level radiation wavelengths and a precise magnetic field. Otherwise, it'd destabilize in a few hours and become as dangerous as heavy tap water. Exposure to air would hasten the process to minutes.

Destroying the Dissenters' supply of mutagen was the first step in my mission. It wouldn't do much good to remove Holt from the Dissenters' grasp as long as they had this. It wasn't as much as they needed, but it was enough to cause some trouble.

There was, of course, another reason for wanting to destroy it. To piss them off, let them know they'd screwed with the wrong bot.

In addition to the stalwart technicians, I scanned Doctor Zarg resting twenty-six feet from the device protecting and treating the cylinder. The doctor was like an old piece of forgotten furniture tossed to a darkened corner. He wasn't in a cage, but the Dissenters had removed his legs and arms.

A forcefield surrounded the mutagen container. I found the other field scrambler in my coat. Though I'd taken a beating, the coat had armored pockets, and it'd kept the device from being damaged. Score another point for Lucia.

Three of the techs ran from the lab without doing anything stupid.

The closest technician, a bird-like alien, drew a small raygun and leveled it at me with a shaking hand. He was a little guy, barely five feet tall, but he stood his ground as he interposed himself between me and the mutagen. Trembling, he couldn't make himself pull the peashooter's trigger, but I respected his guts.

"Scram," I said.

He dropped his weapon and dashed toward the exit.

I fixed the scrambler on the forcefield and activated it.

I recorded the demolisher distantly still struggling to right itself. It was a hell of a racket.

"Thought they'd have scrapped you by now, Doctor," I said.

"My superior intellect made destruction inadvisable," he replied. "My defense protocols make reprogramming impossible. Since I cannot be forced to comply with their current operations, I have been rendered immobile until I am more cooperative."

The scrambler did its job and shorted out the protective field. I reached through the radiation bath, a charged barrier capable of incinerating flesh and liquefying most metals. It didn't do anything to my alloy beside vaporize the paint job, and the cuffs of the illusion suit blackened and crackled. The suit didn't burn, but it started to melt again. I'd have to get Lucia to fix that problem.

I ran my fingers along the transparent vat, assessing it through my tactile web. The material was a thin and flexible plastic.

I threw a punch into it. The vat chimed and wobbled but didn't break. I wasn't surprised.

"It is not indestructible," said Zarg. "But highly durable. Might I suggest a low frequency molecular agitator?"

"Don't have one of those," I replied.

I threw a series of seven quick punches. The vat continued to ring. It quivered but didn't crack. I pressed my palm against it and detected surface irregularities. The thing was breaking, but it was taking its own sweet time.

I launched a jackhammer series of blows with my left arm. Four strikes a second. Could've doubled the rate except punches from my damaged right arm wouldn't have accomplished anything. The vat's tone grew louder and louder, higher and higher, until it was beyond human hearing range and my ability to record. After twenty seconds, small cracks appeared on the surface.

"In its current state, the mutagen is highly corrosive," said Doctor Zarg. "While your alloy is chemically neutral, I would still advice caution, as it will dissolve most any other inorganic material on contact."

"Thanks for the advice."

I recorded the rapidly approaching thudding footfalls of the demolisher. The pilot had gotten it upright and was approaching. A drip of chemical was leaking from the cracks. I was almost through.

An audio analysis warned that the demolisher was less than twenty feet behind me and rapidly approaching. I didn't turn around. I threw five more punches, and the drip became a dribble. One more solid blow would do it. I pulled back my fist to unleash a haymaker.

The demolisher snagged me by the arm. It yanked me into the air and clamped the other pincer around my torso. I pushed my servos to the limit, and nothing happened. The demolisher's grip was beyond my ability to break. Maybe with both arms available and my systems undamaged, I'd have stood a calculable chance, but that was a purely hypothetical maybe.

It squeezed at my elbow joint and nearly sheared off my forearm. Though my chassis was indestructible, my joints weren't. It was rare for something to have the power to pull me apart. My diagnostics warned if I didn't do something fast, I'd lose that arm. But there was nothing I could do. Nothing logical.

"I'm going to enjoy taking you apart piece by piece, you stupid malfunctioning technomorph bastard," said Warner. He was the pilot. He had to be. He wouldn't allow anyone else the pleasure of scrapping me.

A plan came to me. It didn't come from my logic lattice or battle analyzer. I didn't know in which program it originated, and I didn't care. It was my only shot, so I took it.

"You can scrap me, if you want, Warner," I said. "It doesn't change the fact that I almost made it. One defective robot almost ruined it all."

"You've ruined nothing. You've accomplished nothing."

I tried to turn up the smugness rating in my vocalizer. "I made a fool of your security forces. I got into this room, nearly broke the vat. I wouldn't want to be you when your bosses hear about this."

"Shut up." He increased the pincer pressure. A warning flashed on my tactile web. Wouldn't cut me in half, but eventually, it'd start crushing internals.

"Just look at Doctor Zarg over there," I pressed. "Poor guy didn't screw things up nearly as bad as you, and now he's the world's smartest paperweight. Hate to see how a disagreeable asshole like yourself will end up."

"Shut up!" The pressure creased a shallow dent across my torso. "Why don't you shut up?"

"All your work, and you'll end up pushing a mop by the time they're done with you. Couldn't happen to a nicer guy."

The demolisher pivoted and hurled me into the floor. I bounced once, crashed into a bank of computers with a shower of sparks. I wasted no time on a diagnostic report as I quickly pushed my way to my feet.

All Warner had to do was hold onto me, but biologicals were emotional, illogical creatures. They didn't learn their lessons very quickly. Warner was smart enough to maneuver the demolisher between me and the mutagens. He didn't take a step, waiting for me to make the first move. If he got hold of me again, he wouldn't be so stupid.

I barreled forward, and he took one step to meet the charge. As expected, he hadn't taken into account all the factors, including the much higher ceilings in the lab. I waited until I was within six feet of it, until its pincers were poised to seize me once again. Then I boosted. I couldn't assume Lucia's belt still worked. It'd taken quite a few hits, and it was a prototype. I never had any doubts. Lucia hadn't let me down yet, and she didn't this time either.

The pincers closed around empty space as I soared over the demolisher. I landed on the other side and, with my servos cranked to the limit and every bit of momentum behind me, I drove my fist into the vat. I dodged to one side as unstable chemicals exploded from the pressurized container in a geyser. I wasn't fast enough, and my left arm was soaked. The cloth dissolved away. Spray sizzled on my coat, burning dozens of holes, some as large as two inches in diameter.

The demolisher caught most of the chemicals, and true to Doctor Zarg's word, the mutagen evaporated the chassis like ice under boiling water. The demolisher melted into smoldering sludge. In four seconds, the bulk of the demolisher was nothing but a puddle.

The pool of compound spread as more sprayed from the vat. I grabbed Doctor Zarg and moved him away from its edge.

In the center of the compound, covered in molten steel and dripping in mutagen, lay Warner. His skin was scarred and smoldering. He was gurgling and moaning at the same time. It was not a pleasant sound.

"The effects on biological entities should eventually prove fatal," said Doctor Zarg.

"Eventually," was the operative word. Warner, poor, miserable bastard, wasn't dead yet.

The floor, eaten away by the compound, dropped away. Warner fell into the lower floor.

Humbolt radioed me. "We've retrieved the package."

That was the signal. Jung and Humbolt had gotten Julie and April out of the building.

"Any trouble?" I asked.

"Nope. You were right. Nobody cared much about us or them once you were in the building. How's things on your end?"

Seventeen security guards and three ravagers charged into the lab.

"I'll get back to you on that," I radioed back.

Security moved slowly toward me.

"Do we really need to do this, guys?" I asked.

Something growled from the pit in the floor. It sounded pissed off.

A giant hand raised out of the pit edge. Warner pulled his deformed body up. His skin was still red and boiling and dripping away. As much as he was losing, he seemed to be rapidly replacing it and then some. He was growing. While he still had a vaguely humanoid configuration, his symmetry was gone. He was a malformed lump of flesh. And he'd grown a tail.

He spoke, and his voice was raw. "What did you do to me?"

21

Security froze. Even the single-minded ravager autos were surprised.

Warner raked a clawed hand across his oozing chest, and glanced down at the flesh in his hands. His face was little more than a scarred lump with two bleeding eyes and a mouth that had migrated six inches too far to the left.

"What did you do to me?"

He lurched toward me. He hadn't adjusted to his new weight distribution. It was easy to step back, then clobber him between the eyes. It was like punching pudding. His head collapsed beneath the blow, and clumps of hair and slime splattered on my faceplate.

He seized me and lifted me in the air. I activated my gravity clamp to discourage him, but he didn't even notice. Though he was a gooey mound of shifting flesh, his overactive DNA had made him absurdly strong.

"What did you do to me!" he screamed.

I would've apologized if it would've made him happy.

None of the biologicals dared to make a move, but the

ravagers tagged Warner as a threat. They jumped him. Silently, Warner threw me across the room to deal with this new threat. There was the harsh sound of tearing metal. By the time I got up and turned around, five seconds, he'd already crushed two of the autos. The third one he stuffed in the huge maw in the side of his face. He sheared off its cranial unit with one bite, then tossed it aside.

Warner made a snorting sound and spit out the masticated bit of ravager. Yellow and black drool dripped from his jaws as he ran a speckled pink tongue across twisted fangs. He fell over, gasping for breath. His rate of dissolution exceeded his growth. He was slowly oozing to death.

"The strain on his biology is proving too much," said Zarg as calmly as if studying a dying microbe under a microscope. "His cellular structure should break down soon."

Warner fell to his knees. He raised his crushed face toward me and moaned. He couldn't have been aware of much now, only pain and chaos.

"Pity he will not much live much longer," said Doctor Zarg. "It would be invaluable to study the effects. I must remember to collect a sample."

I walked toward Warner.

"It is inadvisable to approach the subject in his current state," said Zarg.

I ignored him. Zarg was a decent enough joe for a robot, but Warner was just another test subject to the technomorph. His suffering was an observable phenomenon to be recorded and studied. There was no compassion in Doctor Zarg's reasoning. Neither was there malice or resentment for all the trouble Warner had caused. Only a clinical, logical detachment.

I, with all the mysterious workings of my faulty prototypical brain, thought Warner was an asshole. I didn't exactly feel sorry for him, but he'd suffered enough. More than enough.

Warner raised his eyes toward me and whined. Maybe he couldn't ask it aloud. But he was dying and he just wanted to get it over with.

I caved in his head with one blow, and his oozing corpse slumped to the floor. I turned to the lead security guard. He was either a Pilgrim or a mutant because he had red-and-blue-striped skin and three eyes. I seized him by the throat with my slime-coated hand. The acidic sludge burned his throat with a sizzle. I assumed it smelled bad, too.

"Now, are we going to have a problem here? Because I'm not in a very good mood anymore."

He motioned for the guards, and they all dropped their pop-guns.

Behind me, ragged breaths registered in my audios while a shadow fell over me. I turned to scan a giant, melting, alien mutant behind me. Its eyes showed no sign of intelligence. I'd killed Warner, squashed his brain. But the thing must've grown a new one. Maybe even two or three. None of them seemed real happy at the moment.

The twelve-foot mutant thing grabbed the guard from my hand and batted me aside. Silently, except for its painful gasping, it stuffed the squirming guard down its throat. There was a lot of shrieking and crunching in the three seconds it took to swallow the guard whole. It had to chew a bit to deal with the wider portions. Four seconds later, stripes formed on its skin and a third eye opened on its forehead.

While eating the first, it'd seized another guard which it immediately gobbled down. As it'd taken on qualities of its first meal, it now grew patches of scales. It wasn't simply eating them. It was somehow absorbing their DNA.

The remaining guards were already off and running. The four at the rear didn't make it seven steps before the mutant leapt upon them. It jammed them down its throat with ruthless speed and efficiency, not even stopping to pick the bits from its teeth from the last before starting with the other. With each meal, it grew bigger and absorbed more random characteristics.

Zarg said, "Surprising. The aberration is apparently attempting to correct the accelerated metabolic rate and genetic instability by assimilating more organic tissue."

"Is this going to be a problem, Doctor?" I asked.

"Unlikely," replied Zarg. "While it might slow the process of decay, it will not stabilize the—"

"How long until it dies?" I asked.

"Seven minutes." He didn't approximate or estimate, and since Zarg was supposed to be a genius, I figured he was right.

The mutant finished the last of the four. It was fifteen feet tall now, and I estimated it must've weighed at least four or five tons. It was less gooey, having gained some stability from the DNA it'd absorbed. It'd also become a mix of seven different aliens, with a crab-like claw, scales, and tiny wings on its shoulders. It didn't seem to hold any particular characteristic long though, and shifted back and forth among the various qualities.

It turned its eyes toward me, and growled. It didn't really look at me. Its pain and rage had been overwhelmed by its tremendous appetite, and Zarg and I were mere lumps of steel.

Its breath grew ragged again. Lesions broke out across its skin. With a bubbling rasp, the thing turned and loped from the lab in search of undamaged genes to refresh its own genetic decay. It didn't use the door but burned its way out by smearing its own corrosive shedding on the north wall.

If it escaped the facility and reached the surface, it could eat a lot of people in a few minutes. On the other hand, the mutant would certainly help to jam up the gears of Dissenter security, which I'd done a pretty good job of jamming myself already.

Holt remained my priority. The aberration was a minor inconvenience in the larger scheme. It might eat a few people, but if the Dissenters escaped with Holt and started mixing up a new batch of mutagen, we'd be back at the beginning of this mess.

I plotted the course on my map files. From here, it was a thousand, six hundred feet north to the panic room where automated security protocols would have removed Holt for safekeeping.

The aberration had gone north.

Could've been a coincidence.

"Doctor, hypothetically, what would happen if that thing managed to assimilate Holt's DNA."

"Postulating." Must've been a doozy of a postulation because Zarg took a full nine seconds to run through the simulations. "It is unlikely that anything can correct the genetic instability."

"How unlikely?"

"The variables are too many to calculate precise odds."

"Take a wild guess."

"I do not guess."

I grabbed him by his armless shoulders and lifted him up. "Zarg, what are the odds that this thing is going after Holt?"

"Unknown."

I sighed. Had to know how to talk to a robot. Even one as intelligent as Zarg.

I said, "Assuming the aberration is smart enough or aware enough to go after Holt, and assuming that by assimilating his DNA it is able to stabilize its decay, how hard would that thing be to kill?"

"With the assumptions given, it can be assumed that the aberration might be statistically impossible to destroy, short of an atomic explosion or other such cataclysm."

"Thanks, Doctor." I set him down. "Was that so hard?"

I set the most direct course to the panic room, moved to the other side of the lab so I could build up some momentum, and went into battering ram mode. I thrust my damaged shoulder forward to absorb the trauma as I smashed through the wall without losing a step.

I hypothesized that I was merely being paranoid, that the thing Warner had become was no longer Warner. Just a thing driven by hunger, rage, and agony. A mindless, unthinking beast fueled by instinct without intelligence or memory. It was only an assumption, and that looked less and less likely to be true as I noted that the creature was burning its way in the exact same direction with single-minded purpose. It was moving fast.

Halfway to my destination, I finally caught up with it. It'd happened upon a room full of biologicals and was taking the opportunity to feed itself, and doing so with quiet efficiency. By now, it'd grown another mouth in its chest so that it could eat even faster. Except for its raspy breathing, the thing never made a sound.

Its head moved in my direction, drawn by the movement. It was smart enough to know eating me would only give it a stomachache. It returned its attentions to three biologicals trapped in a corner. They blasted it with heatrays, which only seemed to be irritating it. I took advantage of the distraction to pull ahead.

The panic room was surprisingly easy to reach. It wasn't designed to be impregnable in itself, but to be in a well-defended position. The facility was in chaos now. Security was as well organized as an anthill being sprayed by a hose. I ran across few guards. They were either rushing in Warner's direction or, just as commonly, running the other way. I could take some small pride that the Dissenters' agenda had suffered a serious setback.

I kicked in the doors. The room was small, barely big enough to hold a few monitoring devices and a table where Holt lay. Two medical drones tended him. Neither was designed for combat, and happily got out of my way as I approached. There was a sealed tube in the ceiling that led back to the chemical lab where they'd been filtering mutagens from him.

He scanned in bad shape. Doctor Zarg had been careful in the extraction process, doing as little harm as possible, but with Warner in charge, the boy's health was unimportant. He'd lost six to ten pounds, and his scales had lost their shine. There were noticeable scars forming where the tubes and wires had been connected to his flesh.

I very carefully lifted him off the table. He was so fragile. I could've crushed him with one squeeze. This had been my objective. Eliminate Holt, remove the threat of anyone else getting the bright idea to use a little boy to endanger Empire. It would've been so easy. Nothing to it. Holt wouldn't even feel a thing, and this mess would be ended.

That was before. Now, there was a monster on its way here, to Holt, alive or not, to assimilate the kid's DNA. No, I had to get Holt out of here. Alive was as easy as dead.

While the risk of an unstoppable mutant aberration put the whole city at risk, I was suddenly grateful for it. Now I wouldn't have to make a decision and find out what kind of bot I was. Could I kill someone, even an innocent boy, even if it was the most logical thing to do? If I couldn't, did it mean I had that elusive quality of humanity or was I just stupid? If I could, was I every bit the ruthless auto I was designed to be or was I doing what needed to be done? All good questions, but they wouldn't be answered today. And I hoped they never would have to be.

Holt moaned and opened his eyes halfway. He spoke so weakly that it barely registered.

"Mack," he said. "You found me. April said you would. She said I shouldn't be scared."

"Yeah, kid," I said. "It'll be all right."

He smiled painfully, then closed his eyes and went back to sleep. Except sleep was too nice a word for it. He was unconscious, out cold. His breathing was shallow and irregular. I had to get him out of here, find a hospital, and keep him out of the belly of a monster for another five minutes.

The aberration screeched as it hurled itself against the panic room. It'd eaten enough by now that it was too big to fit through the doors. Instead, it pounded on the walls and tried reaching in with one of its arms. I kicked it in the knuckles so that it withdrew the limb, but the walls were dissolving under its acidic touch and buckling under its powerful blows. They wouldn't last more than a few seconds.

I reached up and tore away the seal on the tube overhead. "Hang on, Holt." I don't know why I said it. He couldn't hear me.

I activated my booster and rocketed up the tube toward the lab. It was a long way up though, and the belt didn't have the juice for a single jump. So I dug my fingers into the side halfway up, and hung there, cradling Holt in my damaged arm, still functional enough for that, waiting for the booster to recharge.

Below, the aberration screamed and growled as it tore apart the panic room. It would figure out Holt wasn't there in a second and be after us. The thing had some sort of connection to Holt. I assumed it wouldn't remain confused long.

The booster was taking longer than usual to recharge. It was wearing out. I only needed it to hold out a little longer. Just one more time. That was all I asked.

I switched on my radio. "Humbolt, are you out there?"

"Yeah, Mack," he replied.

"I need to talk to the cops."

"Good news," said Humbolt. "We got cops all over the freakin' place out here."

"Detective Alfredo Sanchez," I said. "Short, furry, looks like a rat. Find him."

"I'm on it."

Below, the aberration grew suddenly silent. Even its raspy breathing ceased. I didn't know if it was sniffing the air for Holt's scent or scanning telepathically, but I was sure it wouldn't take long to pick up the trail.

It raised its head upward, looked me right in the optical, and laughed. I swear it laughed. Played that sound back three times, and every time, it could only be a chuckle. A hungry, wicked chuckle.

It was too big to fit up the tube easily, but it was squishy enough that it could force itself upwards. Its dripping flesh dissolved the sides, making its climb easier with each inch.

"Come on, Lucia. Don't let me down."

The belt reactivated.

I boosted the rest of the way as the aberration threatened to grab me by the foot. I didn't have quite enough power, and I barely made it to the edge. I snagged it with my free hand and pulled myself up without losing Holt in the process. There was no time to congratulate myself. Behind me, the aberration was shrieking. I'd bought a fifteen- or twenty-second head start. Maybe less.

I was still sixteen stories below ground. I needed up fast. My memory file directed me to a nearby section of emergency levitator pods. Intended purely for evacuation situations, they worked one way: up. Which was fortunately the way I wanted to go. With some luck, they hadn't all been taken yet.

One was left, and there was a group of five Dissenters attempting to access it. They jumped at my sudden appearance and readied their weapons.

"We don't have time for this," I said.

The aberration roared, and it could be heard ripping in this direction.

They lowered their weapons, and the leader, a rodent-like woman, pressed a few keys on the security console.

"Invalid code," replied the console in a superior voice.

Her shaking hand stabbed at the keys, and the console said, "invalid code."

Biologicals. Couldn't count on them when the pressure was on. Not most of them anyway. I dug into my coat pocket and plugged another of Lucia's gizmos into the console. It lit up.

The aberration appeared at the end of the corridor. How could something that oddly proportioned and lumbering move so fast? It rushed toward us.

"Oh, flurb," whispered one of the terrified lab techs.

Lucia's gizmo chimed happily as it defeated the security console. I shoved my way into the pod first and the rest jumped in behind me. I hit the activation button as a giant hand reached in and snatched out one of the biologicals. His screams were cut off by a sudden crunch. Then the doors closed, and the pod rocketed upward.

"What is that?" asked the rodent scientist. "What is that?" As if there were really an answer to the question that would make everything better.

I checked Holt. He remained unconscious, despite the bumpy ride and the monster out to devour him.

"Mack, got'cha that cop you wanted," radioed Humbolt. "Patchin' him through now. Just speak into my faceplate, detective."

"What the hell is going on here, Mack?" asked Sanchez.

"No time for questions," I said. "Here's what I need you to do. I'm going to be coming out of the southern side of the building. Have a fast rotorcar standing by, ready for immediate takeoff. I've got a kid here who needs medical attention. More importantly, he's got to be kept away from the thing that's following me."

"Thing? What thing?"

"Big dangerous thing," I replied. "It'll be right behind me, and it'll be hungry. Evacuate every biological from the area. You've got thirty seconds."

"I can't do that, Mack. This is the Nucleus. It's a circus out here right now."

"Find a way," I said, "or a lot of people are going to die twenty-seven seconds from now. Megaton out."

It was asking a lot, and if Sanchez wasted time arguing with me, it wouldn't get done. But he didn't reply, and I assumed he'd handle it.

The pod stopped at the ground floor, and the biologicals scattered in various directions. I ran out the southern exit. Sanchez and his men were still clearing the area. They hadn't even put a dent in the crowd. Tempting globs of flesh and DNA were all around. Even if the aberration didn't get hold of Holt, it could do a lot of damage in the three-and-a-half minutes it had left to live.

Sanchez was ready for me. He didn't give me a hard time, just led me through the crowd to the waiting rotorcar. I handed Holt off to a cop. The car shot off into the sky. I turned toward Carter Centre.

"You have to get these people out of here," I said to Sanchez.

"We're doing what we can, but I must've left my wormhole in my other pants," he replied. "Now, what is this big thing that's after you?"

The aberration burst its way through the glass doors. The thing that had been Warner was now a hulking brute of smoking flesh and malformed limbs, seventeen feet high. Its scrambled DNA could no longer make up its mind. Hairy tufts and scaly patches and hungry mouths appeared and disappeared on its random flesh. Its three eyes moved independently of each other, tracking the crowds.

"Goddamn," said Sanchez.

The monster beat its chest and roared. Its every movement flung globs of dissolving, corrosive flesh through the streets. It hesitated, confused by the buffet of scrambling morsels before it. A brave cop drew his raygun and tried to blast it. He only caught its attention. It seized him and swallowed him in two bites.

The rest of the cops started blasting the aberration. It was their job to try and stop it. But it was also a waste of time.

"How the hell do we stop something like that?" asked Sanchez.

"We don't. Get everybody the hell away from it," I said. "I'll keep it busy."

"Can you kill it?" said Sanchez, but I was already on my way.

I didn't need to kill it. I only had to keep it busy for two hundred seconds or so, assuming Zarg was right. I hoped he was as smart as he was supposed to be.

In the four seconds it took me reach it, the aberration devoured three more cops and two unlucky civilians. And it didn't appear like it was getting full yet.

I threw myself into it, lifted it off its feet, and tried to push it back into Carter Centre, away from the street. It didn't quite work out. The way it shed its skin made a solid grip impossible. I only managed twelve feet before it regained its footing and started pushing back.

The thing was stronger than me, and it had the weight advantage. I tried the gravity clamp, but the belt was burnt out. The aberration shrugged me off, tossing me aside. I slid across the pavement and collided with a parked buzzbug. The aberration turned its back to me, dismissing me as an inedible nuisance.

I dug the fingers of my functional arm into the buzzbug's hood, performed a quick trajectory calculation projection, and hurled it at the monster. It sailed in a perfect arc to collide with the back of the thing's head. The mutant stumbled and glanced with annoyance in my direction.

Annoyance. Exactly what I needed.

I threw a treader, then immediately followed it with another buzzbug. Each clobbered the aberration on its dissolving skull, and while they didn't seem to be doing any real injury, they were pissing it off. A pissed-off monster was a distracted monster.

I was about to hurl a gyroped when the aberration whirled suddenly. Two antennae had sprouted from its forehead as it spontaneously mutated. They crackled with blue energy and unleashed a stream of focused radiation. The gyroped, steel, glass, and all, disintegrated into powder. My indestructible clothing, too. My alloy held up, but my radiation screens were ineffective. A short list of internal failures sprang up in my diagnostics file, and thirty or forty seconds of exposure could've fried vital circuits.

The creature wasn't smart enough to realize that so when I didn't disappear in a poof, it cut off the blast. It dropped to all fours and charged. My reflex model had been damaged, and it was on top of me before I could react. It swatted at me with one huge paw. I catapulted high into the air and bounced into a small crowd of civilians. It was a miraculous anomaly I didn't land on any of them, but not exactly good luck since the thing was plenty pissed at me and now moving this way.

A blaster blindsided the beast and blew off a chunk of its shoulder. The aberration growled curiously, more perplexed than hurt. Its eyes scanned the crowd and found Sanchez standing atop a rotorcar. The little guy was gutsy. I'd give him that. And he was about to be dead.

"Come on!" he shouted. "I'm here! Over here!" He blasted a few holes in the aberration's chest.

The thing's antennae started crackling again. There wouldn't even be enough left of Sanchez to fill a teacup.

Another blast caught it by surprise as Jung fired at it from behind. A dozen cops joined in and a barrage of rayfire punched holes through the aberration's flesh. It spasmed and growled. It didn't die. The antennae on its head glowed brighter, and I detected rapidly rising levels of an unidentified radiation in the air. It wasn't dangerous yet, but it was building fast toward a full-scale disaster.

My reflex model finally kicked in. I dashed forward low to the ground, and knocked its legs out from under it. The aberration tumbled over. I didn't allow it time to recover. I jumped on top of it, grabbed its antennae, and yanked them off. They fizzled, but not before a dangerous burst traveled up my arms, ignoring my radiation screens. Circuits shorted out. Hydraulics locked up. My vocalizer started screeching. My one arm kept working though, and I set it on automatic and kept hammering away.

I concentrated on its lumpish head, trying to keep it disoriented, confused, and on the ground. It seemed to do the trick. I pounded its face flat. Two of its three eyes popped out of its head, and slime coated my arms and front.

Twenty seconds later, the aberration snapped out of its confusion, and rolled to one side. With my legs locked, I fell over on my back. The thing stood, gave me a kick, and roared.

The aberration slumped with a groan. Its skin slid away in smoking chunks. It raised its right arm, and the limb fell off. It lurched to one side, then the other, and collapsed with a gurgle. My chronometer was broken, but Zarg's seven-minute deadline must've finally been up.

My hydraulics came back on-line enough that I could stand.

The aberration was a mound of featureless meat. Twisted bones stuck out of its dissolving flesh, but even the bones began to dissolve into the same sizzling green pool of sludge. It kept breathing for a long time. Shallow, painful breaths, even when it was nothing more than a pool of slime, it kept breathing for . . . well . . . I couldn't say how long now, but it seemed a long, long time.

Then with one final gurgle, it stopped.

Sanchez was beside me. He held his rifle at the ready. "Damn, Mack, is it dead?"

My only reply was the steady hiss of static, the only sound my vocalizer seemed capable of right now.

My diagnostic programs reported one failing system. It was my diagnostics, which meant everything else was up in the air. I didn't know how badly damaged I was, but my opticals scanned the world as flat and gray. I fell over and didn't even realize it until I noticed Sanchez standing at a vertical angle.

He said something. I heard the sound, recognized his voice, but couldn't decipher the noise into words.

"Zzzzzzzzt," I replied.

And then I shut down.

22

I reactivated twenty-three days later. The information verified that my chronometer was working. And hopefully, so was everything else.

One by one, the systems and programs confirmed themselves. My visualizer came on-line, and I scanned a young blond woman standing before me.

She smiled. "Hey, handsome, how are you feeling?"

"Status report: functional."

"Aren't you the sweet talker?"

I was upright, clean and polished, wearing a new suit. A glance around confirmed I was in an unfamiliar laboratory. "Where am I?"

"My personal lab," she replied. "The one under my apartment. Don't remember, huh?"

"Negative," I said. There was still a bit of static in my audios.

"Do you remember me?" she asked.

"I remember you. Just not your name."

"Not surprised. Your internals took a hell of a hit. The

hardware, I could fix, and Doctor Mujahid recoded the basic coordination programs. Your memory matrix took the worst of it, but she was able to recover most of the data files. There are a few bits and pieces missing here and there."

"What kinds of bits and pieces?"

"Oh, nothing too important. You'll have to learn a few things over again, but shouldn't take you long. By the way, you can call me Lucia. Or Ms. Napier, if you'd prefer."

"I think I'd prefer Lucia," I said.

She nodded. "I'd prefer that, too."

"You're out of jail."

"No reason to hold me anymore. Charges were dropped. The whole messy affair has been swept under the rug. Like it never happened." Lucia pushed a stepladder over to me and climbed it to adjust my tie. "Do me a favor and raise your right hand, Mack."

I did.

"That's your left."

"Whups." I inverted the directional definitions and tried again. Got it correct that time.

"Take a step back," she said.

I moved and knocked her off her stool. She was ready for it and hopped safely aside. "No, that's forward."

I corrected that, too.

"Maybe he's not ready for this, boss?" said a talking metal post. A butler auto, my distinguishing software realized. Name recognition failed me again.

"Nonsense, Humbolt." (I filed that away.) "He's got to get out there sometime. Anyway, the doctor assured me that beginning everyday functioning would get him back in tip-top shape in a week or two."

"Step back." I performed a series of test maneuvers, checking wiring relays and servo response. My basic mechanical functions were up and running. Any program glitches would have to be worked out as they arose. "I'm good."

Lucia instructed Humbolt to tell the guests that we'd be up shortly. I wondered who was waiting for us and if I'd remember them all.

"What about the Bleakers?" I asked. "Julie? April? Holt?"

"Them, you remember." She arched an eyebrow. "You could give a girl a complex, y'know."

"Lucia . . ."

"Oh, they're fine. Holt was a little malnourished, but otherwise, unharmed."

"And the Pilgrims?" I asked, realizing that one of the things I'd lost was Grey's annoying little worm that kept me from discussing certain subjects.

Alfredo Sanchez descended the staircase. "We try not to talk about them, Mack. Hush-hush." He wore black slacks, wingtips, and a Hawaiian shirt with palm trees. It was the first time I'd seen him outside of a suit. The first my damaged memory matrix could recall, anyway.

"How's he doing?" he asked Lucia.

"He'll be good as new in no time. I'll let you boys settle a few things. Come upstairs when you're ready." She pushed the stepladder over again and used it to get high enough to plant a kiss on my faceplate. "But don't keep us waiting too long. By the way, Detective, no smoking in my lab."

She sashayed up the stairs, looking over her shoulder and winking before exiting.

"Looks, personality, brains, money." Sanchez whistled as he returned a cigarette to its case. "How'd you end up with a girl like that?"

I almost said she wasn't my girl, but then again, maybe she was. If so, I was a lucky bot. Or at least, I assumed I was.

"Did you know, Sanchez? About the Pilgrims?"

"Not quite. I mean, I had ideas about it. Knew something was going on, that there was someone pulling strings in Empire other than the Big Brains and Learned Council. Hard to do my job and not notice that. But I still don't know all the details. Need to know, loose lips. You know the drill.

"Okay, Mack," he said. "We've got a few details to go through here. I'll be brief. That mess in the Nucleus changed a few things while you were off-line. Forced the Pilgrims to come out. Still keeping them secret from the general public, but now they've opened discussions with the Learned Council. Put everything on the up and up. Hopefully, it'll help avoid trouble from overeager aliens in the future."

I considered the change. The Pilgrims, once content to manipulate Empire City from the shadows, had taken their first steps out of the dark. They were still hiding, and maybe I couldn't blame them for it. Empire might be ready for the aliens walking its streets, but if it wasn't, then showing themselves would be a disaster. Better to play it safe, I supposed.

"Good news is that the Pilgrims have agreed to allow us to create a counteragent to the mutagen. Sort of a good faith gesture. We're doing it slowly, so it's not traumatic to Holt, but soon the Big Brains will have enough to neutralize any threat, should the need arise."

"What about Carter Centre, the Dissenter lab, the giant pudding mutant that nearly ate half the Nucleus?"

"Just another industrial accident," said Sanchez. "Happens every day."

I wondered if people wanted to know the truth. If it even mattered. Probably not.

"Got a couple of things for you here." He dug in his pockets, removed a piece of paper and a data tube. "The Learned Council can't officially acknowledge your service to the city, but as a token of gratitude they wanted to give you this." He unfolded the paper. "Your certificate of citizenship. Welcome to the club."

"Thanks." I scanned it. It was only a piece of paper, but I guess I'd earned it. Maybe I'd get it framed.

He held up the data tube. "This was prepared by the Pilgrims. Say it's for your opticals only. Tells you where you came from. Turns out Professor Megalith isn't really that bright. Only a Pilgrim science tech who can pass for human. Stole a few designs and parts here and there, tried to use them for his own ends." He set it on the table. "Don't know much more than that, but the details are all in there."

Sanchez removed a cigarette and stuck it in his mouth without lighting it. "Well, guess that about covers everything. Any questions?"

"Yeah. Why am I functional? Seems like some could consider me a security risk, what with what I've recorded."

"Don't ask me, Mack. Like I said, need to know. Nobody's enlightened me on that. Maybe it's because you did good. World doesn't always give good guys the shaft."

"Not always," I said. "But usually."

"I can see your cynicism index wasn't wiped clean. So you ready for your party?"

I took a second to drop the data tube in my coat pocket. "Yeah, I'm ready."

The party was a small affair, eight biologicals and Humbolt. I didn't have all the names and half the names I did have were attached to the wrong faces, but it all got sorted out eventually. There was cake and punch for the biologicals, and everyone was eager to say hello. There was a lot of small talk and hugs and handshakes. Mostly, I kept quiet and let everyone tell me how much they'd missed me.

Somehow, I'd made friends. Hadn't planned on it. Just sort of happened. I guess that's how making friends worked.

Even Doctor Mujahid showed up. She and Jung hit it off right away. They sat on Lucia's couch, talking and laughing. I'd never heard the doc laugh before, but Jung could be one charming gorilla.

Sanchez introduced me to his wife. I hadn't even known he was married. She was a norm, and a tall one at that, six feet in heels. Sanchez barely came up to her waist.

"Alfie says such wonderful things about you," she said.

"Is that so?"

"Oh, yes," she replied. "Says you're a stand-up guy. Make a hell of a cop."

"Actually, what I said was that he was a stand-up guy, but a pain in the ass. And he'd make a good cop if he wasn't such an exhaust port." Sanchez snorted. "Come on, Rosa. Let's get some punch."

She shook her head. "Oh, he's so easily embarrassed. If you'll excuse us, Mack."

"No problem. Talk to you later, Alfie."

Sanchez grumbled, dragging his wife away.

Somebody tugged on my pants. I turned to scan April. "Hey, kid. How you doing?"

She tried to smile but wiped a tear away.

I knelt down. "What's wrong?"

She hugged me. "I killed my daddy," she said quietly, choking on the words.

"It wasn't your fault."

"But I knew they'd kill him. I knew it when they took us away. But I let them take us away because I knew I had to. I had to."

She sniffled. She wasn't quite crying, but she was close. She hugged me tighter.

"I knew that everybody would die. And I knew you had to stop it. And the only way to get you to stop it was to let them take us. To let them kill my daddy."

"There, there, kid." I rubbed her back gently. "You did what you had to."

Hollow words, I knew. Especially to a little girl burdened with the power to see the future. I got it now. That was why she hadn't asked for my help. Why she'd slipped me a note she'd known I wouldn't scan right away. She'd seen the future, a future where Empire burned in its own technotopic madness, and known no one would believe her. Not her mother or the cops or me. She'd set it up, as best she could, so that I'd end up in the middle of an alien conspiracy. She'd done so knowing it would get her father killed.

That was a tough choice for a little girl to make, but she'd made it. Now she had to figure out how to live with it, and that was even tougher.

"What happened to Gavin . . . your father, it shouldn't have happened. But it's not your fault. You didn't hurt him. Some very bad people did."

"But my daddy . . ." She pulled away and wiped her snotty upper lip with her sleeve. "I knew—"

"Shhhh. Come on." I picked her up and walked over to the balcony. "See that city? See all those lights. Every one of those lights is a person, somebody you helped. Can you count them all?"

She shook her head.

"That's a lot of people, isn't it?"

She nodded.

"A lot of families. A lot of fathers, I bet."

"Umm hmmm."

"And your brother. What about him? You helped him, too, right?"

"Yeah."

"And your mom. And me. You helped me, too."

"I did?" She narrowed her eyes suspiciously. "How?"

"You showed me that I can help people, too."

She smiled, very slightly.

"You did the right thing, kid. It's not always easy to do the right thing. In fact, it hardly ever is. Most grown-ups can't make themselves do it when it comes right down to it. Your father would be proud of you for being such a big girl."

I scanned Lucia at the balcony entrance. She was smiling, too, and her eyes were teary.

I wanted to wipe the tear from April's cheek but wasn't confident enough in my fine motor control to try it yet.

"Do you really think my daddy would be proud of me?"

"Yeah, kid. I know he would be. Because your mom and your brother and me, we're all so proud of you. Lucia, too."

"That's right, sweetie." Lucia came over and took April from me. She gave April a tight hug. The kind of hug I wished I could give her without risking crushing her. Then set her down and hugged her again. "Now why don't you get yourself a piece of cake?"

April wrapped one of her tiny hands around my thumb. "Mack, I love you."

"I love you, too, kid."

She glanced to Lucia. "Are you Mack's girlfriend? You're pretty."

"Smart, too," I said.

Lucia leaned over and gave April a pat on the bottom. "Scoot, kiddo."

April went off to join her mom and brother in the apartment. She still hadn't gotten back the bounce in her step or the light in her eyes. But she was young, and kids were resilient. She wrapped Holt in an embrace. He hugged her back.

Julie looked across the apartment, and she was crying a bit, too. Seemed to be a lot of that going around tonight. She mouthed the words, "Thank you." I nodded to her.

"You've got a way with children, Mack," said Lucia.

"Yeah. I'd make a wonderful nanny auto."

Lucia leaned on the balcony railing. I stood beside her. We enjoyed the view for twenty-five seconds.

"So are you my girlfriend?" I asked.

"I don't know. Am I?"

She laughed but didn't fill me in.

I pulled the data tube from my pocket. The one with all the answers. They weren't questions I cared about. Never really had been. I crushed the tube with one squeeze, and let the flecks of circuitry and plastic float away on the wind.

"What was that?" she asked.

"Nothing important."

"So, Mack, you've saved the day, become a citizen." She put her delicate hand in my oversized palm. "What's next?"

"I'm thinking of opening a detective agency. Even got a partner lined up." I glanced at Jung, still in rapt conversation with my shrink. I hoped he wasn't telling her any stories.

"I've got an old office you can use," she said.

"Terrific. You'll have to show it to me sometime."

She laughed again, and I got the impression there was a joke I wasn't getting.

"Seriously, Lucia. I don't know if it's something I should remember. Are you my girlfriend?"

She didn't answer, and I decided it didn't really matter. I'd sort it out sooner or later on my own.

Lucia moved closer and put her arm around me. Together, we watched the twinkling lights of the hazy, gray city.

TOR